Mafia Stalker

BWWM Dark Mafia Romance

Boston Irish Mafia Romance
Book 5

Jamila Jasper

Edited by
Haley O.

ISBN: 979-8-3304-1861-9

Ingram Spark.

Thank you to my Patreon subscribers for your support with this book.

❀ Created with Vellum

Boston Irish Mafia Romance Series

Mafia Playmate

Mafia Property

Mafia Surrogate

Mafia Possession

Mafia Stalker

Click here for the complete collection:

www.jamilajasperromance.com/catalog

Contents

Dark Mafia Romance Preview #1

Untitled

Pronounced: *Orr-in*

Chapter One
Odhran Murray

Six is asleep in my arms. I drugged her. She's been getting very annoying lately and the only way to get her to stay quiet long enough for me to focus on my work is for me to drug her. It's easy to do it without her noticing, since she can't end the night without a drink. We're only nineteen, so you would think she might realize she has a problem. But she doesn't, which suits me just fine now that I need her out of the picture. *Alprazolam* is my best friend in this situation – you probably know the drug by the brand name *Xanax* – but it's a lot cheaper to pay an organic chemistry student to synthesize the generic version.

Anyway, I crush exactly 2mg of alprazolam into a fine powder and stir it into her cocktail every night before bed. It's flavorless. She tries to sleep with me each time the drugs begin to kick in, and each time, I kiss her until she falls asleep and throw the covers over her so she doesn't get too cold.

I hope she doesn't adjust to her dosage too soon. It's getting very annoying to pay for the drugs and Six's constant pestering about our pending marriage only makes me want her more and more quiet. *I can kill her. I can always kill her.*

I suppress the thought. Aiden, my brother and the boss of the Murray family Irish mob, would punish me if I killed her, and there's no way I could hide it from him either. It's Aiden. He's intuitive, older, and he understands the cruelty that runs in the veins of our family members.

He would know.

Six is so quiet when she sleeps. And thin. Pale pink skin clings to her bony physique. Her waist-length blond hair makes her look like a silver ghost in the dark room, illuminated only by my cell phone's screen.

My girlfriend takes up so much of my bed. I wish she would go back to her place, but I suppose she lives here now. Carefully, I roll her body out of my arms and position her so she can keep breathing. I live off campus so I can have more space. I need space for my pet snake, Killer Bee, and then my gaming room. I suppose I also need space for Six since she's here all the time and occupies every square inch of my apartment with her college books and clothes.

Once she's asleep, I can spend my time exactly how I want without Six nagging me about wedding planning or "fucking a baby into her", which is the last thing I ever want to do. Football is what I truly love, but I've had to give it up. I chose my family over the game. But I still need something to do in my downtime and video games have always given me peace of mind. Not just video games but… everything about the world of the internet has always appealed to me. Part of my job involves doing research for and with my brothers.

It's much easier to track and kill your prey with the internet now. It never fails to shock me how people are so reckless. They post their location to their public accounts. They post pictures of their schools, houses, friends, cars, vacation spots, commonly visited coffee shops…

All you need is one piece of information most of the time – a first name – and then a location, and you can find everything you need to know about someone.

Take for example, my victim. The one Six can't know about.

. . .

Chapter One

ONIKA COOK. She goes by a screen name in our video game server, but I cracked that code pretty quickly. It's not like she isn't clever. Cracking her code took *some* time, but she left little clues all over the place that only a careful researcher could pick up on. I found those little clues, those little breadcrumbs and determined that *inky-whiterosepetals* isn't an anonymous, mysterious stranger, but a girl who attends my university.

Tracking her wasn't easy, but I'll explain it to you, because perhaps it will explain my fascination with her.

She isn't the sort of girl who attracts much attention. That's what fascinated me about her originally. Once I realized the woman behind the screen name was right within my reach – an unknown, chubby, glasses-wearing video game nerd with messy curls and the least fashionable clothing at school, my fascination turned into an obsession.

It's her first-year and she spent her entire first semester going alone between classes and her dorm room. She started her Tumblr blog on the first day of her first-year and I read all of the 6,531 posts Onika has made since then. I have my favorites in a private folder.

Once I accessed her Tumblr by typing her gaming screen name into a search engine, I uncovered more details about her. White is her favorite color to wear. Roses are her favorite flower. She writes in her journal every morning using a fountain pen. I read her Tumblr page scouring for clues until I learned that she lives in the Northeastern United States. I cataloged as much information as I could, hoping to find the city and town she lives in.

I was desperate to track down the girl behind the screen name, but convinced she'll be a girl in New Hampshire, or Maryland, and my goal would become that much more difficult if I had to leave the city.

Refreshing her blog four times a day, I read every single one of her updates, hoping for Onika to slip up. Then she slipped up in her efforts to hide her privacy. Only another hunter can understand the absolute euphoria of your prey making a mistake and giving you another opportunity to take advantage of their vulnerabilities.

She mentioned a coffee shop on her blog. *I know the coffee shop.*

That means she lives in Boston. Right now. To attend my university, she would have to. But what were the chances of her being right within reach?

We joined the gaming community chat site and played some games together. She was really good at *Call of Duty*.

Discovering that Onika lives in Boston only made me more curious.

The coffee shop Onika mentions is one right near our university campus. I skipped all my classes for two weeks just to sit in the coffee shop and research in case I could use the clues to match a name to the screen name. I don't need to attend classes to keep my GPA over 4.0, so it's just a matter of making sure Aiden doesn't find out that I'm wasting my tuition money by sitting in a cafe to track down a girl from the internet. College should work on being more interesting.

If he knows why I chose her, he'll be even more furious.

After two weeks of taking notes, I separated and color-coded my notes on my phone, putting all the clues and pieces together until one particular person stood out. She visits the coffee shop at the same time, three times a week and as the fall semester turns into a blistering Boston winter, she always wears a white coat and a white pair of Chelsea boots.

But this girl... the one I believe to be *inkywhiterosepetals* isn't white. I don't know why that gets me more excited. Maybe it's the tattoo I have on the inside of my forearm of special Celtic words to match the brand on my wrist from my final initiation into *the family*, which both demonstrate my commitment to racial purity. Dad had to beg half my brothers to get the words tattooed, but I proudly asked when I was fourteen because of my commitment to Six.

There was never going to be a girl who wasn't Irish in my life because I had her.

AND NOW, I'm going to change that. Callum wants to stop me from acting out my fantasies, from chasing down this girl and turning the pixels into a person for my own pleasure. He doesn't understand why

Chapter One

I've been stalking her and how deeply this need to discover her identity propels me. He doesn't understand that this time, I have a perfectly reasonable motivation for my dark urges.

Once I have a face, I have all I need. I scour student records and public student social media profiles for anyone who knows her. There's a bookstore near campus that sells a bunch of social justice garbage for people who give a crap about screaming in the streets and getting nothing done, and that bookstore has an online page featuring Onika Cook holding up a book for a promotional post.

They tag her public page and I have her. *Almost.*

BREATHLESS AS I view her page, I glance over at Six, lying asleep in bed with me. I'll have to deal with the Six problem eventually, but leaving her isn't as easy as it seems. We might not be married but in the mob, engagements like ours are more serious than marriages. My life has been pledged to hers since we were kids. *I can't abandon her.*

I glance at the pillow where she rests her head, wondering if it would be a mercy to kill her instead of putting her through this. Too messy. Instead, I scroll through Onika's page again, finalizing my plans to stalk her, make her life a living hell and push her to the point of murder.

I WANT to watch her kill for the first time and I want to see if it breaks her. I want to own her completely. Control her. Possess her. Turn her into nothing more than my plaything, my servant in every sense of the world.

There's nothing sexual about it. I couldn't possibly break the vow I made to my family. Unlike my brothers, I still believe in our family's teachings. This is blood lust, nothing more. It's about the psychological and emotional control I've always craved over another living thing. Onika awakens those urges in me more powerfully than any other woman. Identifying her in person only strengthened the obsession I fostered in secret.

Odhran Murray

She doesn't know how much I know about her. She doesn't know that the screen name that shows up to every game she plays, *celtics-fan55* is me – Odhran Murray, the youngest son in the Murray mob family. Everyone is anonymous on the internet, which she thinks works to her advantage, but it only works to my advantage. Not hers.

Chapter Two
Onika

I feel sick to my stomach getting ready for English class. Five roses sit on my desk in a vase. Someone has been sending me roses every week and they're pretty, but not pretty enough to calm me down about going to my college English class.

Because of my scholarship, I don't feel pressure like some of my other friends to get a degree in something 'marketable'. My parents support me enough to let me study what I want. I don't want to give up on my dream of being a writer. I've written fiction and non-fiction on blogs every day since I was 12 years old. My writing has been my lifeline through all the hardest parts of growing up.

When I was a chubby middle-schooler, I wrote fanfiction about Edward Cullen ending up with a plus-sized girl like me. I started writing my own fiction after middle school and posting it online. I love fantasy, horror and all that stuff. All my fiction has a romantic element, but it has also always been dark.

When Kalani's best friend Sophia died, and she went into a depression, everything was hard for our family and I wrote through that too. I've written my way through all the hardest parts of my life, including feeling isolated at my new liberal arts college. Writing helped me come to terms with the first few months here and I stopped expecting more out of college.

Everything about my classes at my new university would be perfect honestly except for one person.

It all started when our professor picked my essay over hers for 'best in class'. Ever since then, Six has never forgiven me. I just wish she would leave me alone but the last time I saw her, she made herself pretty clear.

"You say one word during that English class and I will fuck you up…"

At a normal school, you could report someone like Six to the dean of students, or some other authority, but this is a private school that caters not just to Boston's wealthiest students, but the students whose parents seemed to get their money through particularly unsavory means. I knew about my private college's reputation when I applied, but the English program…

All my favorite authors went to college here at McGraw College, a small liberal arts college on the outskirts of Boston. They all say they had the best professors and the best experiences here that "shaped them as writers". Growing up in New York City, I always dreamed about leaving and going somewhere similar but different. Boston is perfect. It's more lowkey than New York, but I don't feel like I'm going to miss out on everything in this city.

Unlike New York, I feel like I have a chance to get noticed. My only problem is getting noticed for all the wrong things. I never wanted to attract the attention of someone like Six, who is campus royalty. I don't even know why she feels so threatened by me just because of one essay. She has everything.

Her hair is naturally blond and very thick, and she curls it daily so it hangs perfectly to the middle of her back. She wears only designer clothing and she's dating a guy that everyone agrees is the hottest at our college. I've only seen him a couple times.

Once, I saw him at the cafe I visit just outside of our college gates, but that's the only time I've seen him in person that I know of, because I didn't know who he was until my roommate showed me his social media account. His public account, odhran55 has 345k followers. Every one of his pictures has thousands of likes and comments, even if he doesn't post a caption. His picture was striking and made me realize that maybe I'd seen him around before.

In the café, the one time I saw him, I don't even think he noticed me. I definitely never noticed him at the café before, so I don't think he was a regular there. He had a black notebook out and his cellphone. He seemed busy. Maybe angry.

I wrote his name down in my writing journal, but I would have remembered it anyway because it was weird, and as a writer, I keep a list of weird names for reference.

Odhran. Strange, huh? He must be Irish to have a name like that, although he doesn't look particularly Irish. I don't know much about him, but after hearing so much, I made an effort to see what he looks like. *Intense.* That's the best word I could use to describe him aside from the word attractive. But I don't know. I think he looks a little too evil to be really attractive.

He wears all black and he has black hair, incredibly pale skin and fierce blue eyes. The first time I saw him, his height was the first thing I noticed. He's way taller than average, lean and muscular. I wonder if he ever played a sport. It might be strange, but he looks just like a book character, so I took notes about him when I first saw him. I take notes on people all the time in case I need to use the notes in a book, especially interesting people. He would never look twice at me, so I don't have to worry about him finding out or anything embarrassing like that happening.

Odhran is not *just* interesting, apparently. I don't have any friends here, but the closest thing I have to a friend is an acquaintance in my one required science class (Astronomy 101), and she told me that he's from one of the wealthiest mob families in the Greater Boston Area.

"Each one of his brothers is a multi-millionaire and he's set to inherit millions too. They're crazy motherfuckers though. I would stay away from them."

Her advice almost makes me laugh. Like I would have a choice. Guys like Odhran didn't pay any attention to me in high school and they certainly won't be paying any attention to me in college where there are even more thin and attractive girls.

Being mixed race isn't always easy. I look more black than Asian, unlike my sister who looks like a perfect mix of both. I'm chubby, my hair is kinky and impossible to maintain without an elaborate routine, and I have never garnered the attention of a single boy in my entire life. Any time I tried to make a move myself, rejection was swift and harsh.

"You're too fat, Nik," was a common rejection. Sometimes they just laughed at me, as if I was completely stupid for trying to get out of the friend zone.

The rejections that hurt the most were the ones by guys who led me on for a while. They touched me. They held me. They came so close to kissing me and they made me feel like they really cared about me – like they respected me. Most of them were just using me in the end – either for help with their essays or just for a temporary ego boost before they went after the women they actually wanted.

Odhran is popular, and at our college that means there's absolutely no risk of me running into his path, even if I share a class with his girlfriend. She talks about him all the time. Never to me – she would never deign to have a conversation with me. But she always talks about Odhran with her best friend Maura in our class as loudly as possible.

I could write a book just about their relationship and we're only about halfway through the second trimester. Six talks about how they've been together since she was twelve-years-old, how they're going to get married, how they have matching tattoos, the ring Odhran bought her, the trips Odhran has taken her on, how big his dick is, and more. Nobody else even clears their throat as she speaks.

Everyone fears her because of her mob family and her legitimate reputation on campus. She's the main reason I feel sick to my stomach about going to class. What would normally be my most confidence inducing outfit looks frumpy and lame. I wrote a good essay, which was apparently a critical mistake. I got the popular girl to pay attention to me. In my world, that's not a victory.

Her cruelty scares the crap out of me. I've heard what she's done to other girls in our year. She heard a rumor that some girl spoke to Odhran after his economics class, so she and Maura dragged the girl behind the science classes and shaved her hair off before beating the crap out of her. With her last name, she could get away with murder.

Hell, Six's last name is splattered across half the buildings on campus. If Odhran's family is incredibly wealthy, hers must be nearly as wealthy. I wish she hadn't noticed me. I wish I'd gone undetected. But it's not my fault that our English teacher chose my essay. *Don't worry, Nik. You can get through this.*

I DO my best to gain my composure as I walk from the first-year dorms to Cunningham Hall, the building that houses the language department. I'm alone in the halls, even if I'm not late. There aren't many people in my English class and or afternoon classes either.

The only seat open in our English class, where we all sit around a round table, is the one between Six and her best friend Maura Walsh. I freeze in the doorway and consider cutting class because this seating arrangement feels purposeful. But I can't move because two boys who left their backpacks in their seats appear behind me and then our professor appears. Professor Sarah Gemmell swoops into the room, moving us all forward and preventing me from any final possibility of cutting class and escaping.

I have to move forward into the classroom, acting normal, like I'm not terrified to be near Six and Maura as they glare at me. Pretending I don't notice, I sit down between them in the only available seat. My anxiety is through the roof. Maura taps her acrylic nails impatiently on the side of her white Starbucks cup that emanates a strong scent of pumpkin spice. Six smells like she bathed in a very expensive perfume. The strong scents make my nausea worse.

Professor Gemmell seems oblivious to the tension in the room, but the boys across the room elbow each other, cast a glance in my direction and chuckle. I imagine they're making a cruel joke about my appearance, my skin color, or something else. They certainly don't sympathize with me and I've long since lost hope that anyone will. I can take care of myself without anyone's sympathy.

I set my tote bag on the ground and throw my white puffer jacket over the back of the chair. Professor Gemmell opens her laptop and begins shuffling printed essays at the front of the class. As shuffling through essays takes Professor Gemmell's attention off the classroom, Six flicks long hair over her shoulder and reaches over to my notebook with her red fountain pen and writes in red ink.

Walk with me after class.

Calmly, I take my cheap ass black ballpoint pen and write back.

No.

I underline the word three times, even if internally, I'm dying. That's how you get rid of bullies, right? You stand up to them? That advice might work if you're dealing with normal bullies. Maybe elementary school kids. For someone like me, who attracts bullies like honey, that never works. They just enjoy the challenge of tearing me down even more.

I just count on nobody noticing me. It's always worked, but it looks like my time is up, because my sharp rejection hardly affects Six. Why would it? She has all the power.

Six looks annoyed, but she doesn't reply with as much violence as I expected. She snatches my pen back just so I don't have one to write with while Maura digs her fingernails into my thighs.

The acrylics sink into my flesh and I bite my lower lip to fight back pain. I notice Professor Gemmell hand the essays to Tyler Collins to pass them back to the class. He's a guy from Boston with a gross beard. He looks confused at the task, probably because he's a D student who spends the majority of our class time picking his nose and uploading stories to Instagram on his phone.

Unfortunately, Professor Gemmell turns her attention to her PowerPoint after handing him the essays, which guarantees another few minutes of torture as she struggles to work out the new technology.

Chapter Two

Maura's fancy acrylics sink deeper into my thigh.

"Say anything and I'll gut you, bitch," Maura hisses into my ear. Her breath smells like pumpkin spice and it almost burns.

I haven't personally fallen into hot water with Six, despite her hatred of me, but I've heard rumors about her and her friends and what they do. What they've done in high school.

She's from a mafia family and I'm nobody. My sister owns a bookstore and she just married a retired NFL player, but that doesn't exactly allow *me* any hype and status. I don't get tuition money because of who my sister sleeps with or has a baby for. Nobody cares about me – no one ever has really.

Kalani has a big personality, but I don't. I've never been boisterous or popular or cute. I've been the chubby sister that everyone ignores. The one who sits up in her room playing video games all day and all night. I don't like anyone paying attention to me and it's been to my greatest advantage. I've been free to create what I want and get better at my art.

Solitude isn't as bad as people think. Six scratches her next message across my paper.

You don't have a choice or I'll have my boyfriend rape you with a rusty kitchen knife.

SHE PUNCTUATES her threat with a small heart and then rips my paper away so I can't show it to our teacher. Six leans over and whispers, "Don't. Fight."

I'll never stop fighting, but physically, I have to give in. Class begins and I struggle to focus on Professor Gemmell's lecture about the sexual symbolism in Macbeth. I have to participate in class to keep my grades up – this is a liberal arts college – but it's hard to focus with Six glaring at me and occasionally scribbling nonsense over my notes just to demonstrate her power over me.

I don't know if Six will make good on her threat, but it wouldn't be the first time something horrible like that has happened at our school. This place is a playground for rich kids that happens to have the best writing program in the country. I *need* to be here if I want to be a successful writer, but now I have to dodge the landmines I hoped to avoid.

Bullies.

I thought I'd left bullies behind in high school. I was fat back then too, and I definitely didn't know how to dress for my shape, which girls like Six were more than happy to inform me of. I told myself college would be different. I wouldn't try to make friends. I didn't need friends. I have my games and chinese takeout and that's all I need to be happy.

I don't know what to do except listen to Six – this time.

AFTER CLASS, they link arms with me. It looks non-threatening and Professor Gemmell gives us a smile as we leave together, imagining that the three of us are close friends. I try to speak, but my throat tightens and I'm too nervous to say anything. I just go with them.

These girls are terrifying and it's not just that they're all tall, unnaturally blonde and even more unnaturally fit and athletic. They have real power – families of murderers and lifelong criminals. They belong to some of the wealthiest families in America and they know I'm not one of them.

We walk around to the back of the school building together where there are no witnesses before Six shoves me against the wall hard. She knocks the air out of me so I can't yell, but if she wants a physical fight, I'll give her one. Sometimes, I wish my older sister hadn't fought all my battles for me growing up. I can't throw a punch like her and right now, I wish I was a fighting champion because my first punch misses Six.

Maura shoves me back again. "Stop fighting, stupid! We're just trying to talk to you."

It doesn't feel like they're just trying to talk and my fear heightens.

I shouldn't have gone with them to a second location, but they scare me. I've *seen* what they've done to other girls.

"You're not just trying to talk," I say to her, trying to sound tough and puff my chest out. "She pushed me and we're hidden behind a school building. What do you want?"

Six steps back, glowering at me with a scowl on her face. I press my back against the wall, gasping for breath and trying to find the fastest way I can get out of the situation. Their bodies block me from leaving and they clearly knew exactly what they were doing, since we're completely isolated. I don't think screaming would help. They're both athletes and they look like athletes. I'm already out of breath and sweaty.

They could kill me if they wanted to.

"Stop it right now," Six hisses. "I didn't even push you that hard. We're trying to help you."

"Help me do what?"

"Become a great artist," Six says. "Since that's what you fancy yourself, teacher's pet."

She sneers the words and I know they aren't trying to help me. I glance for an escape attempt and I try to run again. Maura is so much bigger and stronger than me that it doesn't work. She shoves me against the brick wall again and Six lands a hard punch in my stomach.

I might have a soft tummy that cushions some of the blow, but the hard hit makes me feel like I'm going to lose all the food on my stomach. My hands curl into fists.

"What do you want from me?" I yell at them.

"I want you to kill yourself, Onika," Six says, grinning at me. Her smile seems more sinister now. "We're going to drive you to the cliffs, and you're going to jump off. Maura will sit with you in the backseat while you write your suicide note."

"I'm *not* going to do that," I say to her. I don't care anymore. I reach into my pocket for my cell phone and unlock it. Without missing a beat, I press 911. As I press the phone to my ear, Six and Maura move as if a single unit. Maura hits me in the stomach far harder and more effectively than Six, who grabs my cell phone and throws it as far away from us as possible before grabbing my hair and slamming me against the wall.

I scream loudly, yelling this time as I fight back. They're serious. Holy fuck, they're serious. Maura presses her hand over my mouth and nose, holding them both shut. The last thing I remember before the world around me fades into fuzzy patches and then into complete darkness is Six smiling at me and laughing.

"This is too easy, Maura. Too fucking easy."

I WAKE up because of the cold. The girls must have taken my jacket off. I recognize the cliffs immediately. They're a few miles outside of the city and a popular spot for students at our school. Unfortunately, it's popular for only two things: lovers and suicides. Some of the famous writers who have gone to our school come here for inspiration. The energy here is dark and powerful.

I've never been brave enough to go to the cliffs, but here I am with two girls, and as I wake up, I know they're going to kill me. Six has a knife, but her friend Maura has a gun. I shiver as Maura slides open the barrel and loads a bullet into her pistol. Six holds the knife at her side as she shakes me awake with one hand.

"You're going to go to prison," I groan as I regain consciousness. I feel really light-headed and like I lost a few brain cells too. I don't feel good. My ability to fight back has been compromised even more. There's never anyone out here – not in the bitter autumn cold with the wind blowing over the cliffs loudly enough to drown out any sound.

Six rolls her eyes. "How could I go to prison when you're the one who chose to kill yourself?"

"We should duct tape her mouth," Maura says. "I don't want to hear her screaming as she jumps."

Chapter Two

Six glares at Maura like she's an idiot, but Maura is totally fixed on me, and she's aiming her loaded gun straight at me.

"Don't be an idiot, Maura," Six sneers. "If we duct tape her mouth, that would ruin the video."

"Whatever," Maura says. "Let's hurry up then. She's fucking disgusting. If I had a stomach like that, I'd kill myself too."

I don't want to kill myself because of my body. I don't want to die at all.

My stomach twists in a horrible knot because I can't fight back and if I attempt to run, I can either go towards the cliffs or towards Maura's bullet. There's no way for me to take control back and adrenaline surges through my body in an utter panic.

I try to stand against the lone tree they leaned me up against. Maura's hand trembles and I raise my hands submissively, focusing all my energy on not soiling myself. It's easy to pretend you will know exactly what to do when you find yourself on the wrong end of a firearm, but I could have never prepared from the paralysis in my muscles, how my body doesn't react how I want it to, but how it thinks we'll survive. I don't want her to shoot me. That's my first problem.

I wish someone knew I was here. But no one except my roommate and a few of my acquaintances in my classes know who I am. There's no one here I would consider a friend. They're mostly Irish and if they're not Irish, they're ridiculously wealthy with powerful families and powerful connections. I'm nobody. I've grown used to being the person no one pays attention to, but I thought I would at least get *some* reward from my life on the sidelines.

I thought I would at least get a life where I could create art forever. Write a novel. Submit a poem to a magazine. *Something.*

I've barely lived and now a crazy rich white girl in my English class wants to make me jump off a cliff. It's not fair that there can be people in the world worse than high school bullies.

"Well," Six says smugly. "It's too bad you won't be able to write a winning essay about *this.*"

"You're going to kill me over an English teacher's opinion?"

"No," Six says. "Her opinion got my attention. Her *wrong* opinion, I might add. I want to kill you, Onika Cook, because I don't believe girls like you belong at our school and it's offensive to me. I'm at the right age, and in my family, something like this gets a pretty big reward."

"New car," Maura says, a smile glinting across her face. "I bet your dad will get you a brand new Mercedes."

"I already have a Mercedes, you dumb bitch," Six snaps with more aggression than necessary. "I want something better. *Real* luxury, like a red Ferrari Daytona SP3."

My stomach drops even further. She's going to kill me so she can get a new car from her presumably racist family. I assume that's what she means by girls like me. Unless she has a problem with short women. Or poor women. She *is* six feet tall, but my instinct tells me that she means my skin color. There are only fifteen black students on our campus, probably because of the school's reputation. The admissions officer assured me the rumors were exaggerations, one angry student who went viral. *Our school doesn't accept racism.*

"Who cares what car you get," Maura says. "You'll get new ink and money. That's more than enough reason to kill a nigger and film it."

Chapter Three
Odhran

This isn't part of the plan. I've waited twenty minutes for Onika Cook to return to her dorm room after her English class. I have a perch from the woods in the cemetery behind her dorm – a camouflage deer stand in a maple tree – where I've been watching for her. Waiting.

This was the day I planned to take her under my wing – to turn Onika into a complete slave to my wishes. To turn her from a good girl into a killer. *Where the fuck is she?*

I've never been this anxious about her. Once I tracked down the username, the girl behind the video games who played better than all the guys in the game, it didn't take me long to track down Onika's phone number so I'd have all the information I needed to keep tabs on her.

Once I had her phone number, it was easy to find her phone coordinates at any given time. But her coordinates have been planted in the same place for several minutes and it's not like Onika to separate from her phone, or to stay in one place unless it's her bedroom or the library. I check my notes twice.

Onika hasn't deviated from her routine five Fridays in a row. She probably hasn't *ever* deviated from her Friday routine since she started classes here. *Something happened to her.* My phone vibrates and plays the special text message tone I have for my girlfriend. My neck tightens. What the hell does Six want now? I have to track down Onika's cell-phone and I don't have time for Six and her whining.

I'm hunting.

Six: Our world is perfect.

WHAT THE FUCK is she talking about?

Odhran: Yes. Where are you?

IT'S ALWAYS useful to know where Aisling is, even when I want her to be as far away from me as possible.

Six: Playing with my new toy.

I ASSUME she's talking about a new handbag, or a sex toy, or something like that. Aisling doesn't have much of a sex drive and she's never enjoyed sex except when she needs to use it to get something. My jaw tenses. I assume she wants something now. But I'm her boyfriend and when she gets like this, she expects more from me than a standard response.

Odhran: Show me.

Chapter Three

. . .

SIX SENDS me a picture of her new toy, and my stomach sinks. *What the fuck?* She's at the cliffs, and Six, who I assume takes the photo, stands far from the edge. In the photo, Six extends a knife, a long eight-inch serrated blade. Celtic knots woven with Aisling's initials decorate the handle of her family's ritual hunting knife.

Every man and woman in Aisling's line of the family has their own and they only use their knives for killing. The girl she has at the edge of the cliff? Onika Cook.

I'm shitting myself. Does Aisling know about my obsession? Is this her way of expressing her jealousy? Blood rushes past my ears and panic floods through me. Adrenaline. How fucking incredible that our bodies can produce such a rush without any drugs.

Odhran: Interesting.
Six: Bitch in my English class. Do you know her?
Odhran: No.
Six: Good. I want to watch her bleed and then make her jump. Does that turn you on?

I BITE MY LOWER LIP. Is this why she's doing this? She thinks the way to keep me happy is to appeal to my darker side – the sadist, the mobster, the man who started killing when he was just a boy. Maybe it would have worked if she had anyone else in her clutches. But it's Onika. *And she's my toy, not Six's.*

Yes, I eventually realized they shared an English class, but I covered my tracks. I kept my secret. Onika doesn't even know that I know about her. She doesn't know how long I've been watching her, and Aisling doesn't either.

Odhran

I LOCK my phone and climb out of my deer stand, jumping to the ground and tearing towards our campus parking lot as fast as I can. I missed my chance to play college football, but I've always been the fastest of my brothers. Still, it's no guarantee. I might not get to the cliffs in time.

I don't even know what I'm doing... Six is not just my girlfriend, she's my betrothed. Our lives have been intertwined since we were children. Everyone expects us to walk down the aisle together. We're a "perfect match" and we always have been – cold, sadistic, Irish mob royalty.

And she knows me. She understands me. Six might be a cold-hearted bitch, but she's always been *my* cold-hearted bitch – the girl my family assigned me from birth. I've never questioned my family and I'm the only one left standing in our traditions. I know what my father would tell me. It's my job to keep my family Irish.

It's also my job to stop Six from doing something foolish. I get into my car, a brand new black Lexus with a custom plate – ODHRAN. It's not subtle, but I'm not looking for subtle. I can park my car near the cliffs where no one will see it and do what I need to on foot. Even if guns aren't allowed on campus, I have a 9mm pistol in a gun safe beneath the passenger seat of my car.

I unlock the safe with my thumbprint and set the 9mm pistol on the seat. I don't know how I plan to use it or what I plan to do, I just know I might need it to stop Six from committing a murder. My phone buzzes with Six's text message notification again and I glance at the message.

SIX: She's crying. It's the perfect high.

· · ·

Chapter Three

SHE SENDS me a video that's a close up of Onika's face as she cries. Her round face takes up the majority of the frame as Six shoves the camera even closer.

"Why do you want to die, Onika?" she asks her.

"My life is worthless," Onika says, her voice cracking. "I don't mean anything to anyone. Nobody cares about me…"

Six laughs. Her laugh makes me sick to my stomach. "Good. You sound like you believe it this time. Don't worry, Nik. Your life is almost over."

Six moves the frame of the camera so it's facing her now. She has a cruelly beautiful face – high cheekbones, enough lip filler to make even the thinnest lips look as full as a celebrity's, blond hair and eyes like the summer sky. I could tell she was Irish even without the little claddagh tattoo on her exposed collarbone.

It's hard to imagine this woman was the one made for me from birth. It's what I've always been told and never questioned it. Her cruel smile does nothing to arouse me and neither do the tears on Onika's face.

She's helpless. If she's at our school and she isn't part of a mob family (which I know she isn't), she must have a scholarship. Kids on scholarship don't get special treatment on our campus. Why pick on her? It's too easy to push her around. Onika's position as an outsider drew me to her too, but I'd rather make her strong than tear her down. Six thinks she understands me but… perhaps she doesn't.

Recently, I've been questioning things that are not my place to question. I drive like a maniac as I get to the cliffs, paying little attention to the road as Six's face in the video flashes into my head and I white knuckle my steering wheel on the way to the cliffs.

Six is perfect and my feelings for her just aren't as strong as my brothers' feelings for their wives because I've been broken from birth. I've always been the broken one. I can't expect to feel anything for Six, I just have to do my duty and care for her.

. . .

Odhran

Even if it's not what I want. I text her back quickly so she doesn't panic and push Onika off the cliff before I can get there if she doesn't like that Onika won't jump on her own. *I hope she doesn't.*

Chapter Four
Onika

Maura holds a gun while Six awkwardly holds a knife to my stomach and gives me the script she wants me to read out loud on camera to prove that I took my own life. She cuts the video to the perfect length in front of me and forces me to log onto my social media accounts on her phone before she posts them all.

"Even if you survive," she says smugly. "You'll wish you were dead."

She's clearly never been in the position I have. My desire to live pulses through me, sending adrenaline pumping into every part of me. It's supremely ironic that I've never felt more alive. *Maybe I can talk my way out of this.*

That obviously only works in the movies, but I want to live, so I do what I think will keep me alive the longest, which is keeping Six talking.

"What happens after I die, Six? Have you thought about that?"

She ignores me and frames my face in her camera as she starts filming. "I have. I plan to watch the video every night. I'll play it on my television and fuck my boyfriend while I watch the last minutes of your life. Maura, lead her to the edge."

Onika

Her boyfriend. Odhran. I shudder. From what I've seen, he probably would enjoy something creepy like that. But I don't think he put Six up to this. I don't bother protesting, but I won't give them the pleasure anymore of watching me scream and cry. I have to accept the truth that there's no escaping my campus bullies.

I never thought I'd be in this position – the victim of a genuine crime. Nobody takes bullying seriously. Hell, I didn't take it seriously enough either. I thought they might push me around, hit me a bit. I didn't expect this. I also didn't expect to feel so calm about death.

But it's settling in that it's going to happen and there's nothing I can do about it.

It's going to hurt, Nik. The bottom of those cliffs is both jagged and wet. If you survive the fall, it'll be slow and painful. And what about Kalani and my unborn niece? What's going to happen to my big sister? I don't think she can lose anyone else... But this is it, isn't it?

My grandma always used to say, "It's your time when it's your time and ain't nothing you can do about that."

I FACE THE CLIFFS.

"Keep walking," Six says.

I walk forward. I can feel my will to live yanking on me from somewhere deep inside me and despite Six's commands and my intention to obey her, I freeze in place, four feet from the edge. Close enough where they could push me if they aren't satisfied with how 'entertaining' I'm making this for them.

There's a part of me that wonders why I'm drawing this out. Six and Maura want me dead and they won't stop until it's done. I clench my hands into fists and then I hear a gunshot. I gasp sharply, partly because I assume it's Maura. Instinctively, I drop to my knees. My hands roam all over me, but I don't think it's me...

I hear a scream. A very loud scream. I can't tell if it's Maura, or Six, but I throw my hands over my ears and crouch down, curled up on the ground as if that could save me from a bullet. I hear running and then another gunshot. And another. More screaming. A car engine starting. Another gunshot. Blood rushes past my ears and I think I'm going to pass out.

I stop hearing anything at all. I don't move even after the shooting stops and it goes quiet. Not completely quiet. Footsteps thud towards me. I'm shaking and frozen in my crouched position, unsure if my bullies are dead, or if this is just another attempt to scare me.

A hand presses firmly against my back and I scream. Not just any scream, an ungodly loud scream that releases all the tension inside my body. But it gets me moving. I press my palms to the ground and shoot up to my feet. Unfortunately, that makes everything worse as I face a large man wearing all black and a mask, so I can't tell who he is. But he's holding a gun in one gloved hand and I know he's going to kill me.

I turn to run, but he grabs me with a free hand and yanks my body against his. I don't recognize his voice, but the second he opens his mouth to speak, his voice is smooth and low, buttery as hell.

"You aren't going anywhere, Onika. You almost died. You're coming with me."

I find my voice despite how much his firm grasp around my wrist hurts. "I'm not going anywhere with you. What did you do to them?"

How does he know my name?

He tightens his grasp on me, clearly displeased with my defiance.

"I scared them."

"You didn't kill them?"

"It doesn't matter," he says, his voice turning icy. "I saved your life, Nik. I want something in return. I want your lips around my cock."

Why is he calling me that? Only a few people call me that and none of them are very large and imposing men.

I force myself to look at his face, despite the mask. It's a rabbit mask with black, smooth plastic and long ears that point up, making the male figure in front of me look like a male demon. He can't be serious. This man can't seriously expect to save my life and then... *assault me.*

"I'm not doing that," I say firmly. I haven't even had my first kiss. I'm the furthest thing from a slut and I don't want to get on my knees for some guy I don't even know before I've ever had a kiss.

"Why not?"

"Because. You could have a girlfriend. Or AIDS. And I didn't ask you to save my life."

It's too dark for me to even notice the color of his eyes. They look black and shiny in the dim light, and there are no other features for me to discern.

"I don't have a girlfriend," he says softly. "I ended things recently. This payment is not up for discussion."

I don't know how he hits me, but he smacks my legs in just the right way that I wobble and lose my balance, falling to my knees in the grass and pebbles near the edge of the cliff. We're still four feet away from the edge and I'm still shaking with terror and adrenaline. I don't want to believe this is truly happening to me, that one torturer creeps in to replace another.

"What's the big deal?" he asks. "Haven't you sucked cock before?"

"I HAVEN'T," I stammer out, staring at the ground as my heart pounds nervously.

"That makes me very happy," he says. "Are you a virgin?"

To me, the conclusion would be obvious. Yes, I'm a virgin. I've never been near a naked penis. I've never had a guy show any interest in me whatsoever. I don't know why I confess the truth to him. I think it's because I feel so close to death, that there doesn't seem like there's any sense in hiding from him.

"Yes. I haven't even been kissed," I answer nervously. Hot shame rushes through me at the confession. It really feels like something I shouldn't confess to a stranger who wants to shove his dick in my mouth.

The stranger's response is aggressive and immediate. He shoves his gun into his jacket pocket before he reaches down for my cheeks and drags me to my feet. I yelp in surprise and pain from the force of his large gloved hand squeezing my cheeks. He pulls his mask up just enough that I can see his lips for the first time. It's the first part of his body I've seen aside from his eyes.

He's pale. But his lips are so pink. Before the thought can sink in, he drags me against his muscular chest without hesitation and kisses me.

His lips force mine apart and he gives me a first kiss that I'll never forget. It's terrifying, completely wrong, but his lips are soft, they taste good, and he kisses me with fierce desire. Inexperience doesn't stop me from losing myself in the kiss. *No.*

The part of my brain that holds my dignity screams at me to pull away from the stranger's kiss. I can tell from kissing him that he's a terrible person. He kisses me like a movie villain, pushing his tongue into my mouth, taking control of my lower lips with his teeth. I don't even know who he is, but he's kissing me like he owns me. *Like I'm his property.*

I make another attempt to pull away from him, which my rescuer and attacker doesn't like. He grabs my cheeks so forcefully that I yelp.

"You don't resist me when I kiss you," he says. "I saved your life and from now on, your body and soul belong to me."

His words send a shiver of terror through me, but unfortunately, my body has another response that's more unfamiliar to me. My panties feel strangely wet, almost like I'm having a strange, sticky period.

He leans forward and licks me. He runs his tongue from the bottom of my neck all the way to my ear lobe before he bites on it.

"You are mine," he whispers forcefully in my ear. "And to make you understand that properly, I need you on your knees."

"I don't even know your name."

"My name doesn't matter," he says. "You'll know it when I'm ready. Now get on your knees, Nik."

My nickname. He's calling me my nickname like we're friends. But I don't recognize his voice at all. I've never heard it. I can't even guess at the face behind the mask. I'm terrified. He looks physically strong, dressed in all black with a tight hoodie and joggers that outline well-defined, bulging muscles.

He could easily overpower me. He already has.

"I can't do that with a stranger."

"I'm not a stranger," he says. "I know more about you than you know about yourself. I know who you are, Nik, and I've been *very* patient. I need your lips around my cock."

I drop to my knees. What choice does he give me? Even if I run away from him, where would I go? He came here for a reason and there's a part of me terrified that I'm the reason. *I know who you are, Nik.*

There's not a single guy on campus who has so much as asked for my name, far less my Snapchat or social media. I'm a nobody, and I've started to cherish the power solitude has to help my art. *I don't know him.*

Air rushes out of my lungs as my knees hit the ground. I hear him unzipping his pants and I glance at the bulge in front of me for the first time. By the time I have the courage to glance at the stranger, he has his cock out. It's big. I mean, I have nothing to compare it to, but my expectations were that he would have a much smaller one.

He's white.

That's my second thought after noticing the size of the cock protruding from the otherwise clothed torso in front of me. The large man who rescued me from Six and Maura on the cliffs is white. I wonder if he goes to my school. *How else would he know me?*

In high school biology classes, we learned the average male penis was five inches long. No way that's a penis, then, because it's as long as my forearm. I don't have the longest forearms, but surely this can't be normal, right?

"Open your mouth, Nik."

His voice is so deep and the stickiness down there feels more intense. He doesn't give me much of a choice about opening my mouth. He pushes the head of his dick against my lips and spreads them open. Before I can gasp or protest, he thrusts his cock into my mouth as far as he can push it. I gag and brace myself against his thighs, but he wraps his hands around my hair and takes my mouth, fucking it slowly, giving me a chance to adjust, but very purposeful with how he's fucking me.

He's rough about how he uses my mouth, taking me for his pleasure and grunting with each deep thrust, especially as his gigantic cock brushes the back of my throat. Each time I gag, he pumps into my mouth harder. He never stops groaning in pleasure. His moans provoke a horrifying response in my body. The wetness between my thighs turns into a tight knot and I feel super self-conscious and aware of the wet spot between my thighs and where the tightness centers.

"I'm going to cum," he says. "I'm going to cum in your mouth and you will swallow every drop."

He doesn't stop pumping into my mouth as he talks to me and I willingly accept every inch of him, running my tongue along the underside of his thick shaft, tasting him, losing myself in the experience. I don't know what I feel. This is wrong. Everything about this is wrong. But I'm so aroused that I can't ignore it. I grab his thighs again, but not to push him away, to draw him deeper into my mouth.

The sound he makes when I take him deep makes my heart race. It's so hot. I don't know why I'm yielding to him. There's no explanation for why I would participate in my violation.

"Fuck…" he grunts, surprising me with an eruption of hot creamy fluid from the tip of his gigantic cock.

I'm a virgin, but I just let a stranger cum in my mouth. I try to pull away from him but he grabs my hair tightly again and sinks my lips all the way down the length of his shaft.

"I said you're going to swallow every last drop," he says sternly. My lips tighten around his cock with every intention of obeying him as I run my tongue over the tip of his cock and let his release slide down my throat. It's warm and salty, but it doesn't taste bad. Once he finishes, he roughly removes my face from his cock.

"I ruined my life for you," he says. "So I'll definitely be back for your cunt. Here's a phone. New number and everything. You can download your personal crap later. Call a taxi and return to campus. Six and Maura won't bother you again."

He reaches into his pocket and tosses my phone a few feet away from me. I don't think before I scramble for it. I don't even know how he got my phone.

"If you call the police, the Irish mob will kill you, so don't bother. But you don't have to worry about your safety again, Nik."

"Who are you?"

I grab the phone and turn around, shining the light from my phone on him. That doesn't reveal anything. He's done his best to cover himself up. All I know is that he's tall, muscular, and completely fucked up.

"It doesn't matter who I am. What matters is that you stay out of trouble."

I watch him walk away towards a black car before he climbs in. I stand there, frozen. I want to call the police, but I don't know what I could even tell them. I have this man's semen in my mouth and I'm a mess. How could I explain to the police what happened? They would never believe that two college-aged girls drugged me. Maybe when they heard the name of my college, they would guess my attack was mafia related. The police wouldn't help at all.

Because I'm scared, I'm shaken up, and I don't know what else to do, I listen to him and quickly download the app and get a ride-share back to campus, logging into my account and paying without having a wallet on my person. Shoutout to actually remembering my complicated passwords..

Chapter Five

O DHRAN

Six: You can't break up with me via a text message. We're engaged.
Me: I can do whatever I want.

I PUT my phone down and exhale, my fingers running smoothly over the controller and then hammering the buttons quickly until I kill four of my enemies. Nice. That was too easy. I move around the screen, casting a glance at Onika's icon in the gaming server. *Online.*

She's been online almost as much as I have this week – seven full days since the incident at the cliffs. *Painful days.*

I don't want to deal with Six right now. I know what I did was impulsive, but I had to do it. My disgust and desire to get away from her was too intense. I know you can't just *end* a relationship the second you don't want it anymore but... those are other people's rules.

Aiden is going to flip that I ended this engagement without warning him, but I couldn't help it.

The words just flew from my fingers and I broke up with her minutes before I got to the cliffs. Yes, I texted her while I was driving. I don't even know if she saw the text message, honestly. She *was* on her phone, but she was also a bit preoccupied.

The decision would obviously have aftershocks, but Six is overreacting. I need to focus on Nik right now. *I'm not done with her.*

I'M sure the news of our breakup has reached my family by now. I temporarily blocked notifications from my brothers, so if they're upset, they'll come find me in person. Shit just hit the fan and I need a break from all of them to figure this out. It's hard to balance all of this difficult work with school.

Six has been furious all week, but she hasn't touched Nik again. That won't last long. It'll be a matter of time before she suspects me, even if I went to great lengths to fake an alibi.

Leaning back in my large black bean bag, I stare at the 50" curved monitor projecting the glow from Call of Duty into my apartment. After my injury, I wanted a change, so I moved to the penthouse. It's close to campus, but quiet with a great view of the skyline and plenty of room for all my things. I hired a few of Declan's old buddies to build Killer Bee's enclosure and to bring him over safely.

His room is always locked. I have the largest bedroom and then a guest room in case Aiden wants to saddle me with any family responsibilities. There is always an Irish cousin who needs a place to sleep or hide out from the cops.

The living room, dining room and kitchen are open concept, so you can see everything from the kitchen including the skyline. The living room has a wall of floor to ceiling windows that let in plenty of light. It's a nice place, but Six always hated it. "Too much light". Not to mention, she thought Killer Bee should be "rehomed" at the Franklin Park Zoo.

I thought I would be lonelier after the breakup, but my apartment is just as cold without Six's crap everywhere. It's quieter than I'm used to, but I don't mind the quiet. Growing up with a big ass family like mine where nobody knows how to shut the fuck up – especially not my sisters – you come to appreciate quiet.

I can't just leave Nik to her own devices. I have to keep an eye on her too. It's harder now that Six is furious and breathing down my neck. She's not close enough for me to drug her to sleep.

Nik doesn't know I'm the one who rescued her, and I know Six still wants to hurt her, but our break up has temporarily provided her significant emotional distraction. Unfortunately, distracting her from hurting Nik has made my life a lot more difficult. I have to manage her extreme emotional response to something that she should have seen coming.

Our relationship has always been destined. We've been together since we were young. But that commitment has always felt more like a duty than an expression of any humanity or passion. It's not like I have those things – humanity or passion. I don't see the point in them. I want to feel like other people. I *want* to be more like my brothers. But I'm just different even if I try to be normal. I don't think I can be normal with Six. She's too much like me. Possibly worse. *I don't want to be different anymore.*

After the cliffs, I don't want to go back to her. I don't want to suffer for duty anymore. I've tasted something different and my obsession surges through my veins and occupies my every thoughts. I think of nothing but Onika Cook. *My precious little Nik.*

Onika hasn't handled our encounter on the cliffs well. She skips all her English classes and spends most of her time on our gaming server playing Call of Duty. I thought she would handle it better. Her lips felt so good around my cock. And kissing her...

I don't normally like kissing. I couldn't even tell you what provoked me to kiss Nik. Her lips look so full and different from the lips I'm used to. I've never cheated on Six, so I'm only used to one pair of very fake lips. But they're familiar. They're home. They're nothing like Onika's.

Claiming her so quickly after letting my girlfriend go definitely bordered on immoral. But I got drunk off her lips the first time they touched mine. So thick. I've never seen lips so big up close, but I'm obsessed with them. Sliding my cock into her mouth was spontaneous and impulsive. I wanted so much more from her.

I restrained myself.

But everything that happened on the cliffs has clearly affected her, and now she doesn't leave her bedroom. I play a few more rounds of Call of Duty while I wait for her to sign-off at around 10:30 P.M. She's more disciplined than I am about video games. And homework. And sleep.

I get out of bed and drive to campus. I don't live far away – just a five minute drive – and Nik isn't going anywhere tonight. She lives in the first-year dorms, which are adjacent to a cemetery. Very convenient for me. I park in the cemetery and walk through the graves up a hill towards the first-year dorms. Nik's room is on the first-floor and I can easily climb in through the window.

I haven't done it before, but I've considered how easy it would be. Tonight, I'm wearing all black again, but fresh clothing. I've waited too long for her since the night on the cliffs and I need to know how she's doing. Why she skips her classes. Why I haven't seen her walking around with that white puffy coat and her long hair...

There's no one around Nik's bedroom window, no security, no students passing by. It's not *that* late, but we attend a small, liberal arts college so there are large parts of campus that are isolated enough for me to pull this off. I push my hand against the window and slide it up slowly. After what she went through, you think Nik would have locked it.

I should feel nervous as I slide the window up, but I execute it in perfect silence. This isn't my first time breaking in somewhere, and a dorm room at a liberal arts college is probably the easiest place I've entered. Climbing up proves slightly more difficult, but Nik has her bed on the opposite side of the room, so I don't have to risk waking her immediately.

After hoisting myself up through the window, I land on the hard-wood floors too softly to make a sound. My eyes have never struggled to adjust to light. I don't enjoy light very much anyway. It's a standard issue dorm room, which means that Nik must have a roommate. I glance between the two beds and it's easy to spot which one is hers. Nik's roommate isn't there, which helps a lot. During my research, I learned a lot about Nik's roommate.

Her parents have a connection to the Murray family (the mob family, not our biological family). She poses no threat to Nik and seems to only pose a threat to dining hall cinnamon rolls. Even without prior research, I would have known Nik's side of the room even if there were two human-shaped lumps asleep in the separated twin beds.

Her bed is covered with fluffy white sheets and blankets and her desk is set up for video games more than studying. She does most of her studying in the library, so this bedroom is her safe space. At least it was until I climbed through her window. She still doesn't hear me as I walk around her room slowly.

I touch her desk. There's a little stuffed Pusheen cat balanced near the keyboard. Empty Chinese takeout containers with soy sauce scented lo mein and pieces of beef. I don't eat garbage like that, but the smell reminds me of Callum who was practically addicted to takeout while he was in college.

After taking inventory of the items on her desk, I move closer to the twin bed where Nik sleeps, snoring gently. My heart quickens as I approach the bed. She looks so peaceful. Her hair is in some kind of strange shiny covering and a giant blanket covers her body completely. Protecting her.

Why are you in this bedroom, Odhran? You can't take what you want from her. You just can't.

I glance over at her roommate's bed again. I might have less time than I think. Her roommate could return at any moment. Maybe she just stays up later than Nik. I take small steps to approach Nik's bed and stand over her, watching her for a few minutes. She looks so peaceful. So *small.* Yes, she's curvy, but she's a very short woman and despite her ample physique, she's short.

"Nik," I whisper. She doesn't budge. She'll be awake soon enough. I lean forward and then clamp my hands over Nik's mouth, an action which awakens her with a snap. I feel her hot breath against my palm as she makes a failed attempt to scream.

"Hello, Nik. I told you I would come back for you."

She thrashes around in bed and I quickly subdue her, using her comforter with one hand and keeping my other hand over her mouth so she's pinned to the bed. She still attempts to struggle, but even using all her strength, Nik doesn't stand a chance against me.

I climb onto the bed and use my body to pin her to the bed this time. I still keep one hand over her mouth, holding tightly against Nik's sweet, soft lips. Her lips are wet and trembling in fear. The fear and the softness get me instantly hard.

"I miss your lips. Ever since that night at the cliffs, I haven't stopped thinking about you. I didn't get enough from you, Nik. I want your cunt…"

The word cunt provokes an intense and violent reaction in her. She pushes her hands against my chest and her body struggles against mine to no avail. I push her harder into the bed and pin her down so she stops struggling.

"Fuck, Nik. I'm not going to hurt you."

I PROVE it to her by removing my hand from her mouth.

"HELP!" she screams and I cover her mouth again immediately. The dorms are made for college students to scream and fuck in. Noise won't attract as much attention as Nik thinks, but I still don't need her yelling and cutting my visit short.

"Do that again, Nik and I'll spank your ass so hard you won't be able to sit to play Call of Duty for a week."

She whimpers and squirms again. I don't think I can trust her, but

I stop covering her mouth anyway. I want to look at those lips. And kiss her. And put my cock in her tonight. I'm tired of waiting.

"Who are you?" she gasps, wriggling her arms against my hold. I let them free, giving her a sense of freedom so she doesn't flip the fuck out and ruin everything for us. Once she has her hands free, she stops struggling against me as much and starts touching my face. I like when she struggles, honestly.

She's curious about me. That has to be the only reason she isn't fighting. If I can use her curiosity to keep her here without struggling against me, I'll do that.

Tonight, I don't bother with a mask, but it's still too dark for her to see who I am. She still can't tell who I am, even if I let her touch me. She *could* turn her light on, but I'll stop her before she gets so far. Nik's small hand touches my jawline and she runs it all the way over the sharp line, all the way over my cheeks.

Then she runs her thumb over my lips.

"Does it matter?"

"Yes. You saved my life. And then... you hurt me," she says. Her voice sounds so small and soft. She's doing her best to hide how much I terrify her, but I can smell it on her.

"Is that why you skipped all your classes this week?" I ask, running my hand slowly over her cheek. Touching her is just as exhilarating as the first time. This time, my excitement builds even further because I'm so close to her.

Nik's body completely surrenders to mine in the bed as I press my body firmly into her, feeling the softness of her curves against my hard, muscular body. I refuse to believe this desire is purely sexual. It has to be a part of my blood lust – what I'm known for. Because I know I'm not like my brothers.

She's quiet for nearly a minute. "How do you know I skipped my classes?"

Her silence wasn't just out of terror. She's thinking. What a lovely little mind she has. Nik's a creative, which is more than Six or anyone else from my world can say. We play our roles. We do our part within our family's organization. But we don't make art. Not *real* art. Not like what Onika makes.

I press my nose into her neck and feel her squirm nervously as I do so and answer her question earnestly.

"I told you on the cliffs that you were mine. That means every part of you belongs to me entirely. That means you don't take a step without me knowing about it."

"No," she says fiercely. "That's not possible. You don't even know me. You *can't*."

"That doesn't matter," I murmur, running my tongue over her neck. "I didn't come here to talk, anyway. I came here to touch you. I came here to finish what we started."

"What about my roommate?" she says, stifling a gasp as I slide my fingers inside her panties and crudely explore her lower lips. My dick feels like it's going to burst.

"When is she coming back?"

"I don't know."

"Then you'll have to cum quickly…"

She squeals as I hike her thick thighs up and scramble beneath her blankets and between her legs. Nik sleeps in an oversized t-shirt, a comfortable wire-free white bra and pink panties completely swallowed by her ample ass cheeks. I've watched her get ready for bed through her window (and once, her webcam) enough times to know without removing her shirt.

Once I have her thighs over my shoulders and I can get completely drunk off the scent of Nik's musk, I have a brief moment of hesitation.

I shouldn't do this. Getting between her legs pushes the boundaries of my vows. I can't justify eating her pussy as an act to break her. If I put my tongue between her legs and make her cum, I'll have to punish her even harder than I initially intended. My breath quickens as my desire for Nik swells to an impossible heat.

Without thinking, I rip her panties to the side. She yelps, but then quickly quiets herself, instead making soft whimpering noises somewhere on the spectrum between pleasure and terror. I can smell her cunt from this position and as I rip her panties away from Onika's voluptuous thighs, wetness from her underwear dribbles all over my fingers.

She's soaked through her panties completely and I haven't even put my tongue in her cunt yet. Her protests and whimpers conceal the heat and desire emanating from between her legs. She confessed that night on the cliffs that she was a virgin but now that my face is inches away from her cunt, it's almost like I can smell that she's completely untouched.

I want to claim her.

I need to claim her.

Chapter Six
Onika

The intruder slides his tongue between my legs, using his mysterious tongue to urgently spread my lower lips apart and directly stimulate my clit. I don't want to squeal in pleasure, but I can't help it. There's never been *anything* down there and nothing I read about in books could have prepared me for the immediate burst of pleasure.

He licks my lower lips and then sucks on my clit, forcing me to moan again. Then he starts teasing me with a rhythm and I lose control. With no boyfriend in my past or present and no potential guys in my foreseeable future, I had no expectations of what a man's tongue between my legs might feel like. It's heaven. His tongue is pure fucking heaven.

A part of me feels dirty for not pushing the stranger away. But what's the point? I can tell from his voice that he's the same guy who put his dick in my mouth. At least this time, I feel euphoric. He slides his tongue over the most sensitive parts of my pussy until I feel an incredible tightening between my legs, like something big is about to happen.

I moan again and try to squirm away from him. It feels too good. Too intense. I don't know what's going to happen, but I can't breathe.

Chapter Six

My head is light and out of my control completely. He controls me. The stranger. I moan out loud again and he focuses more attention than before on my clit. I'm so weak. I should fight him. Instead, I gasp, "Please…"

It sounds like I'm begging for more. He pushes one finger against my entrance. I can feel him working his way in. Terror surges through me. But then his tongue rolls over my clit again as his finger enters me and the terror vanishes in an instant, replaced by a euphoric explosion that knocks the sense out of me.

"YES!" I cry out, begging a man who climbed through my window to continue his ministrations between my thighs. I'm crying out for him now. Wanting him. Craving him. He doesn't stop licking my pussy and his finger begins moving gently in and out of my entrance. I need to feel that explosion again. I want it. There's nothing I can do to stop him, so I tell myself that I have to surrender to him.

He owns me.

"Please…" I whimper again, but instead of using his tongue and finger to fuck me to the orgasm I just begged for, he pulls both away and disappointment crashes into me like a tidal wave. A defeated moan escapes my lips followed by a shiver of hope as he kisses my inner thigh.

"You came a lot," he announces, kissing my thigh again. I moan softly, begging him for his tongue again without words. He can't leave me like this. It's bad enough he fucked my mouth on the edge of the cliffs and then left me there. He can't give me one and a half orgasms, leaving me on edge and yearning.

"More…"

He smacks my inner thigh so hard that I yelp. Why? I don't question it. I just shudder and wait for him to tell me what I did wrong.

"Not yet," he says sternly. "Don't be greedy."

I don't feel greedy. It's simply not fair for him to show me that much pleasure and then take it away. He had his finger in my pussy. Surely he can't leave me hanging after that. I feel empty. Needy. I don't feel like a virgin anymore, even if technically I still am.

"If you want another orgasm, you need to get your shit together," he says. "No more skipping classes. No more running away from Six and Maura."

My breath catches. It's really him. The figure on the cliffs. My body tightens from the memory of his large cock thrusting urgently into my mouth. He grunted like a beast with each thrust into my tight orifice. He took sick pleasure in owning me. He said things that made me feel terrified and drawn to him at the same time.

He must go to this school.

"Why do you even care?"

"Because you're mine and I have a purpose for you."

Does he mean fucking my mouth with his cock? Or fucking my pussy with his tongue? I shudder in fear. I don't know if I want this. There's a part of me that wonders if I can handle more of him. I don't even know who he is.

"W-what purpose?" I ask him, searching for clues as I beg my eyes to adjust to the darkness. I have terrible vision at night.

"I want us to kill together," he says. "But you're not ready, Nik. I need you to be stronger."

The way he says my name sends a jolt of pleasure straight to my pussy. I feel fucked up and wrong for my body's response, but it's out of my control. The rest of his statement fills me with dread. It's like he's giving an explanation that doesn't explain anything at all.

Why would anyone want *me* to kill? I'm nobody.

"That doesn't make any sense."

"You're a writer, aren't you?" he says. "I've read your work. It's good, but it could be better. You write about blood and violence, you toy with it in video games, but you have no real experience with it. I want to change that."

How does he know that I play video games? No one on this campus except my roommate knows that. Everything he says only brings me more questions than answers. It's like he wants me to figure out who he is on my own. But how the fuck can I do that?

"Are you in my psychology class?" I say, hazarding a guess. He moves his hips forward and I can feel the big cock in his pants rubbing against my thigh. He's so hard. A gush pools between my thighs and I shift my body against his, almost forgetting that I should be fighting him.

That he's a maniac. And even the craziest creative trapped in the back of my mind shouldn't let a sick freak like this get in my head.

Even if he's a good kisser.

Even if he just made my pussy gush.

EVEN IF HE'S read my writing. And for some reason, he wants to encourage my fascination with the macabre. But he doesn't get it. What I write is just fiction. I'm a boring, regular, plus-sized college student. My plan is to learn about better fiction from college classes, not by turning my life into a real life horror movie.

"No," he says. "You'll know who I am when I'm ready. For now, you listen to my every word or I will find you and punish you for disobedience."

"What kind of punishment?"

His voice suddenly sounds dark and terrifying. "You don't want to find out."

"Okay. Fine."

I don't know if I'll listen to him yet, but I know I'll at least have to pretend.

"You change your relationship status to *taken* on social media the second I leave this room. I'll contact you and give you instructions. You are no longer to skip classes or avoid living your life as a normal college student. If anyone messes with you, I'll handle them."

"I can't be in a relationship with someone I don't even know."

"This is not a relationship, Nik. It's something deeper than that. *Much* deeper than that," he says seriously.

He kisses his way back up my thighs and then kisses me on the mouth, forcing me to taste myself. The taste makes me feel light-headed again. He runs his tongue over my lips, licking me off myself. There's nothing he won't do. No impulse he won't follow. With his cock still pressed against my thigh, I'm incredibly nervous, despite my traitorous body gushing with his every movement.

"I wish I knew who you were."

"If you prove that you can obey me, I'll tell you. But right now, it'll be more trouble for both of us if you know. Just trust me, Nik."

"How can I?"

"Because I made you cum and even if my cock is about to burst, I'm not going to fuck your virgin cunt until you stain your sheets. You're welcome."

I shudder at his idea of kindness.

"You're Irish, aren't you? That's why you don't want me to know. Because I'm... black."

Technically, I'm mixed race – Chinese and black – but most people don't care about the Chinese side of my family because my appearance doesn't make it obvious. I got my mother's eye shape, but not much else. I still have dark, coppery-red skin and I guess my hair isn't as kinky as Kalani's, but it's definitely not straight either.

He takes too long to answer, which tells me that I'm right.

"It doesn't matter," he says. "Promise you'll obey."

I hesitate.

"Promise," he snarls. "Or you will regret it."

His hand slides up around my neck. He doesn't squeeze, but the threat is implicit. I agree to his demands, or he hurts me. I just wish the fucked up things he was doing to me didn't turn me on. I squirm beneath him, hoping to appear resistant. Hoping to give him what he wants.

"I PROMISE," I whisper reluctantly.

"Good," he says, running his tongue over my cheek possessively. "The next time I come back for you, that pussy will be ready for my cunt."

As he climbs out of bed, I'm frozen. Technically, I could grab my phone. I could call someone. I could scream. But I don't. His large, dark form walks calmly towards my window and he jumps out, closing it behind him almost respectfully. I'm gasping for breath, half-panicked and half-exhilarated.

Chapter Six

.   .   .

Your owner: Update your relationship status. Now.

I DON'T WANT him coming back. Now that he's gone, I can recognize how fucking crazy my body's reaction to him has been. What the hell is wrong with me? The buzzing from my phone instigates me into action. I update my status across every social media platform.

Taken.

Your owner: Thank you.
Your owner: Get some sleep, Nik.

I DON'T BOTHER to text back. His message was clear – he wants me asleep. And I don't want to be awake a moment longer. Maybe if I close my eyes, when I wake up, this will all be a dream.

Chapter Seven
Odhran

Her pussy was begging for me. I could smell her desire in her sticky juices and smeared all over her inner thighs. I'd never tasted pussy before that night. I didn't know a woman could get so fucking wet. Six hated sex that wasn't rough and violent. She didn't have the patience for my tongue between her thighs.

Thinking about what I used to have no longer interests me. My mind is singularly fixated on a woman I should have never touched to begin with. I'm in big trouble now. Aiden and my brothers are driving over to my apartment, which means I have to clean up, pull my books out and pretend that I've been living on the straight and narrow the past week instead of neglecting my classes and keeping Nik under close observation. I also need to feed Killer Bee a frozen squirrel from the freezer. *Fuck, there's too much going on.*

They would never understand what I'm going through. None of them work the way I do. They're not obsessive. They don't have my dark instincts. I don't know if it's just because they're older, but they've always felt more responsible than I could ever be.

When my doorbell ring from the apartment's guest entrance, which is down a hallway from the private elevator which opens into the living room, it couldn't be anyone else. Six has English class right now with Nik, which doesn't exactly bring me lots of comfort. She's avoided Onika for the past week, but that's only because her outrage with me has kept her completely occupied. And apparently, she has also involved my brothers in our breakup. That's probably my mother's fault. I can't imagine my brothers intervening in my love life without her involvement.

I walk to the door wearing white socks with a black Nike logo on the ankle, black Bruins joggers, a white t-shirt, silver chain and an oversized black hoodie. I keep the hoodie up to obscure my roots, growing in an annoyingly pale color compared to the black dye I prefer. I look more Irish with pale skin and dark hair – at least I think so.

My eldest brother doesn't wait one second after I open the door before he begins berating me.

"You ended a nearly decade long engagement over text message, Odhran. Have you lost your fucking mind? The Cunningham family wants fucking blood over this. *Blood.* These people are not rational."

To my great annoyance, Aiden doesn't arrive to chastise me about my love life alone. Rian walks into my apartment behind him, glancing around in surprise because he's never been here.

"What is he doing here?" I grumble, giving Rian a dirty look, which he ignores.

"It's clean in here," Rian says, giving me a sarcastic and condescending smile. "I'm surprised."

"Focus, Rian," Aiden snaps before quickly turning his attention back to me. "What the fuck were you thinking, Odhran? I want fucking answers."

Aiden's tendency to overreact and fly off the handle for every little thing used to entertain me when I was younger. Before I grew old enough to become the target of his ridiculous temper. I run my tongue over my lips, trying to come up with something that will cool the temperature of the room.

"I'm tired of her. I don't love her. I don't want to get married.

Look, isn't breaking up with her better than drugging her every night so I can get some alone time?"

My brothers look at me like I have two heads. Haven't they ever drugged their girlfriend's for some peace and quiet? Perhaps it's a generational thing. Aiden has always struck me as very old fashioned, aside from having a black wife.

"You have problems," Aiden grunts in frustration. "Not just psychological problems. I'm not fucking playing around, Odhran. These people want blood."

My brows pinch together as I consider how much to confess to my brothers. I doubt Aiden would approve of me stalking a fellow student or plotting to turn a good girl into a killer.

"Then they can have it. I wasn't going to let Six hurt an innocent person."

"Explain that statement," Rian interjects before Aiden can express the same sentiment more harshly.

"This is personal," I grumble. "I'd rather not get into it."

There's no logical explanation for my fixation with Onika. All I know is that my duty to Six feels like an anchor. It's not something that I want around my neck anymore. The strange sensations I have when I think about Onika overpower me. The incident on the cliffs only made it worse. *I want Six gone.*

My brothers stare at me like I have two heads. I'll admit that my fixation with Nik has escalated out of control, but it's nothing that my brothers haven't done. They left our family vows behind. I'm not saying I'm going to marry Nik. I don't plan on marrying anyone. I just want this stupid obligation gone. I don't want to be with Six anymore.

"Have you lost your mind?" Aiden asks. "This isn't like you, Odhran. You love Six. You have been joined at the hip since you were in middle school. What happened?"

"I haven't lost my mind," I tell Aiden, careful to hide my frustration. My brothers all overreact to my negative emotions, like I'm going to snap and kill someone for no reason. I've always had a reason for killing, just like them. I hate that they don't trust me and I don't even know if there's a point in telling the truth.

Chapter Seven

"Then explain yourself," Aiden says. He seems almost kind, making me want to open up. "If you wanted to end your engagement, you should have come to me. I understand what you've done, but you've also created an enormous fucking problem."

"She hurt someone."

"We've all hurt people," Rian says, doing a horrible job of hiding his frustration with me.

"I mean… what she did was a hate crime. An Irish mob ritual. And the girl they hurt is… a friend of mine."

"You don't have any female friends," Rian says. I can't blame him. Six isn't exactly the sort who encouraged it, so he has a point. I don't know how else to describe Nik without my brothers probing too deeply into my personal life. I want to protect her from them almost as much as I want to protect her from my ex-girlfriend.

"Since when do you care about hate crimes?" Aiden asks. He sounds solemn and pensive, and it occurs to me that he doesn't think I'm telling the truth. He thinks I'm making up a story to appeal to them and to get out of marrying Six.

"It doesn't matter. You can ask her what happened, or better yet ask her friend Maura. I don't want to be with her anymore and I don't see why you two should push me to stay engaged to a racist."

"Aren't you racist?" Rian asks. "Does it really matter? You're creating problems, Odhran. If Aiden won't say it, I will. I don't buy your story."

I wiped the videos of their torture off Nik's phone, but not before sending them to mine. There's a part of me hesitant about showing my brothers the evidence. I still want to protect Nik.

"I have proof."

"Then show me," Aiden says, standing supportively next to Rian. They would scare me more if I wasn't telling the truth. I hand my cell phone to my brothers and let them watch Nik's torture. Hearing their voices and her screams that night tugs at my heart-strings. I try not to show them how much hearing her in pain affects me.

When I'm done with her, she won't ever feel that much pain again.

Odhran

. . .

MY BROTHERS APPEAR SUFFICIENTLY CONVINCED by the video evidence. Rian suggests showing it to Six's father, but Aiden points out that he would most likely support his daughter's activities.

Maybe he even pushed Six to do something like this knowing it would get back to Aiden eventually. Not every mob family agrees with the diverse array of wives my brothers have married. Aiden, the boss of the mob, married a very dark-skinned woman he rescued from traffickers. Rian married his plus-sized African American nanny. Callum and Darragh both married their best friend's black younger sisters.

As the youngest brother, I haven't been in the habit of speaking up often, but now seems like the right time. I'm not a little boy anymore.

"Maybe her family pushed her to do it," I suggest. "It's no secret what our families have believed for generations. Perhaps one spouse the other families might have ignored, but not four."

Both my brothers consider my idea seriously. I feel better. I'm used to being the shithead kid getting in trouble, not earning respect.

"I'll talk to her father. But you should have come to me."

"That's it? I'm off the hook?"

"No," Rian snaps. "Six is furious with how you've ended it. Callum and Darragh are holding her brothers at bay by keeping them busy with extra work at the casino and the new nightclub."

"I can't make it better."

"You have to," Aiden says. "Find a way to make it better."

I do have one idea, but it's not one that Aiden would approve of.

"Yes, Aiden."

Reluctantly, Aiden purses his lips and responds. "You did the right thing. Is that girl really your friend?"

Lie. "Yes."

"Then you had better keep her close," Rian says. "From everything we've heard, Six doesn't know you were the one who stopped her that night. I'd keep it to myself if I were you. That girl already has a target on her back."

"I'll take your advice."

52

My brothers don't stick around my apartment much longer. Rian gives me advice about how to work out with my injury, but without football, I haven't been in the mood for much more than calisthenics and video games. I should have been playing college football this semester and I'm friends with most of the team, but family business came first and I got shot. I'm well enough to work out but my varsity football days are over.

Once my brothers leave, I log on, anxiously waiting for Nik to come online. She's normally online at this time. Next to her icon, the line of text reads, "Last seen 14 hours ago."

Where has she been?

I TEXT HER URGENTLY.

Me: Where are you?
My Pet: My room.
Me: Your bed?

I KNOW I'm fucked up, but just imagining her in that bed again gets me instantly hard. But she doesn't reply instantly. One minute. Two minutes.

My Pet: Yes.

I IMAGINE her holding her phone up, breathless, waiting for my response. Fearing me, but curious all the same. She gets so wet when I hold her. Tasting her made her cum so hard. *It's just not safe for either of us right now…*

Odhran

· · ·

Me: I want a picture of you.

THREE MINUTES. Five minutes. My frustration builds as my erection grows. I want to see her.

My Pet: You first.
Me: Clever. Send a picture in your underwear.
Me: Now.

IT TURNS me on that she pushes back against my commands. Everything about her turns me on. I glance from my phone screen to my computer screen. She's online. *Oh fuck no.*

Me: Nik.
My Pet: Be patient.
Me: No. I would rather not be patient.
My Pet: Fine.

SHE DOESN'T PUT up as much resistance as I expect. Several minutes later, she sends a picture, without her face, of the softest, prettiest body I've ever seen. I love her curves. Soft orange light bathes Nik's cinnamon skin. I want to touch her. Smell her skin. Make love to her.

Chapter Seven

Me: Gorgeous. Fucking gorgeous. Now touch yourself.

Chapter Eight
Onika

Ever since he started texting me, my life has been a blur. I keep my head down and strategically work to avoid Six and Maura, which has been much easier than I expected since I don't want to go out in public much anymore. It's not like my room necessarily feels safer. He could break in at any moment. My nameless, faceless, terrifying rescuer slash stalker.

Trying to figure out what I feel for him has been part of the blur. The only thing that makes sense anymore is writing, so when I'm not in class or playing video games, or having Chinese food delivered, I just write. When I'm out there in the world, I feel so confused and numb about everything happening. Sitting down to write is different.

I connect to the parts of myself I want to hide from when I'm writing. It's terrifying and exhilarating at the same time. *Just like the stranger.*

It takes me an entire week to recover from our first sexting escapade which happened after he texted me. *Now touch yourself.* I didn't know what to do at first.

Touching myself and experiencing that kind of pleasure didn't come naturally to me, but his commands were firm. Insistent. And as always, I find myself obeying him even when I don't want to.

Chapter Eight

· · ·

Your owner: Record yourself moaning as you cum.

57

I DON'T EVEN KNOW his name. He could be anyone. All I know is that he isn't associated with Six or Maura. He couldn't be, or he wouldn't have saved my life. It's getting harder to get through the day without knowing who he is.

So I plot a way to expose his identity. I know he's deeply controlling and beyond confident in himself. But I also know he's deeply protective of me, even if I don't know why. If I can keep him sure that he has a tight hold on me, I can get what I want – the truth.

For one week, I submit to the stranger's demands. He tells me what to wear to class, what to eat, how much coffee to drink, and if I didn't know better, I would say he was keeping very close watch on me. If I even dare skirt the truth, he knows. But there's never anyone around who I suspect. All the guys at this college are normal Boston kids with Irish heritage. No one seems different. *I'm the only one fucked up in the head over what happened.*

The kids around me are all the same even if my world seems completely fucked up. They keep to themselves and go out of their way to ignore my existence for the most part. My acquaintances and those sorta-friends you have in college don't notice anything wrong with me. But I'm a complete mess. Emotional. Obsessed with writing. Hooked on the mystery of the man who saved my life. And hurt me.

I send him pictures in my underwear every night and wait for my roommate to sneak out to be with the new guy she's hooking up with. She never gives me any details about who he is, but she leaves me alone every night now. The first couple nights, I was worried someone would break in again. But now that I've gained confidence being on my own, I push my so-called owner a little further. I do something different and out of the blue. I text him first – at 10:30 p.m. – half an hour after my roommate leaves for the night.

Onika

. . .

Me: I'm alone in my room and scared.
Your owner: Doors and windows locked?
Me: Yes.

I WANT TO TYPE *obviously,* but I don't want him to be suspicious.

Your owner: Unlock your window.
Me: That'll help.
Your owner: 10 minutes

MORE INFORMATION. Wherever he is, he's not more than ten minutes away. Is that a coincidence? Does he live ten minutes away from me, or does he just watch me that closely? I walk to my window and unlock it.

THEN, I set my booby trap.

My heart races. I can't believe this is probably going to work, especially if I keep the lights off. I have to move quickly. I take the baby oil off my dresser and pour it on the floor at the base of the window, coating the hardwood floors in a thick layer with it.

I borrow my roommate's decorated paddle from her initiation with just her name on it and some designs in light pink and white, her sorority colors. It's the best weapon I can find and I just need to hit him in the back of the head.

This can't be that much different from what it's like in video games...

I crouch between my dresser and my bed, waiting for the mysterious stranger to come. I don't know if he will, if he's messing with me, or if he suspects me and he's coming back armed or with some way to punish me. My booby trap isn't exactly Albert Einstein levels of genius, but it'll surprise him and hopefully that will work. If he doesn't trip on his own, my roommate's paddle should help do the rest of the job.

Ten minutes takes a painfully long time to pass, but then I hear footsteps. It's strange, but I recognize them. Having never seen his face, I have several other ways to identify him. How he breathes. How he moves. His voice. I tighten my body between the bed and the dresser, waiting for him to slide my window open.

He opens the window and I watch his arms flex through his black hoodie as he hoists his body over the window sill. His feet land on the ground and then his balance gives way. He yells out a series of loud expletives as my trap works and he falls precariously to the ground. I leap out of my position behind the dresser and as he attempts to scramble to his feet, I hit the man who climbed through my window in the back of the head. He makes a loud grunting noise and then he lies there in the baby oil completely limp.

I need to make sure the man lying on the ground isn't awake before I tie him up so he can't escape. My body shakes as I approach his body to check the man's pulse and make sure that he stays unconscious until I'm ready. It's still too dark for me to see his face. It looks like he has a mask on or something. My heart pounds so loudly I can hear blood rushing past my ears. The adrenaline rush in real life is much more intense than in my fiction.

I have to cross the room to my desk to get to a lamp, so I don't want to bother with that until the intruder is completely tied up. I don't want him waking up and getting revenge while I'm fumbling for the switch. At least I know the stranger is unconscious even if I don't know who he is, so I work with that first. *He's huge.*

I drag him out of the oil, or at least try to. It doesn't really work. The oil gets everything sticky and the man lying on my floor must be at least 6'5" tall. I still have to tie him up before I get the lights on. I take the rope from my bathrobe as well as the one from my roommate's and fix his wrists to the frame of my standard issue freshman dorm Twin XL bed.

Tying him up in the dark takes a little effort, but my eyes adjust to the light a little better and I can make out slightly more of his features. He has a nice face shape, beneath the mask. Not like that matters. He's a psychopath. He might have saved my life, but he's kept me on edge ever since then and I can't wait any longer for the truth.

I yank on his arms once and then twice to make sure he's secure. I can't believe he doesn't wake up. I must have hit him pretty hard, but I didn't feel any blood on the back of his head, just baby oil soaking through his ski mask.

My anxiety is through the roof as I walk over and turn my light on. I almost don't want to turn around as if the man who climbed through my window could suddenly break free and turn into a horned demon. He's always had the upper hand. Now it's my turn.

When I turn around, he's still slumped over how I left him with his arms outstretched almost painfully. If I don't wake him up eventually, a cramp in his arm probably will. He's breathtaking, even sprawled out on the ground with his face and hair completely covered.

The man has a solid, muscular body apparent beneath his black joggers and matching black hoodie. I prefer wearing white and red clothing, since I already have jet black hair, but he clearly has an obsession. I shove his shoulders again to see if he'll wake up, as if I'm looking for some excuse to back out of raising his ski mask.

Thankfully, he doesn't wake up. I still don't have any clues. Slowly, my fingers reach beneath the mask and make contact with his skin. As I move the fabric away, I can smell his sweat and feel scratchy stubble.

His scent makes my stomach flip as my body reacts to the powerful memories of this strange man's muscular body on top of mine. I pull the mask away, but I still don't recognize him as I reveal more of his face. It's only when I take it off completely, and push the black hair away from his face with my hands that I identify him.

I've only seen him a couple of times in person, which is why I don't recognize him at first. And I'm surprised. Obviously.

Chapter Eight

. . .

"ODHRAN..." I whisper.

THIS CAN'T BE POSSIBLE. He doesn't even know who I am. I don't want to believe this is possible and I can't wrap my head around it. He's not in any of my classes even if he's a freshman. He doesn't live on campus – our school is small enough that it's easy to tell who lives on campus and who doesn't, but that isn't common for freshmen. He must be super rich since housing around here is expensive. Most students wait until at least their junior year to move off campus.

I thought learning the identity of my rescuer would make things better, but now I'm sick to my stomach. He's a member of a powerful Irish mob family. And I just hit him over the fucking head with a sorority paddle.

When he wakes up, he could hurt me. For all I know, he has back up. For all I know... he has a gun. In a panic, I reach for the sides of his joggers and pat him down. With my heart beating so quickly and my panicked search proceeding furiously, I don't notice that he wakes up until he says in a booming, terrifying voice, "Are you searching for my cock?"

I shriek and jump backwards, stepping right into the puddle of baby oil and flying into the air. I'm sure I didn't *fly* exactly, since my ass and head land painfully on the hardwood floor with a thud. I'm typically an uncoordinated mess, but my body couldn't have chosen a worse time to give way.

I yell again and search for something to grab hold of, finding only a floor full of baby oil while the man tied to my bed stares at me without making a sound, as if I'm the animal in the trap, not him. Maybe he's just eerily calm like that. Always in control.

Grunting, and struggling to maintain anything close to dignity, I slide myself across the floor, keeping a safe distance away from him and create some tracks of baby oil as I pull myself to my feet using my roommate Rylee's bed. He doesn't stop staring at me, which makes me feel like I'm not in control.

Of course I'm in control. He's the one tied up. I'm here and I'm sure that my roommate won't be coming back, and it doesn't matter if he's staring at me with intense, creepy blue eyes.

"That was graceful," he says, the hint of a smile curling at the corner of his lips. I don't find it funny.

"You have a girlfriend."

"No," he says in a voice that's quiet, but not whispering, like he's forcing me to listen closer, somehow commanding my attention with quiet power. "I don't."

He shifts his weight a little and I'm nervous he'll break free, but he doesn't even try. I stare at him like I would if I'd tied up a panther or a snow leopard. Odhran doesn't seem scared, but I am. My hands are sweaty. I don't know who I expected, but I didn't expect the girl who picks on me to have her boyfriend...

"Is this some kind of sick game?" I snap at him. "Did you tell her to hurt me? I don't understand. Why. Are. You. Here?"

He slowly tilts his head to the side, his black hair with two-inch blond roots falling over his eyes. They're such a gorgeous shade of blue – not a dark cobalt, but a pale blue, so light it's almost clear. They're icy and highlighted more because Odhran's skin is so freaking pale. Even if this isn't the first time I've seen him, this is the first time I've seen him this close.

He's sexy for a monster.

"I saved your life. I *was* protecting you. But now that you've done this, my job will be a lot more difficult. Congratulations on getting me to fall for your little trick. I promise not to underestimate you in the future," Odhran says. His muscles bulge out of his joggers as he moves his long legs again.

I take a step closer to him, skirting around the mess of baby oil, hoping that it makes me seem like I'm less afraid of him.

"Don't expect me to thank you," I reply. "And that's still not an explanation. Nobody knew I was at the cliffs. Nobody *knows* how much Six and Maura hate me. Unless she told you... Unless this is part of your secret plan to gain my trust and... I don't know!"

I know I'm babbling and rambling probably makes me sound insecure and silly, but at least I have him tied up and even if I'm a mess, once I calm the hell down, I *will* find out what the fuck is happening

He must have deleted the videos they posted to my account, because after the stranger handed my phone back on the cliffs, the videos were gone. I was in too much shock to properly realize it until I got home and didn't wake up to an embarrassing nightmare unfolding on social media. *Your owner.*

"Since you already went to such great lengths to get to the truth, I'll tell you. Although I thought you enjoyed your games."

He smiles for real this time and his smile is just wicked. But hot. So fucking hot. Odhran's sharp, masculine features are softened by his smile and he has a dimple in his right cheek. I try to ignore the fluttering in my chest when he smiles at me, especially because *he's crazy.*

"You think I enjoyed having you violate me on the cliffs and in my bed?"

"You came every time except at the cliffs," he said. "It was hot. Very hot."

Every inch of my skin warms instantly. My mouth feels frozen. I don't know what to say to a comment like that. I'm not one of those women born with innate seductive skills. I'm just a slightly more fashionable version of who I was in high school – the awkward, chubby, overlooked dork.

There's a lump in my throat as Odhran keeps burning into me with his intense gaze. Doesn't he get tired of staring?

"That's not the point," I stammer weakly. He makes me feel utterly exposed, even if he's let me do most of the talking. And the pacing. And the panicking. It worries me more that he's so calm and certain of himself.

"What is the point, then? If you like a girl, you want her to feel good."

"You don't like me. We're strangers."

He chuckles, and that laugh sends an unwilling gush straight between my thighs. Thank goodness he's not *actually* in my head, because if Odhran could tell how my body responded to these small details about him, he would probably only use it to his advantage.

"We are not strangers."

"I don't know anything about you."

"Yet you confidently asserted my relationship status a moment ago, even if I made it abundantly clear where I stand with you."

My throat tightens. Okay. Be calm, Nik. Yes, a 6'5", unreasonably attractive man just climbed through my window and now he's announcing we've already gone further than I've ever gone with a man. It's terrifying. I don't even know why I'm still standing here instead of just running away from him. He doesn't seem to think anything he did was wrong.

"Shoving your dick in my mouth isn't the foundation of a healthy relationship."

"I also put my tongue in your pussy and ate you out so well you had the best night of sleep you've had in weeks."

"I still don't understand. You *can't* know me."

"But I do. Your favorite colors are white and red. Your favorite flowers are roses. Your favorite video game is Call of Duty, and you've played over seven hundred hours. You're a writer – probably the best at this school. And you're... strangely attractive."

"How do you know that stuff? We've never had a conversation."

He continues, "You were born at Mass General, you're a Taurus sun with a Taurus rising, born on May 7th. Your father is black, and your mother is Chinese. You graduated from a small private Catholic school called Saint Hubert's Academy as the salutatorian, missing valedictorian by 0.5% percentage points thanks to a math test. But it was just luck that you were *here*. At my school. In my ex-girlfriend's class."

There's no point in denying anything he said. It's all true. But he still doesn't explain how he knows all this information.

"You sound like a stalker."

"More like a researcher. I have nothing to hide from you anymore, Nik. Untie me so we can talk. It's urgent."

Chapter Eight

He is definitely trying to trick me. What the hell could be "urgent" about me needing to untie him? He came here because I tricked him, not because of anything urgent going on. Odhran will have to be a lot more clever if he wants me to let him loose in my room.

He's crazy, Nik. Don't let him play you.

"Are you crazy? I'm not untying you and there is nothing urgent about this situation."

"You will," Odhran says confidently. "Your roommate will return eventually, which makes this urgent, and you can't exactly stuff me underneath your bed. I've tried hiding there before and I can't fit underneath there with all your winter clothes. Plus, I don't want to hurt you. If I wanted to hurt you, I could have done it before."

Chapter Nine
Odhran

Nik exceeds my expectations and impresses me with her wit, even if she has me tied to the bed and currently uncertain of whether I'll extract her obedience easily. She considers me with the utmost suspicion, refusing to take more than her obligatory step closer to prove that she doesn't fear me. Nik is clever. I've always known she was clever, but I assumed she would focus most of her cleverness on writing since our first encounter on the cliffs.

She's been far busier than I could have anticipated, but judging by the expression on her face, I have a bit of work ahead of me before I convince her to untie me.

"I'm *not* untying you," she repeats.

"I want to help you. I've helped you before. My ex-girlfriend hasn't bothered you in weeks."

I haven't let go of the idea that Six might be plotting something else. I hope if she is, my brothers uncover it soon, but if they don't, as soon as I get out of here (and punish Nik for this extreme reaction) I plan on keeping a much closer eye on Six. I won't have to bother going through so much trouble to hide my identity anymore.

"That's just pure luck. Or maybe she's afraid because you're a psychopath."

"I would love to believe that Six fears me. But she doesn't. And neither should you. Now *untie me.*"

"Yelling at me won't make me more likely to untie you."

"What will make you more likely to then?" I grumble, giving Nik a cruel look. "Because you're being unreasonable."

Does she really expect me to believe that she went through all this dressed like *that* because she hates me? She knew I was coming. She could have worn anything. But she wears the sexiest nightdress in her closet – I've broken into her room before to rummage during one of her classes. One that exposes her thighs. I shouldn't stare at her chubby thighs and immediately imagine running my tongue along the insides. I want to push my tongue between her legs again to taste her pussy. She's wasting time. Once I get her punishment out of the way, we can get to more important things. Like tasting her pussy.

She doesn't realize how much she makes me think of sex. How she burns inside of me. How it hurts to be away from her, to not know exactly what she's doing. I threw my whole life away for her. I still don't regret it and I haven't even made love to her yet.

"How is this unreasonable? You have been *controlling and stalking me* and you won't even explain why," she says. "I've sent you nudes. You have a girlfriend and I sent you *nudes.*"

"I told you that I don't have a girlfriend," I repeat. "I also told you that I'll explain myself if you untie me."

"Why are you doing this?"

"This is getting annoying," I mutter.

"I don't believe you," she says, at last addressing her emotional state. She doesn't trust me. That'll have to change. I haven't done anything to deserve a lack of trust. I haven't hurt her. Every time I've touched her, I've made her feel good.

"I swear on my ancestors," I promise Nik, giving her a deep, intense look. Slowly, she's getting more calm as she adjusts to her discovery.

"Pardon me if that means nothing to me," Nik says.

"It means everything to me," I say to her sharply. "And I promise you, Nik. I haven't done any of this to hurt you. I thought if you knew who I was, it would make things worse. This would have been *much* easier if you hadn't somehow attracted Six's attention. That was your fault."

"You are unbelievably egotistical," she hisses, rolling her eyes and crossing her arms, unintentionally pushing her breasts together. I try not to get distracted, but it's almost impossible to think straight around her. Especially with her thighs exposed. I don't want to admit that my feelings for her have become more than a strange, dark obsession.

I need sex. I've never realized what I crave before her.

"I care about you, Nik. And you're smart enough to know that I'm right. I could have hurt you if I wanted to. I don't want to hurt you. I thought you were scared and I came here to save you from whatever might be scaring you. I would have killed anyone who tried to hurt you. Six and Maura barely escaped with their lives. I... Untie me and I *swear*, I will help you."

"If you mean sex stuff, that's not the type of help I need."

Judging by her completely agitated state, I'd say Nik definitely needs "sex stuff", but I'm willing to postpone my raging desires if it will calm her down long enough to untie me.

"I understand."

I try to calm her down with a gentle look. She takes a step closer to me. *It's working.* I can't reveal to her at all that I intend to punish her, so I try not to act too excited as Nik approaches me. When she gets close enough that I can smell her, I close my eyes and try to lose myself in her scent. *She's perfect.*

Without much drama or fuss, she unties me and my hands slump to my sides. My shoulders are sore from the uncomfortable position and even if I have every intention of punishing Nik for this little scheme, I plan on both of us feeling a lot better first. I rub my wrists and give her a smile that I hope will put her at ease.

"How did you get so good at knots?" I ask her.

"You can learn anything on YouTube," she says quickly before taking a few steps back. I don't bother moving and not just because I don't want to contend with the sea of baby oil that wiped me out in the first place.

"I'm impressed."

"I don't do anything to impress you."

"Right," I say, rubbing my wrists.

She keeps staring at me.

"Why are you here?" she asks, wrinkling her nose. "If you just want to torture me, Six already did that."

"I'm here for personal reasons."

"What kind of personal reasons? We don't know each other."

She sounds suspicious, which I guess I can expect. Maybe if I explain myself more clearly, she'll understand.

"I found you through video games."

There isn't much of a point in hiding anymore.

I would have preferred to lurk in the darkness for much longer, but maybe this was meant to happen. She seems very confused, though, which is strange because I thought I was being clear.

"Video games?" Nik asks.

"I found you online. It's a coincidence that you go here. To my college. I… found you here by accident. Your connection to Six is… a nightmare."

But it's a nightmare I'll thoroughly enjoy. School is too easy. I don't have football anymore. Why not make it more entertaining?

"I'm not connected to her. She's the one who wants to kill me. I wouldn't have even gone to class if you didn't make me."

"Your education matters. You can't let Six ruin it."

"You were there when she tried to kill me," Nik says with an accusatory tone, as if I went through all the trouble to save her life because I don't care about her. I've gone through great lengths to protect her and I don't plan on stopping any time soon.

Just when I was losing hope, Nik pauses to consider her next statement and says out loud, "She'll probably try again."

"Yes, she will. That's what I meant when I said I wanted to help you. I think it would be easiest if we just… you know… killed her."

Odhran

Onika's eyes widen with an almost melodramatic expression and I can tell that I just said something that she finds extraordinarily taboo. Nik doesn't have particularly large eyes, they're shaped like upside down crescent moons and *dark*. But her strange appearance only adds to the taboo allure that I should never have acted upon.

But there were so many coincidences with Nik. I had to get closer. I couldn't imagine how it would hurt both of us and possibly hurt the rest of my family.

It's hard to believe that we weren't destined to have this entanglement, even if she's the wrong skin color. So wrong that I can't stop staring at it. Fantasizing about it. I can't help but admit the smallest amount of relief that I no longer have to hide myself from her and when we finally make love I can watch my pale cock disappear between delicious, cinnamon-colored folds.

I should be keeping a clear head but the momentary thought of my cock disappearing inside Nik distracts me completely. I told myself this wasn't sexual and certainly wasn't romantic, but now that I'm in her bedroom and the floral scent of baby oil encompasses the room, my thoughts are constantly interrupted by a desire for sex.

"I'm not going to kill your ex-girlfriend," she says slowly, considering me with greater caution than before.

Great. I thought she would be onboard with this. She's already realized she's in danger. Surely she realizes that Six wouldn't hesitate to kill her. That she almost *did* kill Nik.

I patiently wait for her to gather her thoughts for a couple seconds.

"Would you rather she killed you?"

"There are other ways to solve your problems aside from murder," Nik says. "If every time a writer didn't know what to do with a character, and they killed the character off, people would get annoyed pretty quickly."

"Then it's a good thing this isn't one of your creepy short stories, Nik."

She glares at me. "Right. My creepy short story has come to life and is now sitting against my bed."

"If it makes you feel any better I'd rather be in your bed with my fingers inside your cunt."

Clearly, this does not make her feel better. I wait for her face to go through several emotional changes before she stammers out, "You are nuts. And you aren't getting anywhere near me or my bed. You promised you wouldn't hurt me and…"

She doesn't bother finishing her sentence, like she fears drawing attention to my cock will only make me more eager to use it on her. Because of what happened on the cliffs and how wide I stretched her mouth and filled it with my dick, she knows that taking my cock inside her virgin pussy won't be easy.

"I said I won't hurt you and I mean it. But I still want you and more importantly, I want you safe. You have no idea what sort of people you have crossed and the trouble you caused."

Technically, I caused some of the trouble by ending my relationship with Six, but if the incident on the cliffs had never happened, I would have waited much longer to pounce on Nik.

"I haven't done anything," Nik says. "I feel like I'm caught up in some twisted game and I don't want to play it anymore."

She might not want to play anymore, but I definitely don't share the sentiment. Balancing myself carefully using her bed and my dresser, I rise to my feet and pull off my slippery shoes, carefully padding across the floor in just white Nike socks.

Nik keeps her distance and she keeps her eye on me closely. If I want to win her trust, I'll have to win it slowly. I raise my hands in surrender to her.

"I'm tired of sitting," I tell her. "I don't want to hurt you. I never *meant* to hurt you. I found your writing first. Your poems. Your essays. I fell in love with your words and that love became an obsession. Something deeper. I spent months searching for your true identity, assuming you were some Irish-American girl from Idaho or Chicago or something."

"Surprise, I'm nothing like your precious Irish girls."

I can't blame her for sounding so bitter. I don't hide from my beliefs, even if they confuse me. They are fixed. Unchanged… I think. I don't know if my obsession with Nik has changed me. I don't feel different. The only thing different about me is my desire.

I tell myself that it doesn't matter why I want her. I just do. And I'm not in the habit of abandoning any of my goals.

"I only need you to be yourself," I respond calmly. "I told you, I'm not going to hurt you and that includes not involving you in a twisted game. This isn't a game to me."

She looks like a cute but angry beaver as her face twists with frustration.

"You couldn't have found me from my video game profile. That's ridiculous."

"I got injured. I spent hours and hours on the internet. I was bored. And apparently, very lucky. You're different from other people, Nik. You have talent."

"Flattery won't get you what you want," she says, trying her best to sound tough. I love when she fights back. I love feeling her get stronger as she pushes against me, beginning to fear the consequences of inaction more than she fears my response to her.

"I don't need flattery to get what I want. I just need to take it."

She dramatically reaches for that greasy sorority paddle again. Now that she doesn't have the element of surprise, Nik will have a much harder time taking me out with a weapon that I could easily snap in half. It's difficult to be as strong as my brother Callum without committing to being a freak of nature, but being the youngest of my brothers doesn't mean I'm weak.

Nik clearly doesn't think that considering the way she's looking at me with fierce determination, as if she's working up the courage to smack the shit out of me with that paddle. To fucking destroy me. I can't say I blame her for wanting to hurt me considering her perspective on our encounters.

She'll have a change of heart soon. It's already a step in the right direction that she untied me. Deep down, Nik is a good girl. Her goodness drew me to her in the first place, especially because of the subject matter she writes about. It's gritty. Dark. Terrible.

Chapter Nine

It's a life that Nik doesn't know, but she will soon. Even if she disagrees with me now. We'll get out of this together.

"If you take one step closer to me, I'll hit your knees," she says to me, refusing to break eye contact.

She's so strong.

Chapter Ten
Onika

He raises his hands up like he isn't going to hurt me, but Odhran is out of his mind if he thinks I'll let my guard down around him permanently. I untied him because I think he'll keep his word this time, but that doesn't mean I trust him unconditionally.

"I won't take another step," he says. "But you will. And you'll let go of that silly paddle."

"I have no reason to listen to you."

"Your floor is covered in baby oil," he says. "Effective. But ridiculous. I'll help you clean it up before your roommate gets back."

"I don't need your help cleaning up. I need answers. So no."

Rage flashes across his face every time I defy him. Odhran does his best to suppress it, but I can tell he's extremely unfamiliar with the word *"no"*.

"I already gave you answers," he responds tensely. "My ex-girlfriend is trying to kill you and ending our relationship has repercussions that could very well end your life too. I *want* to protect you, but you have to let me. You have to trust me."

"And cleaning up my floor will make me trust you?"

"It'll probably help. Did your last boyfriend scrub your floors on his hands and knees?"

I can tell he's trying to catch me off guard and even if I can see his game for what it is, I feel like I'm falling for it.

"Okay," I answer him calmly. "I'll go get some soapy water from the dorm bathroom. I have washcloths in the top drawer of my dresser."

He nods and then adds. "Don't try anything stupid."

While the thought of running away from him appeals to me, or maybe going for help, I know I won't. If he wanted to hurt me, he could have done it already and now, he has my curiosity piqued. Not about the murder thing. That pathetic attempt to terrify me won't work. It's everything else about him. He seems so similar to Six and everyone from my college who completely ignores my existence.

But he's different. Sometimes.

I don't know what to make of it and I don't know what to make of Odhran. He's a stranger in pretty much every meaningful way, but there's a part of me that knows him so intimately. It scares the crap out of me, especially knowing that he belongs to my worst enemy. I can't trust that he's single until I get confirmation, and I won't be able to get that until Odhran gets something that he wants.

If he just wanted to make sure I was safe, I'm sure I'll be able to convince him to leave by making a few "concessions".

I return to my bedroom with the soapy water and notice nothing out of the ordinary except Odhran made my bed and he's sitting on it with his legs extended and three washcloths next to him and he's shirtless.

My breath catches as his muscles pulse slowly with each breath. My stomach does that little flip thing and the gush between my legs totally embarrasses me. My body has this inability to behave itself around Odhran.

"I'm disgusting," he says, referring to the baby oil all over his body. "You could have killed me."

"You aren't even bleeding," I grumble, not wanting him to play the victim considering what has happened every time we've encountered each other. I set the bowl of water on the ground near where we have to clean up and glance behind me expecting Odhran to join me with the washcloths.

"You're staring," he says, smirking arrogantly and gazing down at his perfect ab muscles.

"I'm not. Just making sure you're not going to pounce."

"I won't," he says and then he takes his sweatpants off, exposing the tight, thigh-hugging boxer briefs beneath them. I stare at him, utterly mesmerized despite myself. I *think* I want to say something, but I just stare at him, dumbfounded. He's the type of guy you fantasize about. Damon Salvatore meets real life – instead of being a forty-year-old playing a teen on TV, Odhran is actually age appropriate. More importantly, he's real.

His package bulges out of the front of his underwear lewdly. He rakes his fingers through his obsidian hair and examines his body for God knows what. Baby oil? It occurs to me that he's admiring his physique, not examining it. Of course he is. He has more tattoos than I expected. I guess I've never seen him in this complete state of undress before and it surprises me that he's not just covered in black ink, but he isn't uncomfortable in the slightest.

"Why are you undressing?" I finally stammer out, although I have clearly already lost all semblance of control in this situation. "You're going to get too cold without clothes on."

It doesn't seem like a good idea to be near him while he's basically naked. Odhran ignores me and takes the washcloths, joining me on the floor. I only notice how enormous he is in comparison to me when we're side by side.

His arms are gigantic and covered in tattoos that all seem to blend together into two sleeves. He doesn't have any tattoos on his back or chest, but it seems like that's only the case because he hasn't had time to sit for more ink. His thigh has a tattoo of what looks like a terrifying mask. It's hard to see when he crouches next to me, but I noticed it as Odhran walked over.

He dips the washcloth into the warm water, his large hands sinking into the bowl. His knuckles are bruised and there are scars all over his hands and all the way up his forearm like he has spent a lot of time fighting.

"Are you going to help or keep staring?"

"I'm just saying you're going to get cold," I grumble, annoyed that he called me out for staring again. I'm not staring for the sake of it. It's in my best interests to keep an eye on Odhran since he could strike at any time.

"I'm fine."

He works quickly and efficiently, like someone well used to cleaning floors. It's weird to say, but maybe you have to see him clean up to understand the strangeness. He moves in a neat pattern and then after washing and drying the floor, he runs his finger along it as if there were someone stopping by later to check for trace amounts of baby oil.

Odhran barely allows me to help, since he cleans over the parts of the floor that I try to clean, much to my irritation. Once we're done, he sits back on his ankles, still side by side next to me, and he looks over at me with a big smile on his face. It's still eerie to see him smile and to know that he's the same person who shoved his cock into my mouth on the cliffs.

"You will do a *much* better job of this when we're done with my ex."

My heart sinks again. So he still hasn't let his little murder plot go?

"Whatever, Odhran."

"You're right," he says. "This has been unpleasant enough without bringing up more unpleasantness. You smell sweaty."

"Thanks," I grumble, suddenly self-conscious. I have never been one of those dainty women who could exert herself and stay looking perfect. If my heart rate increases even slightly, I look a damn mess. I can't imagine how bad I look now. My hair feels puffy, untamed and clumped up in random tangled knots.

Odhran looks perfect. He doesn't look like a sweaty hot mess.

"I meant it as a compliment," he says. His expression changes and even if I'm new to romance, new to dating and new to everything, I instinctively recognize the expression on his face. Maybe I learned it from movies. He wants to kiss me. I can tell and then his hand rests on my chin, tilting my face up to his.

Odhran's eyes are beautiful and intensely terrifying. They're so pale and his pupils are tiny black dots in the center of the expanse.

"I like you sweaty," he says and then he kisses me. It really happens. I can see his face, feel his lips and know that he is exactly who he says he is. I could never mistake those lips for anyone else's. I could never forget what my first kiss felt like, even if I tried.

Everything about that night was so intense, but adding to that exhilaration was *those* lips. Odhran's hands move around my jaw and he squeezes my cheeks possessively as our kiss continues. His hands are strong, but he doesn't squeeze me hard enough to hurt me.

Knowing that he could hurt me if he wanted to quickens my heart rate and I kiss him back more intensely. He likes the more intense pace that I set, even if I don't know what I'm doing and I half expect him to leap away from me in disgust.

My inner voice tells me he's a bad person. He hurt me. He wants me to *kill* his ex-girlfriend. If I'm looking for red flags, Odhran is soaked in crimson. Kissing him turns my common sense on its head. He helped me clean my room. He hasn't hurt me yet. He gave me my first orgasm. He dumped his girlfriend and saved my life.

He pulls away from me and my confused emotions intensify.

"You don't want to become a killer, but I won't have you in danger, so you must agree to *something*."

"That depends on the 'something'."

"You have to obey me. And no more tricks."

"That's a pretty broad command."

"It's intensely frustrating that you don't trust me," he says, scowling.

"That sounds like your problem," I say, finally sounding confident. He still has his hands around my cheek and it hasn't escaped me how close those hands are to my neck. I breathe slowly, desperate to appear cool and collected.

"You're right," he says. "It's my fault. That will change. You already belong to me, it's time for that to become more… apparent."

"Your ex-girlfriend will *love* that."

"Six isn't your problem," he says. "She's mine."

I feel a strange disappointment that he says "She's mine" about her. That's the point, isn't it? We can't *actually* be together.

"Right."

"Not like that," Odhran says sternly, his fingers tightening their grip on my cheeks. "Let me make myself clear, Onika. From this point forward, neither of us are single. I have never done partial commitments. I don't know what we are, but we are *not* available. Is that understood?"

He doesn't loosen his grasp on my cheeks until I nod and whisper, "Yes."

"Good," he says. "And I mean it. Six is my concern."

"Whatever."

He releases my cheek and rises to his full, impressive 6'5" height. I stand up, even if my height is far less impressive. I'm still not comfortable enough around Odhran to give him a complete advantage.

"I don't want to leave you tonight," he says. "You brought me over here. So, even if this is an uncomfortable dorm room that reeks of beef lo mein and baby oil, and has very little room for me, I'm staying."

"You can't fit in my bed. You're a giant."

"You will sleep on top of me," Odhran says haughtily. "But not before you shower."

"Thanks," I grumble, embarrassed that Odhran points out my sweatiness again. He doesn't seem like he wants to make me feel self-conscious despite his bluntness.

"You will be more comfortable if you shower. Plus, I need time," he says cryptically.

"Time for what?"

He pinches his brow together. "To think about what to do with you tonight. Now take a shower and don't do anything foolish like trying to escape."

"I could have escaped earlier and I didn't," I remind him. "Calm down."

"I won't," he says. "You exposed my identity, which means... Six could find out."

"I don't want to talk about your ex-girlfriend."

"Neither do I. So get in the shower and then get your ass back here. I'll make sure no more monsters climb through your window."

Chapter Eleven
Odhran

It surprises me how easy it is to put Nik at ease. She takes her towel, her shower stuff and a change of clothes to the bathroom and leaves me in her bedroom alone. I can't believe my luck. I open her desk and immediately find Nik's journal. She writes everything in that journal using a red fountain pen. I scan a few pages, but there isn't anything interesting, mostly complaints about being single, her weight, her grades, feeling like her writing isn't going anywhere and not having a boyfriend.

Everyone our age has the same concerns. *And she doesn't need to have those concerns any longer.*

My phone buzzes.

Six: Where the fuck are you?

I PULL OUT MY PHONE, annoyed that she's texting me. I assumed my brothers would have taken care of this problem by now. But I need to get her off my back until I'm done with Nik.

Odhran

. . .

Me: I'm home.
Six: Bloody liar.
Six: attachment.jpg

I OPEN the image my ex-girlfriend attaches in her text message. This couldn't be worse timing.

Fuck. Six is in my apartment. Not just in my apartment, she just took a selfie on my bed wearing nothing but an oversized black Bruins t-shirt. *My Bruins t-shirt.*

If she's going through my things unsupervised, it's a matter of time before she finds information about Nik. If that happens, this problem will explode into a bigger one. Fuck me. How did she get in there?

Me: I recommend you leave. Now.

IT'S TOO LATE, honestly. Even if I could teleport across town, Six would have already had plenty of time to trash my place completely. She can't get into my guns or ammunition and thankfully, she can't get into Killer Bee's enclosure anymore. But she can definitely fuck my shit up. *That would be a terrible fucking idea.*

Six: Cheater. Liar.

Chapter Eleven

I TURN MY PHONE OFF. I have a choice now. I can leave and handle Six, or I can stay with Nik. I know what I want to do. She returns after a fifteen minute shower – a quick shower by Nik's standards – and when she walks into the room, the scent of her lotion gets me rock hard instantly.

I remember the first time I smelled the cocoa butter on her skin. My choice is clear. I can't leave this bedroom tonight.

"You look hot."

"I'm wearing sweatpants."

"It's much less revealing than what you had on before," I point out.

"That was on purpose."

"Come here."

She approaches me, but she doesn't get too close to where I sit on the edge of her bed. She has her hair wrapped up in a large t-shirt and no makeup, nothing at all on her cinnamon-colored face. *She's so pretty.*

My stomach lurches. I know I shouldn't think of her as pretty. I shouldn't like her skin, or the way her eyes are so… different. There's no color to them, no summer sky, no murky green. They're black. Terrifyingly deep pools that draw me in.

"Come closer," I command her, my voice growing deeper. I need to touch her tonight.

"You're scaring me."

"I just want to kiss you."

I take her hand and press it to my lips, calming her instantly. I haven't forgotten Nik's punishment, but I can tell that each kiss pushes her fear further away. I kiss her hand again and draw her closer. She allows me to rest my hand on her hips for the first time and spread my legs for her to stand between them.

She's all mine.

Her freshly washed scent is really fucking good and the mixture of girly potions all over her skin and hair drive me fucking wild. What the hell do they put in that stuff? The woman looks like a snack and smells like a fucking bakery. It's pure heaven.

I reach for the towel holding Nik's hair together and unwrap it, allowing the thick mass of coily hair to descend down her back. It's so thick and the scent of her shampoo fills the room as I drop the wet towel.

"Your hair is longer."

"Yes," she says, shaking a little nervously. Maybe she's shaking because of the cold. I can't really tell. I lean forward and kiss her shoulder. Definitely nerves judging by the way she shudders beneath my touch. Luckily for her, I enjoy watching her shudder. I'll enjoy Nik even more when I watch her squirm beneath my grasp and beg for mercy.

"Very beautiful. Come closer."

"How much closer can I get?" she asks, breaking eye contact with me for a split second to drop her eyes to my crotch. My legs are spread because with just my underwear on, there's no point in trying to hide anything. Nik swallows slowly as she glances at my crotch and she quickly looks away as if averting her gaze from my dick could make my erection disappear.

"Much closer."

I take her hand and pull her closer so my thighs are around hers, ready to squeeze her in place if she makes even the slightest efforts to escape. Nik suspects nothing. I rest her hand against my bare chest. She curls the tips of her fingers, digging slightly into my flexed pectoral muscle. Her eyes scan my tattoos but there are no flickers of recognition that suggest she understands any of the Gaelic meaning or the old Irish symbols.

My throat tightens at the contact from her hand. Warmth spreads from the point where she touches me and I can't help staring at her, forcing her to look back at me with cautious consideration. *I can't wait to punish her.*

I push the other emotions coursing through me out of my head. This is about wanting to own her, nothing more. It's not about the intense connection I felt reading her words. It's not about her lips, or her soft skin, or how fucking addictive it was to realize that I could have her. That I could not just think about her all the time, or stalk her online profile, or research her... but I could touch her.

In some ways, I'm wired differently from my brothers, but in other ways, I'm so disturbingly similar that it hurts.

"What do those tattoos mean?"

"Nothing you should concern yourself with," I murmur, placing my palm over hers, giving the initial impression that I'm comforting and supporting her. She doesn't know what's coming. My heart rate betrays no deception and I keep gazing into her eyes, appreciating her precious innocence before I ruin it completely. My cock jerks in my pants.

"If you're going to be in my life, I want to make sure they don't mean anything weird."

"Nik," I say sternly. "I'm not holding your hand so we can talk about my tattoos."

"Okay," she says, drawing out the word slowly and suspiciously, clearly aware of how my hand moves to her wrist and how I'm gripping her very tightly.

She ventures cautiously, "Odhran… Where's the paddle?"

"What?"

"I had it up against the desk when I left and now it's gone."

My grip on her wrist tightens and my thighs squeeze together to hold Nik in place before I answer. "I hadn't noticed."

Before she can react, I quickly maneuver her body and throw Nik over my lap with all the force it takes to get a short but relatively plus-sized girl over my thighs. I pin both of her hands behind her back as I hold her down, disabling her faster than she expects.

Nik lets out a terrified, piercing shriek which she quickly silences by sinking her teeth into my thigh. Her legs thrash behind her as I use all the force it takes to pin her down and position her properly over my lap so I can reach her ass and spank the hell out of her with the paddle I'm concealing beneath her pillow.

I pin her down so she can't move anymore, but that doesn't stop her from biting me again. I smack her ass so hard that she has to yelp and let go of my thigh.

"Stop biting me or you will only make things much worse."

"You said you weren't going to hurt me, you liar," she says, kicking again and making a failed attempt to wiggle away from me. Nik is much smaller than I am, even with her curves, and her body is incredibly easy to control. I can feel her stomach undulating against my cock as she fights me, but it doesn't take long for the force of my weight holding her down to tire her out.

"Liar…" she whimpers weakly one last time.

"I am not hurting you, I'm punishing you. There's a difference."

"Then why does my ass hurt?"

She glances over her shoulder, but the expression on my face forces her to quickly avert her gaze. This is a punishment, not a game, and my sternness resonates through her dorm room. I can feel her trying to steady her breathing, trying to stay calm and think. All prey is the same. My cock throbs against her again and she makes a frustrated grunting noise.

"If you think your ass hurts now, you are about to have a terrible week."

I slowly run my palm over her ass and nearly cum in my pants. It's almost a relief that she misbehaves and that I'm certain I will always be able to count on Nik to misbehave and instigate my incredible passion for spanking. I've tried to indulge in this desire for true punishment followed by sexual gratification, but I've always had to stop myself before getting this far. It never felt right before.

Nik has a particularly unique ass – a plump, voluptuous, round ass that protrudes so far from her hips that it's almost like a shelf of flesh. Just looking at it makes me question everything about sex and what I *really* want it to feel like. The thought of plunging into that softness and feeling the warmth of Nik's folds and those gigantic round ass cheeks pressing into me turns me into a fucking beast.

"This is not fair," she says. "You have to stop, Odhran."

"No. I explained everything to you quite clearly, Nik. You belong to me now. Your pussy. Your heart. Every last fucking inch of your body belongs to me. Your baby oil trick and tying me up like a prisoner are absolutely unacceptable. There will be no more lies. No more tricks."

Nik insults me because she knows it's her last resort. "You're a monster."

Chapter Eleven

Your monster.

"Yes," I tell her. "I am. And I don't fucking mind it."

I reach under the pillow and tease her by touching the paddle to her ass gently through her clothes. I'll have to spank her bare obviously to leave bruises marking her as mine and to ensure that she thinks *very* hard about disobeying me the rest of the week. Once I leave her tonight, I'll have a fucking mess to clean up with Six. Who knows how fucking long that will take and what lengths I'll have to go to keep Nik out of trouble while I clean it up.

"You don't have to do this," she whimpers, pleading with me one last time.

I yank her sweatpants down and then her panties. Nik makes a strained sobbing noise, maybe some mixture of embarrassment and fear. Juices dribble from her now exposed wetness and coat her thick, chubby thighs with clear juices. The splatter from her arousal draws my attention immediately to the apex of her thighs.

"Please..."

Her whimpering sounds are so sad. There's a part of me that doesn't want to do this, that wants to throw the paddle down and protect her. *This is protecting her.* My emotions mixing with my urges confuse me to the point of discomfort.

I steel my voice and stiffen my resolve to Nik's pitiful pleading.

"I want you to remember this very carefully the next time you think of disobeying me," I tell her before cracking down on her soft, bare ass with the sorority paddle.

Chapter Twelve
Onika

I have never experienced anything more painful in my life than the paddle landing on my bare, round ass cheeks. My mom used to hit Kalani, but my sister was older than me by nine and a half years and by the time it was my turn to get spanked, Kalani would get so mad at my mom that she stopped altogether. This is far worse than any spanking my mother could have come up with anyway.

Instead of yelling out loud, I bite hard into Odhran's thigh. The sociopathic beast doesn't even flinch as my teeth leave a mark on his thighs. I let go of him, allowing the spit and a little blood to flow over Odhran's bare, pale and hairy thigh. I'm facing the creepy mask tattoo on his thigh head-on and now the eyes look like they're staring at me. Warning me that I am about to suffer so much more.

But then again, maybe he's done.

I AM MISTAKEN.

I PROMISE myself I won't cry out. No matter how hard he hits me or how many times, I won't cry out and I won't bite him again. Judging by how big his cock grows each time I fight him or bite him, he takes far too much pleasure from my suffering. He hits me again and the pain is even more intense. The third one nearly makes me cry out.

Tears stream down my cheeks soundlessly. My ass is totally numb, so the pain of the fourth hard smack barely registers. I can't imagine I'll be able to sit down tomorrow or the rest of the week. Because English class hasn't been painful enough.

"You aren't making a sound," Odhran murmurs, almost like he's noting the observation for himself and not at all for me. He hits me again and I don't give in to him on his fifth smack with the paddle. I hear him rest the paddle on the bed and then his fingers spread my cheeks apart and he presses them between my lower lips.

I *moan*. Oh my God. Maybe he's done. Relief floods through me as his fingers slip over my clit and send a rush of pleasure through me unlike anything I've felt before. It's impossible to ignore how fucking wet I am. Odhran removes his fingers from my pussy and I clench my thighs together instinctively.

Oh no. This doesn't feel right.

"I'm not done," he says, confirming my suspicions. Juices dribble down my thighs even if I'm terrified. Odhran slowly wipes my juices off on my thighs.

"I'm saving all of you for later," he says again.

"Odhran, no. I've had enough."

"I don't think so," he says. "You haven't had enough until your ass turns purple."

"I'm black," I tell him. "My ass doesn't turn purple."

"Hm. I think you're more of a burned cinnamon color. I can get it purple."

I don't bother threatening him with another bite when clearly threatening to bite Odhran doesn't affect him in the slightest. His weight shifts on the bed as he grabs the paddle again and his hard dick keeps poking into me. I hope he doesn't think we're having sex after this.

Sex is the last thing on my mind when he paddles my ass again, hitting me a sixth, seventh, and eighth time in rapid succession. My ass jiggles and aches as tears continue to stream down my face, but I refuse to give Odhran the satisfaction of a scream.

"You're almost done," he whispers. "You can handle one more. I know you can, beloved."

My throat tightens. Beloved? I can't protest, and especially not now, since I'm terrified of what sound will come out of my mouth if I allow it to open again. My only choice here is enduring Odhran's punishment and submitting to him.

He pins me down completely with his gigantic, muscular arm and I am entirely under Odhran's control, forced to suffer the punishment that gets me so inexplicably soaked between the thighs. His last hit with the paddle feels especially painful and cruel. But I don't scream.

I exhale and shudder as he releases his grip on my torso, allowing air to flow freely through my lungs and giving me the freedom to escape. I'm in too much pain to escape. My body just wants me to lie here and let the air flow through me, even with Odhran's cock crudely pressing into me.

He touches my ass gently, but I flinch from the slight contact.

"Oh, fuck," he says. "Your ass is perfect."

"It hurts," I shudder.

He slowly caresses my ass as I fight back whimpers. His warm touch would otherwise have been welcome, but now it just stings and brings me the most confusing emotions I've ever experienced in my life.

"Good," Odhran responds without the slightest hint of sympathy. "I wanted it to hurt."

"You're a sadist," I complain, still plastered to his thighs even if he has given me plenty of time to escape.

"Maybe," he says. "I also know this is the fastest way to curb your disobedience."

He runs his fingers down my thigh and picks up my juices on his fingers, sliding his bare hands over the back of my thighs and then pushing two of his coated fingers inside me. I gasp as he enters me rudely and unceremoniously, purely for his pleasure.

"You are insanely fucking tight," he comments, swirling his fingers around inside me and then withdrawing them just when I can feel my inner walls clamping down on him.

When he removes his fingers, I feel a surge of regret like I would do anything to have Odhran's fingers back between my legs. I should care how fucking wrong this is, but I just don't. *I want to feel him.* I squirm and make an effort to escape him, half hoping he'll pin me down again, but definitely not hoping for more lashings from the paddle.

I slide off his thighs onto my knees and my ass stings as it jiggles and bounces when I find my place on the floor. Since it's more of a fall than a slide, Odhran considers me curiously and stifles a chuckle.

"Graceful," he says in his infuriatingly deep villainous voice. So many local Boston guys have high-pitched accents, but Odhran's voice sounds very deep and old world. I could romanticize his voice if I didn't know for sure that it belonged to a complete monster.

"Whatever."

"I could do a lot of things with you down there on your knees, but not tonight. Come."

He waits for me to obey, watching as if he expects me to defy him. My ass hurts so much I can barely stand up. I turn around to examine it and wince from the stinging pain. Once I'm on my feet, Odhran takes my hand and turns me around so that he can examine my ass closely.

His grasp on me is so firm that I know there's no point in defying him and making any effort at escape. My ass hurts too much for me to think about anything but relief. Thankfully he doesn't bother touching my butt again. He just stares at it for a few seconds, his blue eyes flickering with intense excitement. They're almost shimmering.

"You got a lot more bruised than I thought."

"I won't be able to sit for a week."

He smirks. "Maybe two. Can I take a picture?"

"Absolutely not."

I don't know if he'll listen to me. He hasn't bothered with my feelings about anything else.

"Okay," he says. "Get your pajamas back on. We're cuddling."

It's a constant thought cartwheeling around in the back of my head that Odhran is nuts, but everything that comes out of his mouth is crazier than the last thing that came out of his mouth. He can't possibly think I'm going to climb into my dorm room bed and cuddle with him after he left bruises on me.

"We aren't cuddling. I went through this to find out who you are and now that I know… I don't think we should continue seeing each other. You have or *had* a girlfriend, Odhran. You're just going through a slump with her and once you're done with whatever mind game you're playing here… you'll want her back."

I think I understand him. I'm not a psychiatrist or anything, but I write horror fiction. This allows me to climb into the dark recesses of the human mind. I couldn't hope to imagine a character as confusing, dark and alluring as Odhran. He tosses his straight black hair out of his face and pinches his brows together like he's either angry or thinking.

He's probably some monstrous combination of both if I really think about it.

"This is not a mind game."

"Then *what* is it?"

"A relationship," Odhran says, sounding so painfully genuine that he stuns me into silence.

"Is this how you've started other relationships?"

"I've never started a relationship," he said. "Six and I were always…"

"Okay, forget I asked. I don't want to hear about your ex-girlfriend."

"Jealous?"

"No. Her best friend called me the n-word and they both beat the shit out of me. I just don't want to talk about her."

I see the first hint of humanity on Odhran's face – at least since he helped me clean up the baby oil. To my genuine surprise, he apologizes.

"Sorry. We don't have to talk about her. Sex is easy for me. Relationships are not."

I want to come up with something sassy, but I have even less experience with relationships than Odhran. No guy has ever asked me on a date, or had a crush on me, liked my photos on social media or put the fire emoji under my selfies. I am completely *invisible* to guys. So I really don't know what to do or what to say. I'm naive to this. Odhran touches my lower lip gently and despite myself, my nervousness melts away just a little.

He must want to touch me. No other guy has done this before, so I have to assume that he wants it.

"How can we be in a relationship when I hardly know you?"

"Get to know me," Odhran says calmly. "You already know how my cock feels when it teases the back of your throat."

He's saying the dirtiest possible words, but in his smooth voice, it just sounds delicious and I can't even come up with something clever to say.

"That's–

"No more protests," Odhran says. "This is happening, Nik. I want it to happen. *I want you.*"

If my ass wasn't throbbing in pain, I wouldn't even believe this was real. But there's no way this pain is faked. Odhran's feelings on the other hand...? *No. This is real. For his twisted, murderous purposes, Odhran has a fixation with me.*

"You want to turn me into a killer," I tell him. "Those were your words. The sex stuff is just to get me to do what you want."

Odhran's smirk creeps me out, sending a chill down my spine as he draws me closer to him.

"It's not your job to question my intentions. It's your job to dedicate yourself to me completely and entirely while I sever ties to my old life."

"You have very odd ideas about relationships."

My throbbing ass isn't even the first clue that everything about Odhran's tastes are completely unconventional.

"Maybe," he says. "But my parents were married until my father died and I know a few things about keeping relationships together."

I strongly doubt that spanking was involved in that.

"Okay," I tell him. "But I've never had a boyfriend. I don't even get a chance to think about what I want."

"What's the point of thinking?" he says, running his fingers over my lips again like he's appreciating the fullness, like he's never touched lips like mine before. I feel self-conscious but I can't risk darting my tongue out to nervously lick my lips without touching my tongue to Odhran's fingers.

I swallow slowly and nervously.

"You don't need to think," he says. "You need to obey. Attend your classes. Go to the gym. Eat right. And be ready for me when I come for you."

The first two parts sounded fine, but I've never gone to the gym or eaten right in my entire life. Odhran looks like he spends a lot of his life in the gym, which is funny because he also looks like a vampire who sleeps in a coffin. He's pale, but his skin is taut over extremely firm, thick muscles. How can he find time to play video games, attend classes, have a social life, stalk me to the point where he knows all these little details about me *and* have time for the gym?

"I don't have time to go to the gym and eat right."

Odhran smirks. "You must. I'll go with you if necessary. But let's start with attending classes and getting your ass healed. You won't be able to focus unless you sleep. Come to bed."

If I take a step towards him, if I agree to going to bed with Odhran, I'm agreeing to a relationship with him. If I say yes, I'm agreeing to Odhran in my bedroom. His body. His fingers. His complete and utter control over me. I blame his intense blue stare for the control he has over me, but it can't be just his eyes.

It's Odhran's everything. He kisses the top of my forehead and my throat tightens as he draws the last ounce of resistance out of me with a kiss. He takes my hand and I follow Odhran to bed. My ass hurts as I climb into bed and try to find a position to lie in that doesn't hurt. My butt has always been too curvy for me to sleep on my back, but sleeping on my stomach with my ass protruding seems too vulnerable a position for me to be in near Odhran.

If he chooses to spank me again, I don't think I'll be able to fall asleep at all. Odhran sleeps against the wall, somehow squeezing his 6'5" body into my twin XL bed. He stares at me in the dimly lit room as I lie on my side, facing him. Odhran has a predator's eyes and predatory behavior, so it feels unsafe to look away from him. His eyes are so gorgeous, that I almost don't mind.

This must be a weird, very detailed dream.

"I'm glad I followed this impulse," he whispers, pressing his hand to my face. "I can't wait to fuck you, Nik. But I have my own shit to take care of. Come here."

"Where?"

"My arms," he whispers. "I'll hold you until you fall asleep."

I'VE NEVER EXPERIENCED anything like it before. If my mother or father ever held me to sleep, it was so long ago that I can't remember what it felt like. This feels better than wrapping myself in a down comforter. Odhran is shockingly gentle with my butt as he turns me around so he can spoon me.

He runs his hand over my butt slowly, touching me as gently as humanly possible.

"I'm sorry I hurt you," he whispers. "I don't know how to love without pain. I don't know how to bond. But I like you, Nik. I like you more than I expected."

He presses his nose into my neck, inhaling my scent deeply and then moving hair away from my neck so that he can give me a soft kiss.

"You scare me, Odhran."

He chuckles. "You have nothing to fear anymore, Nik. I always protect what's mine. *Always.*"

I don't fight him. After the intense pain Odhran caused spanking my ass, the relief from cuddling is downright euphoric. I want to agree with him, nuzzle into him and let the exchange of warmth between us continue as long as possible. Everything just feels good, like the aftermath of my adrenaline rush heightens every little moment between us.

Falling asleep has never been so easy for me.

Chapter Thirteen
Odhran

I hate that I have to leave Nik in the middle of the night, but once she's asleep, I have to solve my problems before morning. My phone is completely filled with messages from Six. Pictures. Videos.

I've wanted to end my relationship for years, but now that I've finally done it and all hell has broken loose, I wonder if I've created more trouble for myself and my family than necessary. Maybe I should have done what my father wanted – the only son who would listen to every word he said without question.

There's no point in sneaking out the window of Nik's room, so I leave through her dorm room door. My cock aches with desire for her after I used every last drop of my self-control not to wake her up and make love to her.

I just can't make love to Nik until I properly break ties with Six. Until I get rid of her. I still want Nik to kill her – to do *something* dangerous and dark that will break her creative mind right open and give me access to the parts of her that fascinate me the most.

I know she has a dark side. *I brought it out of her tonight.* Just thinking about how her body reacts to my spankings, my cuddles and every touch exhilarates me more than anything I've ever felt. I can't get her off my mind. It was bad when I became obsessed with her horror writing – her descriptions of blood, gore and the psychology of a sociopath or killer – but this is so much worse.

Touching Nik has turned me into a full blown stalker and I don't mind it.

I SPEED to my apartment from campus, running through several red lights and taking every side street I remember to get to the front desk of my building. There are cameras and there's an intense security system, but Six has everything she needs to enter unimpeded. I take the elevator up to my floor. Once I exit the elevator, I can already hear music coming from the far end of the house – my bedroom.

I have one half of the floor and my cousin owns the apartment on the other half of the floor. Each of us have our own elevators leading into our apartments, but he's never around. We each have a guest entrance outside, but whoever came in used the elevator.

Fuck. Loud music pulses from my bedroom filling every room, and I hear loud voices, screaming, and it sounds like there's a fucking party happening. Thankfully my guns are all locked up, or I would worry about walking in there unarmed. For a moment, I consider calling Aiden, or any of my brothers, but just because I'm the youngest doesn't mean I need them to save my ass all the time.

Aiden initiated me into our Irish mob family. I learned all the skills necessary to handle Six, even if what awaits behind that door is a massive fucking mess. I only have a few hours before I'll have to text Nik and keep her compliant with my instructions. I exit the elevator into an entirely new fucking nightmare.

Pairs of shoes litter the floor in front of the elevator. Two pairs of high heels – Six and Maura possibly – and then three pairs of sneakers. Mens' sneakers. I don't think anyone hears me enter because the music is so loud. They're playing *Promiscuous Girl* by Nelly Furtado. That's the song my brother Callum would play during his morning showers in high school. *So annoying.*

If there are men in here, I need a weapon. The closest one is in the kitchen. I don't even give a fuck about getting caught or anyone noticing me. I stride past the living room, ignoring Maura hooking up with a black guy on the couch. She runs her pale hands along his back as he keeps his head lowered between her thighs. Where the fuck is Six?

Neither Maura nor her new friend notice me, so it's easier than I expect to get to my gun safe in the kitchen. After my father died, my mom gifted me the gun she bought him for their first anniversary – a 9mm Sig Sauer. It's small, but powerful enough to blow a hole through anyone's head. Hopefully that won't be necessary.

I don't need a bloody mess on my hands tonight when I need to make sure Nik gets her ass to class in the morning. The gun safe is in the drawer of the kitchen island. I pull it out without anyone noticing. *I'm too calm. That's dangerous. I can kill everyone in this apartment and not feel a fucking thing.*

The speakers in the living room continue to blare music. That has to stop. I walk over and unplug them, shocking Maura's friend away from her naked body and causing Maura to scream. I raise the pistol at her head and then shift my aim to his head. Maura screams again.

"What the fuck! What the fuck are you doing!?"

I glance down at my coffee table. There's a mirror, three white lines, several hundred dollar bills and a few baggies of different powders – not all of them crystal white. Two used needles sit next to a spoon and a lighter. The more I calm down and let my killer instincts take control, the more I take in the devastation around me. Six and her friends have trashed the place — it's not just drugs on my coffee table or Maura getting head on my couch.

There's blood on the carpet, curtains shredded away from the floor-to-ceiling glass windows in the apartment, clothing everywhere and empty bottles of vodka and gin.

"Shut the fuck up, Maura," I say calmly. "Who's your friend?"

"Don't hurt him."

"I asked his name," I sneer, keeping my eyes on the man who looks like he's about to shit himself. He has clear fluid smeared on his face and his dark eyes sit deeply in his dark brown skin, much darker than

Nik's. If I can get away without firing any shots tonight, that would make my life *much* easier.

"It's Nathaniel."

"Get the fuck out of here, Nathaniel."

Smart man, Nathaniel, has his hands up and he doesn't take his eyes off me. He knows he's in deeper shit than he thought he was getting into. It's hard to suppress my gut reaction to him and Maura. *It's wrong.* Her own family would disown or kill her if they found out about this.

She has an Irish boyfriend.

"If I could just get my clothes," Nathaniel offers slowly, gesturing with a cautious elbow towards a pile of clothing on the floor — emerald green boxer briefs, a pair of black ripped jeans and a black t-shirt with Japanese text on it.

"No," I answer. "You walk out of here naked or you don't walk out of here at all. Now leave."

"You ain't gonna shoot me when I turn my back?" He asks, raising his hands higher as if greater submission to me could stop a bullet if I were really that cruel.

"No. But aren't you worried about Maura and what happens to her?"

Nathaniel glances guiltily at Maura, but only for a flash before he turns his gaze back to me and shrugs. "Not really."

"Right, man. Then get the fuck home. Hope I never see your ass again."

He hops over the back of the couch and Nathaniel flees down the hallway with loud, attention-grabbing thuds. It's a miracle Six hasn't heard us by now.

Maura grabs a throw pillow and once we're alone in my living room, she covers her naked body with it. I don't bother looking at her because Maura's presence doesn't concern me as long as she serves her purpose.

"Where's Six?"

"I don't know."

"Okay, Maura. I'll ask an easier question then. What the fuck happened out here?"

"Talk to your girlfriend."

"I broke up with Six."

"You can't end a relationship like that, Odhran," Maura says fiercely, glaring at me with genuine hatred. "You Murray boys think you'll always own this city, but it's not true."

"Careful, Maura. Those words could get you killed."

Aiden wouldn't have any of us kill a woman, but he wouldn't have to. There are several families in the mob loyal enough to ours that those words could get Maura killed at several different places on campus.

"If you were going to kill me, you would have done it. So right now, you're either going to humiliate me, torture me, or *use* me."

"Don't delude yourself, Maura. I have no interest in you. Nor do I have an interest in Nathaniel, although I'm sure your older brother might."

"You wouldn't dare tell him, not after what Six found out," Maura says, her face reddening in the dim fluorescent light illuminating the living room. The blue light from the city outside gives the room a soft look, almost distracting from the mess and the blood everywhere.

"What did Six find out?"

"That you're a bloody cheater," Maura says. "Though it's not surprising. You deserve what you have coming to you."

Despite my gun pointed straight at her, Maura hops off the couch, deciding against modesty as she flings her pillow aside and picks her dress and underwear up off the floor of my living room. I allow her to dress.

"I was faithful to Six for as long as our relationship lasted. Unfortunately, our relationship is over."

"Whatever, Odhran. She's in your bedroom getting absolutely fucked right now. Have a good night."

I lower my gun.

"Is this a joke?"

Odhran

"Bye, Odhran," Maura says, taking off down my hallway with her shoes in hand. Fuck, she's better than I thought.

I have three choices — chase after her, shoot her, or see if she's telling the truth. Without the loud music, I can hear sounds from the rest of the apartment, but it mostly sounds like low talking. My front door opens and then slams shut.

I know she's here. Her shoes were at the front door. She sent me videos and text messages and threats. But I still don't want to face this. I keep my finger off my pistol trigger as I calmly walk towards my bedroom door, down a much shorter hallway past my living room.

As I draw closer, the noises from my bedroom grow louder. Talking. And then I hear it. Moaning sounds. They sound ridiculous and faked, but that doesn't matter. This is a performance. Six's performance.

I can't afford to overreact when I enter that room, but I also don't know how the fuck I can be expected to keep it together. I push the door open and take it all in. She's naked on my bed, bouncing between two tall, fit looking men who are both members of our college football team.

I know everyone on the team. Fuck, I grew up with half of them. Their names are unimportant but they're both blond haired and blue-eyed with rippling abs and Celtic tattoos. They should know better.

And this is nothing but plain disrespect. The taller one pounding Six from behind notices me first and jumps away from her, swearing up a storm. The other one reacts by stumbling backwards, freeing an average-sized cock from Six's lips as he steps away from her.

She sits back on her heels and glares at me, as if she knew I entered the room but kept on deep-throating a stranger's cock in my bed. If she's trying to upset me, she fails. All this does is irritate me profoundly. I left Nik for this.

"Odhran! Fucking, Christ! Is this your place? She didn't tell us this was your place!"

Six snorts as she fails to suppress her amusement. Her playmates don't seem to notice how gleefully she embraces the chaos. She runs her tongue over her lips as she sits back and glares.

"Hello, Odhran."

"You have gone too far, Six."

I wish I was angrier, but there's more irritation than anger. We were betrothed when we were too young to know what that meant. Six was my first for everything — my first girlfriend, my first kiss, the first woman that I've ever loved.

I've done things for her that I can't even confess to my brothers. I might have been harsh in how we ended things but… *I can't accept what she did to Nik.* There's a difference in being proud of our heritage and what Six and Maura did to her.

I can't allow this to happen.

"Are you fucking kidding me?" Six spits out, her brows darkening. "I know you're cheating on me. The worst of it is that it's the bitch I tried to kill. It's like my heart *knew.*"

The men stand back as Six takes her phone off the bed and throws it at my head. Tears well in her eyes and then she leaps off the bed, not bothering with clothing and definitely not worrying about my weapon.

"You're a cheater and a cunt, Odhran. And when I get my hands on your little pet, I'm going to rip every last inch of her fake ass hair off her head."

"Take a step back, Six."

She takes a step back because she knows I'm serious. The men she has in the room dress quickly. I don't give a fuck about them. If they know what's good for them, they'll get the hell out of here before I'm done with Six and before I tackle the disrespect of this open violation.

In our world, you don't touch a woman who belongs to another — not without assurances that most certainly couldn't have come from Six. She doesn't have the power. My brothers are right. The sands beneath us are shifting and this is a test. An important one.

"You aren't going to shoot me," she says. "I know you, Odhran. You wouldn't kill a woman. You're too weak."

"Weakness has nothing to do with it. Our families are not just about identifying the strong from the weak. We have vows and honor and respect. We have clearly defined standards of behavior."

I hear my bedroom door slam shut as one of the fuckers leaves at my demands. The other stands back, hovering in my peripheral vision as if he's terrified of leaving Six alone with me and he wants to protect her. Fucking idiot. Six is a bigger danger to him than I am. Poor stupid motherfucker.

"You *cheated!*" She screams at me, her face suddenly turning completely red and then purple. She pushes me and I keep my hand on my gun, allowing her to hit me, allowing her to throw fists at my chest. Her new boyfriend or whoever the fuck he is, calls her name in an attempt to lure her off of me, but I give him a sharp glare and he slinks back into the dark corner of the room, waiting for Six, who hasn't given him a second look.

"You fucking cheated with a fat whore!"

I let her hit me and then she steps back, gasping for breath and completely exhausted from cocaine and fighting me and fucking and being a mess.

"We are not together, Six and what you've done will lead to bigger trouble than you're ready to deal with. It's late and I don't want this to escalate any further. You've taken your anger out on me. Get your clothes and get your friend. Go back to your place and if you dare lay a finger on Nik or anyone you think I care about, I will cut your hand off with a meat cleaver and give it to my brother for Christmas."

I watch Six making several hundred calculations in the back of her head. She knows me, she can read my facial expression. She understands my morals, my thoughts, my fears, my feelings. Six knows me better than anyone in the world. *But I don't love her. I don't love her the way a man loves a woman and now that I'm a man, I can see it clearly. The familiarity of a childhood friend, maybe. But now, it's almost nothing.*

Maybe I don't want to be cruel anymore. Maybe I don't want to be like her or my father. *Maybe my brothers are right.*

"I'll kill her," Six says. "I almost killed her that night and maybe I should have. I don't even know how you met her…"

"None of that matters. For the sake of our families and because of my brother's orders, I'm allowing you to leave. I'm calling a truce between us and I will respectfully leave you alone. I will... I'll give you whatever you want."

"I wanted our life," Six hisses. But I've finally pissed her off enough for her to at least get her clothes. The man behind her approaches and tries to hand her a shirt. She snatches it from him and yells at him to get the hell out of *her* apartment. I allow the slip, just because it gets the motherfucker out of my apartment. After giving Six a sad, forlorn glance, hoping for a better reward for all his chivalry, he realizes the futility of earning emotions out of her and leaves.

We're alone and it's so painfully quiet without the music and without the drunk, high idiots. Six looks a mess, but not due to heartbreak. She's covered in sweat with disheveled hair and makeup smeared all over her red, angry cheeks.

"I need you to go."

"I hate you, Odhran."

"I know."

"I should have known something was different between us. I should have seen it."

"Nothing you did could have saved us, Six. And fucking two guys in my bed isn't what will win me back."

"What about bringing you that bitch's heart? I can prove how much you mean to me, Odhran. Our families... Without this engagement... You don't understand the life you've sentenced me to."

"We're too different, Six."

"We're not."

"I saw it for the first time in that video. Nik is innocent."

"She's a fucking whore."

I know she's angry. Some part of her is definitely heartbroken. We had a life. We were promised to each other... But she still gave her body up so easily to other men. If nothing else, it means that she will move on. She *can* move on. Six might want me for her own reasons, but she doesn't need me and she definitely doesn't love me. When you're in love, you can't even entertain the idea of seeing anyone else.

"Don't hurt her. She's not a whore and I never cheated. She's... a research project."

"That's nice. You end our lives for a research project."

"Yes."

"Fuck you, Odhran."

"I don't care if you hate me, Six. But if you do one more thing to violate the rules of our family, I will tell Aiden and I can't tell how he will react."

"If he's as weak as people say, I'll be fine," she says. "Screw you and screw your entire fucking family. If that bitch is lucky, she'll make it through the year."

That had better be all talk. Six doesn't sound serious, she just sounds hurt, but considering what she's done to Nik before, I can't take any threat lightly. I have to fight every urge in my body that I have to hurt her. I *want* to hurt her. My desire to protect Nik nearly overrides my common sense. But the best way to protect Nik is to listen to my brother's commands.

To trust my family.

"Don't do anything to get yourself in trouble and we won't have trouble. I won't even charge you a cleaning fee."

"Fuck you."

SHE LEAVES and I follow her out of my apartment. Once it's empty, I scan every room with the pistol just to make sure Six doesn't leave me any surprises. It's a fucking mess. Everything is a fucking mess.

I WISH I'd never left Nik.

I NEED HER HERE. *I need her.*

Chapter Fourteen
Onika

Bzzt. *Bzzt. Bzzt. Bzzt. Bzzt. Bzzt.* My ass throbs as my cell phone aggressively buzzes, waking me up what feels like hours before my alarm. I don't have class until noon. I can feel bruises and welts all over my aching butt, so the last thing I want to do is get out of bed or risk moving my butt and grazing it across my sheets.

What the hell happened last night? I groan, desperate to ignore my buzzing phone, but it buzzes again. *Bzzt. Bzzt. Bzzt.*

I groan and run my hands over the sheets until I touch my phone case. My entire body hurts even if Odhran technically only spanked my ass. My notifications are all from Odhran.

Your owner: Wake up, Nik. Thinking of you.
Your owner: I can't stop thinking of how pretty you looked last night.
Your owner: Gym before class. See you there at ten.

Onika

THE FIRST TWO texts are crazy enough, but the third text makes my heart flip. The gym? I'd rather spend the morning harvesting pumpkins in Disney's Dreamlight Valley game than getting out of bed and getting clothes on. I appreciate Odhran's compliments, but with class at noon, there's no reason for me to leave my bedroom before eleven.

Except his other texts.

Your owner: Don't even think about ignoring this.
Your owner: Does your ass hurt?

I ROLL my eyes at the barely concealed threat.

Your owner: Wear black leggings, a sports bra and a white t-shirt.

HE'S serious about this gym thing. How can I work out when my ass hurts? I don't even know how to work out. Exercising was always something that needed to happen in front of people at school and it was always the worst part of my day. I tried to cover up and to hide, but being the biggest and slowest girl only draws more attention to you.

The thought of entering my campus gym where girls like Six and Maura go to craft their perfect bodies scares the ever living crap out of me. But I still have three more texts from Odhran. I doubt he's going to give up.

Your owner: Respond, Nik.
Your owner: Respond or I'll come over.

Chapter Fourteen

Is he serious? Doesn't he have anything better to do than show up here? My roommate could be back here at any minute…

Your owner: Nik.

HE IS RELENTLESS.

Me: I'm up.
Your owner: Ready for the gym?

I DON'T NEED an hour to get ready for the gym. Odhran's instructions were simple and anyway, *I'm not going.*

Me: I don't work out.
Your owner: You start today. I'll be there.

I'll be there. I shouldn't find Odhran's presence or his overbearing text messages comforting. I know what's technically right, but whenever Odhran talks to me or messages me, it's like he switches the sensible part of my brain off completely.

Me: My butt hurts.
Your owner: Send me a picture.

Onika

I SHOULD HAVE KNOWN he would answer something like that. Part of me wants to defy him, but another part of me delusionally hopes that if he sees how much he fucked my ass up, he'll take pity on me and let me out of this gym requirement. I'd rather recover from my night with him and maybe write about it. *Definitely* write about it. I can't process what happened between me and Odhran without writing. My fucked up horror stories are therapeutic to me.

I peel my clothes off over my ass and set my camera up against my pillow, using the timer to take a picture of my butt where my giant, bruised ass takes up the entire frame. I quickly grab my phone off the bed and examine another one of my first "nudes".

My insecurity rises to the surface when I look at the picture. My ass has a lot of cellulite and with the bruises all over it, I feel like it bulges out all weird. It's too big. It's too heavy. My big ass has always drawn the wrong kind of attention and lots of bullying.

I don't have a perky little butt like the girls here.

My finger hovers over the white arrow "send" button. My concern about Odhran overreacting overrides the self-consciousness which would have otherwise crippled me. I send it and my heart drops. I shouldn't care if Odhran texts back or not, but regardless of my confused feelings for him, I'm still completely vulnerable.

I take my clothes off since I'm already halfway there and search for the gym outfit Odhran assigned me via text message. It's not hard to find a pair of black leggings and I sleep with sports bras a lot, so that's not too hard either. But a white t-shirt? I don't know if I have one of those, especially not one I can wear to the gym. As I search through my t-shirt drawer, my phone buzzes again.

I'm too nervous to check, but three more buzzes follow and I'm too scared of Odhran knocking on my window right as my roommate walks through the door or some other equally horrifying situation. I glance down at my phone to see the four texts from Odhran.

Your owner: Lovely bruises, Nik.
Your owner: Your ass is gorgeous.
Your owner: See you at the gym.

Chapter Fourteen

Your owner: Don't even think about skipping.

Me: I'll be there. No need to be rude.
Your owner: See you then, beautiful.

I DON'T EVEN KNOW how to respond. My roommate bursts into our
bedroom while I'm completely lost in thought and she lets out a
surprised shriek that I'm standing there in the middle of the room.
Her shriek snaps me out of my focus on my cell phone.

"Ohmygoodness! I didn't think you would be here," Rylee says, her
red, wet hair sticking to her neck. Wherever she just came from, she
clearly showered and dressed there, so she must just be here for
books.

"Yeah. I'm going to the gym."

Rylee gives me a look of complete confusion. "Really? Are you
sure?"

"What? Think I'm too fat to go to the gym?"

I don't mean to sound so cranky. Normally, it's easy for me to
be cordial with Rylee. She's prettier and more popular than I am,
way too popular with boys to spend more than a few nights in a
row sleeping in our dorm room, but she hasn't done anything
wrong and I hate feeling so bitter for something out of her
control.

Rylee has curves and she's proud of them. She posts in her underwear on Instagram all the time holding onto her stomach or showing
off her butt in a new pair and gets hundreds of likes. Her followers
seem genuinely invested in what color she dyes her hair next and she
does her makeup straight out of a YouTube cottage-core aesthetic
tutorial.

The incident with Odhran still has me feeling unhinged and
emotional. Rylee never lets her smile falter. Maybe that's why she has
normal guys chasing after her instead of maniacs. Thankfully, Rylee
doesn't take my harsh tone personally.

"Not what I meant. It's just early. Fuck, I haven't been to the gym in… well, I don't think I've ever gone. Do you want company?"

Her sea-green eyes flash with genuine concern as she shakes her shaggy hair out of her face and searches through the pile of clothing on her bed for a crop top.

"No, I'm fine."

"Well, do you know what you're doing?" Rylee asks while checking out her ass in her full-length mirror and spanking her own butt a couple times to see it jiggle.

Crap. Rylee is way more outgoing than I am and if she takes enough pity on me, she'll probably invite herself along to the gym. I have no idea how Odhran will react to that. I don't even know if he has a plan for what to do when his friends or Six's friends see us together in public. I don't have to risk running into Six and Maura until my first class at noon. English classes alternate – evenings some days and earlier in the day on others. I never let my guard down despite the fact that nothing has happened yet, and Odhran's assurances of safety.

"Not really. I'm meeting up with someone."

Rylee's face lights up. "But you never leave the room!"

She sounds excited for me, rather than judgmental, but drawing attention to my complete lack of friends makes me deeply insecure. I don't know anything about making friends with white girls like Rylee, who doesn't know anything about being black, much less being black and Asian, which is an entirely different experience from most other black people anyway. I guess I've just always been a weirdo who preferred books and typing on my computer to interacting with people.

"I know. It's a bit scary, honestly."

I find my white t-shirt and put it on. Rylee's routine is a lot more elaborate. She dresses in a pair of white-legged lavender pants and a green crop top without a bra on underneath. After painting her lids with thick black liner, Rylee searches for books on her desk and shoves them into a large tote bag shaped like a strawberry.

"Who are you meeting up with? I'm not trying to be rude but I've never seen you talk to anyone in our year."

She's never seen me talk to anyone, period. I study alone, I eat my meals alone and when I'm not doing that or attending classes, all I do is play video games.

I don't want to tell Rylee that I'm meeting up with Odhran. I don't know if she knows him, but if she does, then she probably knows about his relationship with Six. I don't want to be in the middle of this drama. It's hard enough to motivate myself to leave my room.

"You probably don't know him."

"It's a *him?*" Rylee says excitedly, giving me her complete attention now that I'm talking about boys. "Did you meet him in one of your classes? Wait… did you meet him on one of those video game chat apps?"

She isn't asking that many questions, but I'm still overwhelmed and a little embarrassed that I'm known for staying in my bedroom and playing video games. I am the complete opposite of popular athletic girls who meet guys at the gym before class.

This is the longest I've gone without playing video games and considering how sore my ass is, maybe it's for the best that I don't spend all morning sitting at my computer. I could lie on my stomach and play with my Nintendo Switch, but that would only instigate Odhran to climb through my window and do something even crazier than before.

My response doesn't come fast enough for Rylee.

"Answer me, Nik! Who is the lucky guy? I can't believe it. Wait, is it Jamal? Is it Adam? Is it D'Shaun?"

I don't bother pointing out that she only mentioned black guys, like black men and black women are assigned to each other by default just because we're minority students. It's not the biggest deal in the world, so I just shake my head. I don't even know a guy named Adam at this school.

"Who is it then?!" She asks with the urgency one might use to ask the location of a malignant tumor.

Telling Rylee about this might be a bad idea but considering

Odhran asked me to update my social media profile and he seems hell-bent on possessing me completely *and* he didn't tell me not to tell her, maybe it won't seem so bad.

I breathe the two syllables quickly as if I don't really want Rylee to hear. But of course she hears me and she screams his name.

"OH MY GOD, YOU MEAN THE HONORABLE ODHRAN PATRICK MURRAY, AISLING'S BOYFRIEND!?"

She shrieks the entire sentence and then shrugs. "Well, I suppose he's the ex-boyfriend if what I heard from baseball Max is true."

Rylee taps her chin and then gives me a confused look.

"Hold on. I don't get it. *How is that even possible?*"

My phone buzzes and I don't know if I have time to answer Rylee's question. Instinctively, I check the message, even if it's rude to interrupt our conversation with my phone.

Your owner: Waiting.

RYLEE HAS INCREDIBLE INTUITION.

"Oh my goodness, is that him? It's totally him. NIK! How did you pull that off without ever leaving the room? Aisling is going to *kill* you."

Rylee's love of gossip makes her sound a little too gleeful about the prospect of Six killing me. My throat tightens nervously. I can't blame Rylee for not knowing that Six already tried and very nearly succeeded at ending my life. I'm just glad Odhran deleted the evidence. *I just want to move on from this and Odhran's insane murder plan isn't the best way to get away from this, despite what he thinks.*

"I didn't pull anything off, Rylee. It's complicated."

"Wait, aren't you happy? Are you sleeping together? I want to know *everything.*"

"Can we talk later?" I ask her. "I'm going to be late."

"Yes! Of course. Don't let me stand in the way of you and that sexy vampire freak. Is it true he drinks blood? God, don't tell me now. Tell me later."

Rylee gives me an unnecessary hug that doesn't fill me with the same excitement she possesses over my meeting with Odhran. I didn't want to treat this like a big deal, but Rylee's reaction reminds me that I'm dead meat. I'm also running late and I'm sure more than five minutes will be enough to drive Odhran crazy.

Me: I'm on my way.

HE DOESN'T REPLY to my text. I walk as fast as I can towards the gym, which doesn't feel very fast. My phone buzzes about four more times before I get there, but I don't bother checking it in case it slows me down. As I approach the giant glass doors, I can see Odhran leaning up against them dressed all in black.

Even before I can see his face, I sense he's annoyed. I glance at my watch. I'm only one minute late — as in sixty seconds. I wave to him and he puts his hoodie down, shaking mostly-black hair out of his face as he stares at me, but doesn't wave back. *Great. He's pissed.*

When I'm close enough to talk to Odhran, I'm out of breath, which he takes advantage of, launching into his disapproving admonition.

"You're late. What could have possibly held you up?"

He raises an eyebrow as he awaits an answer with frustrating levels of arrogance.

"My roommate."

"Rylee," he says, rolling his eyes. "Don't let it happen again."

"Do you know her?"

Odhran takes one of his hands out of his sweatpants pockets and pulls the large glass door of the college gymnasium open for me. He responds confidently, "I know everything about you relevant to our relationship."

"That's creepy."

"It's research."

I don't even know where to go when we enter the gym foyer

together. Do we just start doing push-ups here or something? Odhran takes a right turn and then looks over his shoulder impatiently. "Come on, Nik. You're already late. We don't have time."

"Can you chill?"

"Haven't you ever been here before?" Odhran says fussily as he shoves his backpack into a cubby. He's acting like this is the most important part of his day or something. My ass hurts and I want to be curled up like a burrito while eating a burrito, not in this giant building that smells like rubber and sweat.

"No. I haven't."

"Oh," Odhran says, his face growing suspiciously gentle. "That's about to change."

"I thought you knew everything relevant about me. I don't go to the gym and I don't belong at the gym." I respond to him sassily.

My throat tightens and my ass throbs as if warning me to keep my mouth shut before Odhran responds with another spanking. I doubt he would do something like that in public, but he's so unpredictable that I can't say for certain. I'm dead serious about the gym. I can't think of anything more anxiety-inducing than huffing and puffing in front of girls like Six and Maura who look like they were born on a treadmill in perfect matching workout gear.

Odhran's brows pinch together and then he recovers quickly, ignoring my protests entirely. "I see. I'll teach you everything you need to know today and over the next few weeks. But no more skipping the gym."

"I don't skip the gym," I tell him. "I don't go to the gym *period*, so I can't skip it."

"You go to the gym now," Odhran says. "And I'd rather not have other men talking to you, so I'll go with you. Every time."

"Wow, that's toxic."

"I don't care," Odhran says, slipping his hand into mine in an oddly comforting gesture. "We're going this way."

I struggle to keep up with Odhran's athletic stride, especially because of his height. I feel like a round little hobbit next to him, especially in the part of the gym Odhran drags me to with all the machines and weights. They look like modified medieval torture devices and just like I suspected, everyone in here is thin, half-naked and grunting semi-sexually.

I try to pull away but Odhran's grip on my hand tightens.

"I'm trying to run away," I hiss.

"I know," he says, drawing my body against his. "You aren't going anywhere. Relax. If you don't… I don't know. Something very bad will happen."

He lets go of my hand in an odd display of trust and then walks up to one of the machines/torture devices and removes his hoodie. Okay, now I see why he let go of me. Odhran taking his hoodie off freezes me in place and I almost drool all over the floor in the most pathetic and thirsty way possible.

It's not my fault that Odhran looks like this. Even Rylee lost her damn mind when she heard I was coming here with him.

"I'm not taking my shirt off," I say to Odhran as he tosses his hoodie on the ground and straddles the machine like a carousel horse.

"No need," he says, grabbing onto a wide-grip handle and pulling weights down to his chest, flexing every muscle on his incredibly sexy back.

"This is a lat pulldown machine," Odhran says. Or something. It's hard to focus on everything he says while his body looks like… *that*. But he forces me to use all these different machines and fires explanations at me that I understand a little bit. When we're done, I'm ready to curl up into a ball and die. But it's not like I didn't have a little bit of fun.

Odhran gets excited about working out and he's hot. So hot that my imagination is getting a workout too, imagining him all sweaty and on top of me. I tell myself it's just all the hormones in the air at the gym, or maybe I'm delirious from the exertion and losing my mind. Sitting on all those machines with my completely sore ass has been painful as hell too, not like Odhran feels sorry for me judging by the look on his face. This is not a look that says we're about to rest and dig into a pint of ice-cream.

"Ready for cardio?" Odhran asks, just when I'm ready to beg him to carry me back to my dorm.

"What? What's cardio? I feel very cardio right now," I gasp.

He just smiles at me. "Fifteen minutes on the stairs. It feels great. I do it every day."

"You really are a psychopath. There's a reason buildings don't have fifteen minutes of stairs between the first floor and the second floor."

"Yes," Odhran says. "But if it doesn't feel good, I'll let you spank me."

"Odhran!"

I look around at the gym to see if anyone heard him. No one did, because no one is close enough to us, but there are definitely people staring. People I hadn't noticed before because if I let myself notice, I would have been too anxious to hop on any of these strange machines after Odhran.

"Don't you care about people hearing you?" I whisper, hoping that the staring college students will eventually stop. (They don't.)

"No," he says. "I'm allowed to leave and enter relationships as I please. There's no way out of this, Nik. Stairs."

I don't know why he's so convincing. I tell myself it's because he promised I could spank him and the hope of getting revenge motivates me forward.

"Why?"

"Because it's good for you."

"You come into my life like a wrecking ball and now you're telling me what's good for me?"

Odhran tilts his head to the side and just when I think he's going to give me a legitimate answer, he just says, "Get your ass on the stairs."

Asshole.

Chapter Fifteen
Odhran

Nik complains on the stairs as long as her physical fitness allows and then she gasps through the rest of the fifteen minutes as dramatically as possible, as if the slight exertion could genuinely kill her. But she finishes. Dripping in sweat, balled up in rage and glaring at me with the fury of a thousand demons, Nik finishes our workout.

"I hate you," she whispers as she hops off the Stairmaster.

I don't let her push past me. She looks cute. On the verge of death, but cute. I grab her by the waist and kiss her hard. Like Nik, I notice people staring, but I don't care. I *really* don't care. She's mine and I'm not at this college for other people's approval.

My brothers just want me to grow up before I start working for the family. I just need to survive my remaining years here and have fun... with Nik.

I grab her cheeks and ignore her protests as I kiss her deeply and possessively in public. She braces herself against my chest, but there's no fucking way I'm letting her go until I'm done with her. *She's mine. She's mine.* My heart throbs with excitement as I taste her lips, her sweat and everything about her.

Odhran

When I pull away, I take her hand and tell her, "I'm walking you to class."

"I don't have anything that I need."

"I have a spare notebook. It's new."

She seems to accept that answer and she looks unhappy about it until I hand her the large leatherbound notebook out of my backpack.

"This is nice," Nik says, running her hands over the cover, barely concealing her lust for the leather. I don't bother hiding my smirk. I knew she would like it.

"Do you need a pen?"

"Yes."

I reach into my backpack and hand her a new pen.

"This is a Cartier ballpoint pen," I say to her. "Be careful with it."

Nik glances at it skeptically before holding onto the pen.

"Cartier. Is that fancy?"

"Yes. But you can keep it."

"How fancy?" she says, holding it back out to me. I close her hands around the pen and push it back to her.

"It doesn't matter. It's yours."

She doesn't argue. Thank goodness. Clearly I got through to her with the spanking. Discipline is *very* effective.

Nik has English class first and considering how things ended with Six last night, I want to *personally* make sure nothing happens to her. Once her professor arrives, I leave for my first class. Multivariable calculus. It's easy enough. I used to help Callum with his calculus homework when he was in college, so I barely have to attend classes to do well on the problem sets and exams.

College is easy.

Nik sends pictures of her ass at lunch. I love how the bruises look. I'll have to wait about ten days for them to heal and I tell myself that I'll hold myself back and take her virginity once she heals. I can't imagine getting through that night without playing with her perfect ass more. She's far too sore for me to mess with her more.

Chapter Fifteen

Each one of the ten days passes painfully.

The first night, I text Nik while she studies at the library. Her roommate Rylee sleeps in her room that night, so I can't come over. While it hurts to be away from her after experiencing my first night of cuddling with Nik, at least I have time to change the locks on my apartment and enhance security so that Six can't get in and wreak havoc again.

Nobody in my family texts me about the incident with her and Maura. I obeyed our rules despite my impulses. I didn't kill anyone.

For three days in a row, Nik and I have a similar routine. She whines and complains about going to the gym but when I ask her to send pictures of her healing bruises, she remembers what happens when she disobeys and the complaints turn into quiet huffs and impatient glances instead of outright bitching. I can see her getting more comfortable at the gym, and my confidence that she can handle an entire night of lovemaking grows with each passing day.

All of those three days, we have breakfast, lunch, and dinner together, breaking the seal on us appearing together in public. A few guys mention wishing they had a girl with an ass that fat, but other than that, nobody says anything. Girls whisper about us and friends of Six give us dirty looks, but nobody dares say a word to me.

Maura and Six pretend neither of us exist, but I don't have my guard down around either of them and I'm still reluctant to let Nik out of my sight for longer than a few hours. Her friend Rylee spends those three nights with her latest fuck buddy, so I sleep next to Onika until 5 a.m. when I wake up to go for a run and handle my personal business before heading to the gym with Nik.

On the fifth day of Nik's healing journey, I leave at 4:30 a.m. for an even longer run. I need to burn off my lust. Sleeping with Nik's ass pressed against my crotch has been fucking impossible. It's so soft, like a sexy pillow and she rubs it against my dick every night until I'm stiff. It gets worse when she falls asleep. The soft cheeks wrap around my dick through my sweatpants and I have to fight the temptation to wake Nik up by thrusting my cock inside her.

Not yet. Not until I take her virginity and make her first night special. The fifth day I can't keep my hands off her. Between her classes, I make her meet me in isolated wings of her class buildings in gender neutral bathrooms and bend her over the sink to eat her pussy from behind.

I send Nik to every single class with trembling thighs and soaked pussy lips. I only bother attending my advanced economics class and my Medieval Irish History class. I got 115% on my last Calculus quiz, so I don't see the point in showing up for the review session when I could be on my knees sucking on Nik's lower lips. It's a miracle that we don't get caught.

It's a miracle that I don't give in to my urge to thrust my cock inside her and take her virginity in an on-campus bathroom. She tastes so fucking good and waiting for her drives me insane and fills me with delirious desire. I'm long past the point of denying my interest in her goes beyond a desire for domination and control.

There are no words for the emotions Nik provokes in me. I want to make sense of my emotional state, but it's too overwhelming. My body just provokes me to keep acting. To take control of her. To keep her firmly within my grasp and to keep Nik as sexually aroused as possible.

Day six and seven are an even more frustrating struggle. Six and I would go to nightclubs every weekend and keep our relationship alive with cocaine and dancing. It doesn't seem like Nik's scene. It wasn't really mine.

But Nik is my girl now and I might not have loads of experience, but when you're with a girl, you take her out. You spoil her. I wonder what Nik would like, but maybe all girls like clubbing and I should start there. So on day six of her recovery, I message her.

Me: Clubbing this weekend?
Nik: English homework.
Me: You need a break.
Nik: Clubbing is not a break.

Chapter Fifteen

. . .

GREAT. I have to be smarter than this. I know everything about Nik.

Me: Used bookstore?
Nik: Is this a weird sex thing?

I DON'T UNDERSTAND what the hell she could mean by that.

Me: No. It's a place that sells used books.
Nik: Okay. What about them?
Me: You take a break from writing. I drive you to one. We spend time together. It's a date. I'll pick you up at 11 A.M.

SHE TAKES way too long to respond. If I have to wait more than five minutes for her text messages, I feel seriously sick. I might know things about her, but I don't know what Nik is thinking. I don't know if she will have finally decided to pack her things up and run away. That would be a mistake, since I installed tracking software on her phone. But I'd rather not use it.

Nik: Fine.
Me: You don't sound excited.

SHE ISN'T EXCITED. But when we get to the used bookstore *Raven's Used Books* in downtown Cambridge, she can't help herself.

"I don't have a lot of money," she says. "I just like looking at all the old books and imagining myself in a library like the one from *Beauty & The Beast.*"

I have to fight the urge to tell her that I could give her that library in a heartbeat. My feelings for Nik are strong, but I still have to be careful. *She might not feel the same.*

"You don't need money," I say to Nik. "You have me."

"I'm not some kind of gold digger."

I take her hand and push the door open. "You're not," I tell her. "You're mine and that means you have whatever books your heart desires. You can even buy them just because you like the smell."

"How do you know…Never mind."

She writes about her favorite smell – the smell of books – in nearly all her horror stories. Many of them are set in libraries or labyrinths or other settings like that. Nik leaves pieces of herself in everything she creates. *She's so different.*

Nik forgets her disapproval with my research methods once she is completely surrounded by books. I couldn't bother her if I tried at this point. She's in heaven. I insist that she gets every book she touches. We have to fill the trunk of my car to get all the books back to her dorm room.

I can't wait to move Nik out of here. I can't stay in her room long without bending her over her desk and then eating her out again. She tastes so fucking good. Her pussy is so damn delicious. She has to kick me out so she can write. I agree – as long as she promises to let me read it.

On day seven, I show up to Nik's room after her roommate leaves in the morning for brunch with her friends, read Nik's essay, eat her out and fight my increasing desire to make love to her.

It feels fucking cruel that I can't have Nik when I want her so badly. With all her activity in the gym, she's too sore to get away from me when I eat her out and her stamina for enduring my tongue between her legs has already showed significant improvement.

I thought touching her would get this obsession out of my system, but her closeness only makes it worse. I have her pressed against her door as I rest

Chapter Fifteen

on my knees with my tongue deep inside her. I can feel her getting close to begging for it. So when I finish eating her out, I leave. Controlling myself physically hurts me. But I can't stay away from her.

We meet for dinner later – in public. I finger her under the table after we have Peking duck at a *nice* Chinese restaurant – not the places Nik normally orders from. She eats a lot, almost as much as I eat, and she looks so fucking cute when she eats. I can't help myself. She looks so pretty that I want to put my fingers in her pussy.

After she cums in the restaurant and struggles not to scream, she's silent the entire drive back to her dorm.

On day eight, she doesn't talk to me at all beyond what's necessary. She kicks ass at the gym and doesn't even smile when I congratulate her on adding ten pounds to her bench press. Her bruises are almost healed on her butt too. I can't get a smile out of her all day and when I text her before bed, her response stings.

Me: How did I screw up?
Nik: It doesn't matter. You don't care how I feel.

I DON'T WANT her to think that I don't care about her feelings at all. I just want her to feel what I feel – completely and utterly obsessed.

Me: I definitely care.
Nik: Whatever.
Me: I can come over tonight.

I WANT her to say yes. More than anything, I want a chance to prove to her that I care however she wants. If she doesn't want oral this time, I'll play one of her boring farm simulator games with her. She enjoys those almost as much as Call of Duty. But she doesn't want me to come over.

Nik: Rylee is here and her sister is visiting from out of town.
Me: Tomorrow.
Nik: Whatever.
Me: I miss you.

SHE DOESN'T RESPOND and I don't demand a response from her this time. I pushed her too far in the restaurant with my fingers inside her. Separating myself from her is painful, but if she needs time, I'll give her at least a day. On the ninth day, Nik sends me pictures of her ass before I ask.

Interesting.

Me: Gorgeous.
Nik: I'll be ready for the gym soon.

STRICTLY BUSINESS. Nik arrives at the gym wearing a scowl and an *incredibly* sexy outfit.

"Where did you get that?"

"None of your business."

"It's very… revealing."

She rolls her eyes. "It's from a video I saw. Now shut up."

"It looks good."

"I'm not wearing it for your approval," she says.

I don't believe her. There is absolutely no way she looked in the mirror, saw her ass looking that damn good and she didn't think I would notice. She doesn't talk to me throughout our entire workout unless it's absolutely necessary. What the hell is she thinking? She drives me crazy. I walk her to English class and for a moment, she lets her tough exterior falter when we walk past Six and Maura together.

Ten days and neither of them have acted, but Nik has an immediate physical reaction to their presence, even if Six and Maura behave like they don't see her. I take her hand and walk her straight to her seat, forcing some other lame freshman out of the seat closest to the professor.

I leave Nik with a kiss, and head to calculus for a change. If I don't distract myself from Nik with classes, I'll do something crazy. *I won't be patient enough.*

She won't care about me if I don't show her how much I care about her. I'm willing to wait. I wasn't before but… I can handle it now.

On our tenth day together, I text Nik for a picture of her butt, but she doesn't send it.

Nik: No bruises. You don't need a picture.

Me: Can I see your tits?

Nik: You can see them when we're at the gym together in about ten minutes.

Nik: I didn't mean that.

Nik: I meant I'll be there in ten minutes.

Nik: Don't read into it

TOO LATE. Nik folds her arms over her breasts when she gets to the gym. I have bad news for her. I want to go to her tonight, and I want tonight to be completely special between us as we celebrate her healed bruises, but my brothers have other plans for me. Aiden texted me at around six in the morning.

Aiden: Meeting tonight. Get your homework done on time. 10 P.M. Darragh's place.

. . .

NO ROOM FOR NEGOTIATION THERE. I don't want to leave Nik alone tonight, but I can't argue with Aiden. My concern is mainly about Six and Maura showing up again. Aiden will never give me permission to do what I want... Not unless I get my act together. If I can get him to see that I've grown up and that I have become a reasonable person, perhaps he'll allow it.

Tonight, I just need to make sure Nik is safe for every second that she is out of my sight. I message him a standard request for a safe house. I don't want Nik at my apartment alone or on campus where she is too vulnerable. I don't know how I'll convince her to leave campus with me for the night and if Aiden can't get her anywhere safe, a *really* expensive hotel in Boston might be an acceptable option.

"You don't have to fold your arms," I tell her. "I can still see your tits."

"Don't be gross, Odhran. I'm exhausted. I don't want to do some intense ass workout. I want to curl up in a ball and die."

"Why are you so tired?"

"I was writing."

"About me?"

"Not everything is about you," Nik snaps, but I can't tell if she genuinely means it or if I've caught her withholding something.

"Hm. Well it should be."

She rolls her eyes, not appreciating my joke.

"Are you still pissed at me for fingering you at the restaurant?"

"Very good, you solved the puzzle Odhran. Let's stop talking out here so I can put my headphones on and have an excuse to ignore you for the next hour."

"I wish you would ignore me instead of staring at my abs all the time when you think I'm not looking."

"Shut up, I don't do that. You're the one obsessed with grabbing my butt between sets."

"When have I ever done that?"

"Your hand is literally on my butt right now."

Chapter Fifteen

I move my hand away from her butt. I guess it *had* moved over there on its own. Nik swats my hand away playfully. When she puts her headphones on and approaches our first machine for the day, I want to rip them off and have her attention on me completely. But I get so distracted staring at her and her pretty hair and nice butt that I forget to be a tyrant.

What the hell is happening to me?

Chapter Sixteen
Onika

Odhran is weirder than normal today. He thinks I haven't paid close attention to him the past ten days the way he's paid close attention to me. He isn't focused today and he seems almost nervous, which isn't an emotional state I normally attribute to Odhran. I don't know what he is so damn nervous about. I stayed up all night finishing an essay for English class and emailed it to my professor last night, so I'm not just nervous, but exhausted.

I know Professor Gemmell will want to talk about our essays today and probably have them graded in record time. Maura and Six have ignored me this far because I've kept my head down and obeyed Odhran's commands as much as possible so I stay far out of trouble. But this midterm essay counts for 20% of our grade for the year and anyone who cares about their writing is a complete slave to our professor's approval.

I guess nervous isn't the word for what I feel. *I'm scared.*

After a couple sets, I notice Odhran staring at me again. He doesn't bother hiding his staring at me when he watches me work out. I make an effort to subtly stare at Odhran's ridiculously large shoulders or his chiseled chest, but Odhran looks like a hungry vampire as he watches me workout. I try to ignore him, but halfway through our workout, it's impossible.

I'm growing a *little* fond of our morning sessions, but mostly because of the benefits of cardio and weight training, and definitely not because of Odhran. Just because he confidently struts around the gym bare-chested looking like a God doesn't mean I'm actually enjoying his presence. His personality is still brutish and commanding. My ass might have healed, but I still remember how he spanked me with Rylee's paddle.

Before I could stop her, she took it away to paint it in her sorority colors, and now it's too late to tell her the truth. I zone out in an effort to push my guilt over the sorority paddle out of my head, but Odhran distracts me by wiping a bead of sweat off my upper lip while gazing *intently* into my eyes.

I set down the dumbbell I was holding and give him a frustrated admonishment. "I was actually focused that time."

"You're done working out," Odhran says with a scowl. "Too many days of the cold shoulder. We're talking."

"Do we have to talk here?"

"There isn't anyone else here except that guy with the headphones."

The guy with the headphones is the nose-picking D student from my English class. Sure, he has headphones on, but I don't need him in my personal business. Before I can protest, Odhran leans forward and kisses me. His sweaty kisses still catch me off guard.

He's a good kisser, but I push him away.

"Not here."

"Fine," he says. "Then we talk."

"Fine."

"You can't stay on campus tonight. I need you at a safe house."

"A safe house?" I ask him, wondering if this is another sex thing, or if Odhran is being serious.

"Yes," he says impatiently. "I'll send someone to pick you up, but I won't be around tonight and I don't want you getting into trouble."

"I don't get into trouble. I play video games, eat takeout and do homework. Rylee will keep me safe tonight."

"Your roommate has sex with a new guy every three days. I can't rely on her presence."

"Don't slut shame my roommate."

"I don't care if she's a slut," Odhran says. "I care if you're alone. You can't be alone tonight."

I stupidly thought Odhran wanted to have a conversation about feelings and maybe *apologize* for fingering me in a public place where anyone could have seen me. Instead, he just wants to boss me around again and make vague threats instead of being clear. Instead of respecting me.

"I can handle myself."

Odhran's hand juts out and he grips my forearm. "Do you really think so? If I hadn't stopped my ex from murdering you, we wouldn't be having this conversation."

I want to slap him so damn bad.

"Don't throw that in my face, Odhran."

His face softens. He lets go of me and then he seems frustrated as he rakes his fingers through his black hair.

"I will kill anyone who hurts you. To spare myself the moral anguish, I'd prefer keeping you somewhere else."

"You can't *keep me* somewhere."

"Only for tonight," he says. "I'll come back tomorrow in time to drive you back to campus."

"Can you at least tell me why you're bringing this up?"

I have a little bit of an answer about Odhran's strange mood today, but there are shadows around him that I don't understand. He must have secrets – dark ones – if he can scare off Six and Maura. He also wants me to murder Six.

"Are you going to kill someone?"

Odhran chuckles. "No."

"Good."

It's probably some kind of dating red flag that I actually have to ask that question, but I just feel relieved that he's not going to kill someone. I know I should fight him more. But ten days of routine, ten days of spending time with Odhran and… maybe he really is the reason I'm here.

"My family needs to meet with me about my relationship situation."

"They know about me?"

"I mean my *former* situation," Odhran says, his cheeks reddening awkwardly. "I have my ideas for how to solve the problem and they have theirs."

"Should we talk about this here? We can talk about it somewhere that doesn't have cameras pointed at us from every angle."

"The cameras don't record sound," Odhran says. "Have you heard of my family?"

"No. Should I have?"

"No. You're not Irish."

The last three words sound a little bitter, but I don't know what Odhran expects me to do about the fact that I'm not Irish.

"Okay…"

"I work for my family when I'm not in school. Tonight, I have to work for my family and I don't know what they will ask me to do. I don't know how vulnerable you will be to Six, Maura or either of their families."

"Are their families super racist or something?" I ask, half-joking, but clearly, it's not a joke.

"Obviously," Odhran says. "Don't you think it took someone absolutely depraved to hurt you like that?"

"I've been bullied before."

Odhran raises an eyebrow, like what I said surprises him. I thought he knew everything about me and suddenly, I feel really embarrassed exposing myself like this. I'd rather not tell him about the type of things I endured as an overweight kid and then an overweight teenage girl.

I didn't make it to college as a virgin because my childhood was easy.

"They are worse than bullies," Odhran says after a few extra seconds of contemplation. "They will hurt you because it hurts me and they will torture you if they could. I can't have that happen."

"I thought you scared them off."

"There are bigger monsters than my ex-girlfriend and her best friend," Odhran says pensively. "I just went after what I wanted. I didn't think about how it would all turn out."

"It seems like it's turning out just fine," I say to Odhran, but that doesn't appear to cheer him up at all. It's not like I don't worry or constantly freak the fuck out about what they could do to me, but the more time that passes, the more I believe they will stick to bullying instead of outright torture.

Hell, I would be scared of Odhran. *He shot at them.* I don't do a great job of convincing him not to worry, unfortunately. He stays hell bent on this safe house, although I don't see the point.

"No," Odhran says. "This is not a discussion. I'll have someone pick you up and make sure that you're safe."

"This is ridiculous."

Odhran's mood shifts and he becomes immediately sullen and sulky, as if he expected me to celebrate his announcement that I'll be sleeping somewhere other than my dorm room bed tonight.

"There is nothing ridiculous about it."

"Can't I go to my sister's place?"

Odhran wrinkles his nose. "I don't know your sister well enough, so she isn't safe. For all I know, she could be moonlighting as a prostitute."

"This is so stupid and my sister is not a prostitute."

"No, it's not stupid. I care about you."

My chest does something weird when he says that. I'm pretty sure he's just manipulating me and trying to get me to accept his controlling ways. I fold my arms and make my best effort to push back against Odhran.

"You can't just waltz into my life, announce that you're my boyfriend and take control of everything."

Great. The nose picker from my English class is officially staring at us and sure enough, his damn finger is halfway up his nose as he stares at our uncomfortable public confrontation over our stupid relationship. The relationship that I don't understand because it's a constant state of either sex hormones or anxiety.

"We're *together*," Odhran says. "We've been together for almost two weeks and you can't deny that every minute we're together has been nothing but exciting for you."

"Whatever, Odhran. I'm leaving."

I'm tired of getting stared at by that stupid kid Tyler, especially because he starts eating whatever the hell he fished out of his nose and I don't have enough on my stomach to tolerate the disgusting sight unfolding in my peripheral vision. I storm away from Odhran, past the guy watching us and burst out into the gym foyer.

Of course, Odhran follows.

"Where the fuck do you think you're going?" he asks, his deep, smooth, annoyingly sexy ass voice bellows in the foyer. The sound echoes because of the good acoustics and stops me in my tracks, completely against my will.

"Take another step and I will hurt your ass so badly, you won't be able to walk for a week."

I turn around, ready to fight Odhran by throwing my water bottle at his ignorant head. He grabs my wrist so tightly that my water bottle clatters to the gymnasium floor and he drags my body against his.

"What the fuck are you thinking, Nik?"

"I hate you! That's what I'm thinking. You show up out of nowhere and suddenly, I'm in danger and I just want to be a normal person and–

Odhran kisses me. Instead of taking me seriously for one second, he kisses me. I squeal and try to push him off, but he takes firm control of my wrist and stops every word out of my mouth with a fierce kiss. When he's ready, he pulls away. He had better not let go of my hand because I am *so* ready to slap him.

"I showed up because you needed me," he says. "I have *always* been there when you needed me. I care about you, Nik. I deeply, profoundly and very intensely care about you. I know my heart belonged to another girl before we met and nothing happened the way I planned it but… you *are* my girl."

"What about my feelings?"

He loosens his grip on my wrist. "What about them?"

"What if I don't feel the same way? What if I don't care about you?"

His blue eyes flicker with cold rage that he quickly suppresses. If Odhran conceals another emotion beyond his anger with me, he does an excellent job at hiding it from me. My heart does a little flip at this display from him. I don't know why I enjoy getting a rise out of him.

"Then break up with me," Odhran says, his body tensing angrily, like the very idea offends him.

He gives me a stern expression like he would never actually allow such a thing and this is just a test. I keep glaring at him fiercely.

Odhran continues, essentially revoking my right to break up with him. "But do it *after* tonight. I don't have time for any arguments. Whether you want to be with me or not, I won't have my family problems affecting you. I won't have Six hurting you."

"Okay, then we'll break up tomorrow," I tell him, my body shaking. I don't know if he's serious. Would Odhran really let me out of this?

He's clearly still upset, but I watch him bury it in an effort to get on with our day. We wasted so much time arguing that I'll probably be late for English class, even if Odhran drives me there.

"Right," he says, raking his fingers through his thick black hair and continuing to glare at me. He runs his tongue over his lips and I become the first one to break eye contact.

"I'll take you to class," he says possessively. "Come."

Again, Odhran doesn't give me the chance to turn him down. He slips his hand into mine and it's almost like we didn't fight because his grasp feels so good and I wonder if I'm being honest with myself or just living in complete denial because of how guilty I feel for wanting him.

I don't know what to do.

Chapter Sixteen

Chapter Seventeen
Odhran

Nik has lunch alone because I have a more advanced economics class – Game Theory. I have dinner alone, something small and light because Callum will probably bring extra Dunkin' Donuts for us if he doesn't eat them all on the drive over. I take my chances on the donuts. Aiden should be arranging Nik's safety tonight, so I have nothing to do but prepare for our meeting. That means video games.

Nik isn't online, which makes me feel better. She's somewhere safe now and I don't have to worry.

One hour before our meeting, Aiden calls.

"HAVE YOU LOST YOUR MIND?!" Aiden bellows into the phone without explaining himself when I answer the phone. I run through the list of potential mistakes I could have made in my head, but come up with nothing. Aiden might be drunk.

"Not recently," I answer. "What's wrong? Too much Jim Beam?"

"Shut the fuck up, jackass. You are involved with Zariyah's best friend's younger sister," Aiden snarls. "How on *earth* did you find this girl?" Jim Beam isn't the problem. *Damn it.*

"She goes to my university."

Chapter Seventeen

That doesn't answer Aiden's question, but it's close enough to the truth that he doesn't dig any deeper.

"Odhran, we need to have a frank conversation about this," Aiden says. "Dad is dead, so unfortunately, I need to speak to you about your choices and your decisions regarding women."

"I would rather die than talk to you about women."

I try to sound as bored as possible in hopes that it turns Aiden off the idea of talking to me about women. How could he give me any relevant advice? His wife showed up on his doorstep. I'll have to be a little more proactive to find happiness. *There was never any happiness with Six. Just drugs. Sex. And cruelty. I'm tired of it.*

Aiden says, "If you're going to die, you will wait to die until after our conversation. You can die whenever you want after that."

"We're meeting in an hour," I remind Aiden. "Was this call really necessary?"

"I want you over here now."

I hope he has better parenting skills with his own kids.

"What about Nik?" I ask him, unwilling to leave my apartment until I know Aiden will look after her. He hasn't explained anything and I have no right to ask for an explanation from the boss, but I need to know that the person I care about will be safe. I have no intention of letting Nik go after tonight – but I won't force her to stay with me either.

I'll show her how she feels about me. Once I claim her virginity, thrust my cock into her cunt for the first time, there won't be more denial between the two of us.

"Don't worry about Nik," Aiden says. "Worry about getting your ass to Darragh's place before Rian and Callum get there."

"I'll listen to you if you promise nothing bad will happen to Nik after tonight. I need to be sure that no matter what happens, she will be safe and I will be able to go to her."

I don't like how Aiden sounds about Nik. If he forbids me from seeing her, I'll have to listen to him. It's foolish for me to push back against him now and I know it, but I can't stop myself from senselessly defending Nik.

"You will listen to me because I am the boss of this family and your eldest brother. I don't know what twisted game you're playing, Odhran, but I know you and our family. You spent all of your teenage years taking vows to forward racial purity. You have the same tattoos I have and others that were special. This girl... I cannot allow you to play a game with her. Choose someone else."

There it is. I knew he would ask me based on his initial outrage, but I expected Aiden to ask me this part in person.

My heart pounds. He doesn't discourage me from playing a game, merely asking me to do it to someone else. From Aiden, that surprises me. He left his past behind him – the violence, the beliefs, the reluctance to interact with or entertain people of different races. He was the strongest believer in our family. *I wanted to be better than him.*

"This isn't a game to me."

I want Aiden to believe me, but I don't care if he does.

"Then what the fuck is it?"

Would Aiden believe me if I told him that this was love? Would he understand how it felt to be alone and hurt, shut out from my future playing football and forced to indulge in my other favorite hobby – video games. I wasn't looking for girls at first, but when I stumbled upon her profile and then clicked the link to her writing...

I felt something.

"I don't want to be the person I was," I answer Aiden honestly. "All of you changed and dad's dead. I just... It's too hard to stay away from certain people and to hate them and... I don't see the point."

"And you see a point to making a murder plot to kill your ex-girlfriend?" Aiden challenges me.

How the fuck does Aiden know about that? Maybe he's testing me.

"Who told you that?"

"I don't need to be told," Aiden says. "I have people watching your movements just like everyone else, Odhran."

"So you don't have any proof?"

"Don't pull that bullshit with me," Aiden growls. "I changed your goddamn diapers."

"A fact I wish you would stop bringing up considering I'm taller and stronger than you."

Aiden grunts in response. I forget that he can read me and that he usually disagrees with my perspective.

Maybe Darragh or Rian would understand me better. Aiden is too much of a perfectionist and sometimes, he can prioritize peace when I would prefer him to allow me to unleash the chaos brewing just beneath the surface.

"Well *I* can't kill a woman," I continue, carefully restraining my temper. Six might not deserve death for anything she did to me. At first, my desire for her death was a matter of convenience to me and frustration with our life together. After she hurt Nik, my desire grew stronger. But spending more time with Nik calms the beast again and I'm utterly confused about *what* I want.

I just don't want Aiden to order me away from Nik before I can win her heart over. It never occurred to me how important it was for her to love me back before today.

Aiden sighs. "I see."

I can't tell what he sees.

"What?"

"That's what this is about. You want Six dead, so you're using Onika to get rid of your ex. You should have just come to me and you should *definitely* stay away from that girl."

No. This doesn't sound like a direct command, but a suggestion, and I won't be leaving Nik alone unless Aiden gives me a good reason to leave her alone.

"I'm not using her and I already explained why I didn't come to you."

Aiden responds gruffly, "Do you expect me to believe that overnight you have fallen out of love with your beloved Aisling and in love with a mixed race black woman? That doesn't sound like you at all."

Odhran

"What do you know about me? You moved out before I was two years old. Maybe I learned how to be a race traitor from you."

"That's not funny," Aiden says, responding with immediate grumpiness to my efforts at referencing the truth about not just one, but all of us.

It's what our father would think about us and it's what Aisling's family thinks about us. There isn't any point in hiding what we are now.

"It's not a joke. It's what we are."

"Let go of those ideas, Odhran. If you really care about that girl, you will *never* let those words come out of your mouth again."

It's hard for me to trust my brother as badly as I want to. I grew up one way my entire life and while my feelings for Nik are strong, I am not in the habit of putting my emotions first. Emotions have never really been part of the equation.

And could this woman really be so important? *To me, yes.*

"It's not so easy to let go of my beliefs," I tell him. "I care about her but... I want to hurt her. I want to punish her for how badly I want her. It's confusing. I just feel so angry."

My brother grunts and I don't expect him to actually say something helpful.

"Get over here," Aiden says. "I'll get you drunk and we'll fix this before our family meeting."

I DON'T ASK him if he seriously wants me to stay away from Nik. I don't want to risk him saying yes. I play Rick Ross on the way to Aiden's place, my mind turning over images of Nik. I text her while I'm driving.

Me: I miss you. Send a pic.

Chapter Seventeen

S HE DOESN'T REPLY RIGHT AWAY, but she might be in a car or maybe she doesn't have the Wi-Fi password or an unlimited data plan... When did I become a neurotic fucking mess? I should be in control here and that is the last thing I feel like I have right now. Everything spiraled out of control before I realized what was happening and now there are too many moving parts and far too many people involved.

The two of us should run away...

But Nik has to text back first before we can do that. She still doesn't text back when I park my car in the spacious lot outside Darragh's brownstone and I consider tossing my phone into Darragh's driveway so they can't reach me and driving back to Nik's dorm room. She is making me so fucking crazy.

Me: Answer me. It hurts not being near you.

I WAITED ten days to touch her. Ten painful days of being near her, smelling her shampoo and her sweat, tasting her lips, and staying far away from her perfect, flawless, deliciously tight cunt. *Why isn't she answering?*

Before I enter Darragh's brownstone, I see his car and Aiden's in the driveway. I assume the other car in the driveway is Kamari's. We are on fairly good terms and she is certainly much kinder to me than my brother Darragh. I text Aiden that I'm outside. Older people love knocking on doors. It's weird and intrusive when you could just send a text message.

I can hear Aiden and Darragh talking on the other side of the door in hushed tones for about five minutes before Aiden sees my text message and opens the door.

"Why didn't you just knock?"

"It's weird."

Aiden rolls his eyes. "Come on in. Rian and Callum will be here soon. Darragh and I want to talk to you."

I give Aiden a suspicious look, but he doesn't seem angry. And apparently this conversation must include my sister-in-law, Kamari, because I hear her voice in the kitchen.

"No killing. No murder," Aiden says as he leads me into the house. "That's where we need to begin today."

"I haven't done anything," I grumble.

"Good," Aiden says. "Come on."

Kamari and Darragh greet me and I exhale with relief as I see the cheese plates, hummus, and crackers Kamari has laid out for us. She raises her eyebrows as she sees me.

"Look at you, Odhran. Have you been lifting weights lately?"

"Yes."

"You look bigger than when I last saw you," Kamari says. "Good for you."

Darragh glares at her and takes one of the crackers off the plate. "We are supposed to have a serious conversation, not congratulate his muscles."

"Don't be jealous, Darragh."

"I don't have to be jealous when I know I can kill any man who touches you."

"I have no interest in touching anyone's wife," I say sharply, earning a snicker from Kamari and blank expressions from my brothers. They frustrate me *deeply*.

Aiden thumps me on the back. "Good. Now, let's talk about your relationship problems."

"I have something to say," Kamari says. My heart fills with dread. But I have no choice. I have to listen to this. I grimace.

"Please, spare me."

"No," Kamari says. "I'm a black woman and you apparently have an interest in black women, so I'm taking the time to educate you. Sit down."

"Thank you for agreeing to do this on such short notice," Aiden says. "Let's get this out of the way before Rian and Callum get here. Then we can get to the real business."

"Can I have a clue about the real business? Because Nik's safety is my business."

"We're getting rid of your problem," Aiden grunts. "Trust me... Now sit your ass down and listen to Kamari."

Chapter Eighteen
Onika

Odhran tells me to expect a car outside my dorm building at 7:15 P.M. Knowing that he isn't anywhere near campus makes me more nervous to leave my dorm alone, so I ask Rylee for support. She helps me pack my things and then offers to come with me, but I don't think Odhran would be okay with that. But she does walk outside to wait with me in front of my building.

A yellow Mercedes coupe pulls to a slow stop in front of me and Rylee. It's not what I would expect for a mob transportation vehicle, but it looks expensive and I know Odhran comes from a family with money, so this adds up. Rylee squeals when she sees the car and doesn't even pretend that she isn't blown away by the tinted Mercedes.

"Holy fuck, you are totally getting laid tonight."

Rylee misses the point when the point isn't hooking up, so I just shrug, even if I don't think Odhran and I are ever going to be together again. *I have to break up with him.*

I hug Rylee goodbye and then I get into the back of the coupe with my little overnight bag. Before I even see the driver in the front seat, the car pulls away, zooming out of the dorm parking lot before I can get my seat belt attached.

Chapter Eighteen

I fly across the backseat of the coupe and then try to steady myself as the car speeds off. What the hell is going on?

Before I can say anything, the driver turns around and now I'm confused. I thought Odhran was in the Irish mob. As in, the mob of Irish individuals who are presumably of Irish descent. What the fuck?

"I'm Heavyn," she says. "Don't worry, Nik. I'm taking you to your sister and once you're away from Odhran, you won't have to worry about anything anymore."

"What's going on? Are you part of Odhran's... family?"

"I'm married to his brother, Rian."

I didn't know about Odhran's brother, Rian, but I guess I don't know much about Odhran aside from what he wants me to know.

"Oh. Okay."

"Don't worry, girl. We've got you."

I DON'T KNOW MUCH about mafia safe houses, but the place we end up in Wenham, Massachusetts feels more like a luxury beach house than a secret safe house.

Heavyn must have noticed my scrutiny, because she gives me a sympathetic smile and nods towards the house.

"Rian and I bought this house last year," Heavyn says. "Nobody knows where it is except the people inside it and my husband. But don't worry about him. By the time they find out what we did, everything will be all good."

"Okay."

This is the second time Heavyn has said something a little odd, but I don't want to read too much into it. I take my duffel bag and follow her down the stone driveway to the immense front door of the mansion. It smells like the ocean everywhere and I can even hear the soft sounds of the waves on the shore.

This is a gorgeous house. Heavyn uses her fingerprint to unlock the door. Holy shit, there are babies in this house. The second I walk through the front door, I hear babies crying and then I hear the last voice I expect. My sister. And it sounds like she's expecting me.

"OH MY GOD SHE'S HERE. NIK IS HERE."

Zariyah's voice follows Kalani's, but Zariyah has a lot softer speaking voice, so I can't hear what she says, but I recognize the pair of voices since I grew up listening to them gossiping. How do they know Heavyn?

I can hear my sister and Kalani both making a ruckus as they stomp down the hallway of the house towards the entrance. Zariyah and Kalani still spend a *lot* of time together. My sister's best friend Zariyah calls after Kalani as they approach the door together, "Can you calm down? Heavyn already told us that she's fine."

Zariyah does absolutely nothing to calm my crazy ass sister down. Kalani bursts around the corner where I can finally see her and not just hear her. She wraps me up in a big hug that threatens to squish me like a jellyfish beneath a boot. I let out a dramatic choking noise as my sister traps me in her tight grip. She doesn't stop holding me tightly.

"I'm fine! What is happening? What are you doing here?" I choke out, eliminating the remaining oxygen in my lungs.

Zariyah puts her hands on her hips and gives me an oddly intimidating look once Kalani releases me from her death grip. I don't think Zariyah realizes how intimidating she is, but she grew up with a football player for a brother, so her toughness is absolutely legendary. I don't understand why they're all here together at Heavyn's house.

"What we want to know is how my best friend's innocent gamer sister got mixed up in the damn mob. Sit down, girl. We need answers from you," Zariyah says.

She's almost as scary as Odhran.

"Nik, the mob boss's wife is here," Kalani adds. "You've rarely ever left your room How is this even happening to you?"

Big sisters have a way of dragging your ass over the coals for no reason at all. Did she have to throw in that jab about me never leaving my room? I have gone to the gym every day this week.

They keep staring at me, clearly bothered by my hesitation. But I'm stunned and I know way less than they think. What answers could they possibly want from me? I'm not mixed up in the mob. I'm a normal university student who woke up one day with a target on her back.

"I'm not mixed up in the mob," I answer, trying to stay calm but suddenly feeling emotional.

At exactly the wrong moment, my phone buzzes. I know it's Odhran, but I don't feel like I can reply to him right now. Great. He's probably going to freak out even if I'm completely fine. My sister, Zariyah and her friends all have a million questions, including the mob boss's wife Valentina, who seems nice enough, but doesn't say very much. I feel like she's analyzing me.

It's hard not to get overwhelmed and it's oddly difficult not to feel defensive of Odhran.

My first encounter with him admittedly scared the crap out of me, but since then, Odhran has taken the time to get to know me. I feel like I know more about him too. Zariyah, Kalani and their friends act like Odhran is this criminal with absolutely no soul. When he spanked my ass so hard it left bruises, I definitely questioned the existence of his soul, but since then... he's been like a dream boyfriend.

That's part of why it doesn't feel real. Nothing about him feels real. I answer them as honestly as I can, telling them I met Odhran at college, we started "dating" after he broke up with Six, I had no idea about his mob connections (although I suspected) and I'm Kalani's uncool younger sister so she didn't tell me Zariyah's husband's last name. (I probably wouldn't have remembered anyway.) Plus, Murray is a common name and with his black hair, Odhran doesn't obviously look like Zariyah's husband who I might have seen once or twice at the bookstore.

I can feel when they're almost done asking questions because the rate of questioning slows down and they give me time to answer without Kalani freaking out and doing the most every time I say something. Heavyn is the only one capable of holding them back.

"Okay, I think we know enough. It honestly sounds like we overreacted. She looks fine. Nik, are you in any way uncomfortable with your relationship with Odhran," Heavyn asks calmly, giving me a gentle look that would have calmed me down under normal circumstances.

But we're talking about Odhran. Nothing about me and Odhran has been normal.

The question makes me deeply uneasy and my sister's presence here surprises me more than anything.

"It doesn't matter if she's uncomfortable," Kalani says. "She can't date a mobster! She's my younger sister, I don't want anyone shooting her up like Zariyah."

"I didn't choose to get shot at," Zariyah says. "Nik will have a much easier time staying out of trouble. And she didn't even answer the question. We have to respect her wishes."

Like the question couldn't get more nerve wracking, it feels like they're all staring at me expectantly and it definitely seems like there's a right answer here.

"I don't understand what is happening between us but... Odhran cares about me and we just started up whatever this is so... I don't know. I want to give it a chance."

The words stumble out of my mouth partially without my permission. Kalani has always been too old and cool for me to bother her with my lame crushes. What would have been the point? Kalani always had a boyfriend and none of my crushes even liked me back. I don't know how to have "girl talk" about guys and I don't even know what's normal in a relationship.

Odhran scares me sometimes, but when we spend time together, I just feel... *better*. He understands me and he doesn't judge me for my hobbies. I know if I'm scared, one text would make him drop everything to fix it. His murder plot and terrifying ex-girlfriend are definitely cons.

Judging by how everyone looks at me, I suspect I've given the wrong answer. The only person to chime up in my defense is Heavyn.

"That makes sense," she says. "Listen, I say as long as he treats you right... maybe we overreacted."

Heavyn glances to her left at Kalani and Zariyah and then to her right at Valentina. The weight of their expressions makes me want to sink into the floor of this beach house and teleport back to the quiet of my dorm room.

Chapter Eighteen

"We didn't overreact," Valentina says, glancing at her watch. "We have plenty of time to get her to the real safe house without anyone noticing."

Zariyah shakes her head, her large mass of curls sitting in a messy pineapple on her head.

With her hands on her hips and a quite pregnant stomach jutting forward, she continues her interview, "I still have more questions. Callum thinks that somebody might try *to kill* Onika. That doesn't sound like a healthy relationship. What about this trifling hoe who wants to kill Nik?"

I have to stop both of them. Did Valentina just say we weren't at the real safe house?

"Wait, what do you mean the real safe house?" I ask them, staring right at my sister who suddenly has the guiltiest fucking look on her face. Zariyah makes a "yikes" face and Heavyn is suspiciously quiet.

"It's nothing to worry about," Kalani says. "Just uh... listen. We gotta wrap up this conversation with a few more questions before we let you run off with a serial killer, get pregnant and die."

My older sister is starting to get on my nerves. Why do older siblings seem to think their younger siblings are babies forever? My phone buzzes again and my anxiety spikes. If I'm not in the right safe house, Odhran will probably find out and lose his fucking mind. He cares about me enough to want me safe tonight.

"He's not a serial killer," I respond far too defensively. Odhran might talk a big game, but my instincts about him feel... *right*. He has had several opportunities to kill and each time he has come close, he pulled himself away from the edge. Even his plot to murder Aisling appears to have taken the backseat.

"Okay," Valentina says, exhaling with relief. "And he isn't trying to get you to murder his ex-girlfriend with him?"

"Well, I'm working on that," I respond. "He's just... confused."

Again, I can feel their skepticism as I defend him. But how can I explain to them that Odhran isn't all bad and despite his dark thoughts and possibly darker fantasies, he's the reason I can get up in the morning and go to class after what I've been through. There's no recourse against Six or Maura, but with Odhran, I've found myself capable of getting past the need for revenge. He's made it easy to just feel like myself and to feel like I can survive them.

"Confused about what?" Kalani asks. "Maybe we should kidnap his ass and torture the information out of him. I don't need a racist white boy messing with my sister's head."

This isn't a game.

I WANT to tell them that this isn't a game, that they're wrong about Odhran, and that I don't care if this is the correct safe house as long as they give me a minute to tell him I'm safe via text message, but I don't have time because there's a loud electrical buzzing sound and then every light in the house shuts off at once, plunging us into darkness.

We all scream together.

"Get your phone out!" Heavyn says. "Everyone get your phones out!"

But I don't have time. It's pitch black and I can't see anything, but I feel a large arm coming around me and assume it's one of the Murray wives stumbling around the kitchen until a hand clamps over my mouth and nose, and everything fades into blackness.

Chapter Nineteen
Odhran

I'm going to be sick. *She's gone.* Just like that. One night, one guarantee from Aiden that nothing would happen to her, and his woman and her friends ruin everything. I've never felt panic like this before. I've never empathized with panic, hardly understood what it felt like to have the threat of losing someone that you cared about.

I thought love was just about duty before her. It's something else, isn't it. Whatever love is, I think it's what I feel for Nik. I don't just care about her. My heart aches. Every part of me aches and I can feel my skin turning red as I grow more desperate to leave.

"I'm leaving," I announce to Aiden and then make an effort to force my way past Callum and Rian, who form an immovable wall. Darragh drags Kamari off to their bedroom and I can hear him yelling at her and her yelling back, explaining that her and the other wives just wanted to help Nik. To save her from me.

My brothers have never hidden their low opinion of me. They view my unfailing loyalty to our father as a personal failing. But I have always been a mobster at heart — cold when necessary, but loyal to whatever boss that I have. Right now, Aiden is my boss. My loyalty lies with him and with his vision for our family. I trust him because that is our ultimate duty as Irishmen.

"You aren't going anywhere," Callum says. "Calm down. We're going to get her back. All of us."

"None of you could possibly give a shit about her the way I do."

Rian scowls. "Stop the theatrics, Odhran. You have been there for all of us, despite being menacing and off-putting. We won't abandon you now. Especially not when all of us have a part to play here."

Callum snorts. "My part to play will be adding to the long list of spankings I'll have to give Zariyah once she's given birth."

"I *need* to go to her," I yell at them. "I should have killed Six when I had the chance."

Whoever took Nik left her cell phone behind at the beach house, so I have no way to track her. She didn't plan this and she's probably scared, alone, and she needs me. I have never felt my heart this painfully before. I hate how much it hurts. When I have her back, I don't know what I'll do to keep her out of trouble but if I need to handcuff her to the bed and only release her to eat and shower, then so be it.

It helps that Callum and Rian are equally furious. Aiden gets on the phone with one of Aisling's brothers.

"It's Six. It has to be Six," I tell Aiden as the phone rings. "I knew she would get into trouble if I left her alone."

"Quiet," Aiden says in a hushed tone. "Not one word out of you. If she really is responsible, we'll find out. But I need you to listen and trust me."

Every urge in my body tells me to disobey my brother, but I know I'll put my duty first, despite the temptation. I have my own car, my own weapons and the complete capacity to end everyone's life who put their hands on Onika Cook. Aisling's brother answers the phone and Aiden wanders out of the room, leaving me with Callum and Rian as my only companions to deal with my conflicting feelings. I've never loved anyone like this.

We are all stunned into silence as we hear Darragh growling, "You make me so insufferably horny, woman."

Rian rolls his eyes and utters sarcastically, "We can reassure ourselves that Darragh's doing an excellent job laying down the law."

Chapter Nineteen

Callum smirks. "Can you blame him? The woman is a goddamn firecracker, always about to explode."

He seems more entertained than angry. I don't blame either my brothers or their wives for this. I only blame the person who took Nik.

AIDEN RETURNS from his private phone call red-faced. I can tell from the way he looks at me that I'm right about Six being responsible for Nik's kidnapping. I don't know how she found her, but one gap in our security was all it took. I promised her that she would be safe. How can I ask her to love me after failing her?

"What did you find out?" I press him as he rubs his growing blond beard impatiently. Aiden locks eyes with me and I see an instinct in him that I haven't seen in a long time.

"We have a whole lot of Irish motherfuckers to kill," he says. "I gave them a chance to make things right and I've made promises to my wife but... Odhran. We don't have a choice anymore."

"What did you learn?"

Aiden ignores my question again. "You need to make me a promise in exchange for handling this. We need an equal exchange. But I need you to be ready for more responsibility."

"I will do anything for her. That's all I ever wanted to do."

"I don't know what the fuck is wrong with you," Aiden says. "I don't know why you love this girl over the one you had but... you're right about that family. They want us to return to the old ways and they want to do it with the *doirteadh fola* ritual."

Blood rushes to my head as Aiden pronounces the old Gaelic word for bloodshed. I didn't think my panic could grow more intense until now. Out of all of us, Rian speaks Gaelic the best since he spent his time behind bars so he reacts before I do. Callum doesn't react at all. He had a pretty Irish girl in class doing all his homework for him and he never even kissed her.

"What does that mean?" Callum asks with genuine confusion. "He's going to daughter-fool her?"

My stomach sinks. I can't even laugh at Callum's idiocy and

155

normally, I find my older brother's foolishness entertaining. Rian gives Callum a look of complete disrespect. "You should go to prison, Callum. I think you could use the free time to improve your Gaelic."

I ignore the two of them for the time being.

"I won't let that happen," I tell Aiden, looking back at him. "If that's what you want me to do, to put Nik in danger, I won't do it."

"Of course I won't let that happen," Aiden says. "This is a direct challenge to my authority and I am fucking sick of it. I have kept peace in this city ever since our father died and I will not have my methods questioned. Our father had his faults, but he was right that sometimes you have to rule with an iron fist."

If Aiden spends much time grieving our father, he doesn't show it, but for the first time since he died, I see a flicker of grief in Aiden's eyes. Maybe it was all those nights they shared a drink at Mulligan's. Maybe it was the way they were close to each other before Aiden fell for the girl in the box on his doorstep.

I already know that I would give anything and everything for Nik. I don't care what I have to do or who I have to kill. I'm ready to join my brother in his vision for our family's future.

"I told you we would have to kill more," Rian says with a sigh. "This would be a lot easier if our wives would sit somewhere obediently for once instead of pestering us and catching stray bullets. Luckily, I taught Heavyn how to shoot in case she pops up somewhere."

Callum snorts. "I would be a buffoon if I taught Zariyah how to shoot. She would kill me in an instant."

"After this, if Six survives, Nik can use her as target practice."

Six already tried to kill her once. I was too complacent about protecting Nik, assuming my threats would be enough. You can kill someone in seconds.

She could already be dead. Callum makes an effort to comfort me, but I barely hear what he says. Aiden commands us to move out so we can search the city and I focus on listening to him, although there is one more question I have.

"Do we know where Six took her?"

Chapter Nineteen

"It's all in the ritual," Aiden says. "They'll need to take her somewhere with a connection to their Irish bloodline. They need dirt."

"It sounds more like witchcraft than a mob ritual," Callum grumbles.

Aiden shrugs. "Half the time it's like there's no difference. But these old superstitions and rituals only cause hate and at one point in time, maybe we had to defend ourselves but this isn't about self-defense anymore. We *rule* this city and we are not victims anymore."

"I just want to find her and I want to kill."

"We could always be sure of that," Callum mutters. "But he's right. Let's move. Can't say for fuck what places around here are connected to their Irish bloodline."

Darragh and Kamari finally exit their bedroom. I suspect their argument transformed into something more judging by the guilty look on Kamari's face and her messed up hair. Darragh has his plain white t-shirt on inside out, which is another clue.

"Did we miss much?" Darragh asks. Aiden looks like he could strangle him, but Kamari clearly notices his murderous expression and steps in between the two of them before Aiden can act on his tempestuous impulses.

"Calm down, Aiden. We were merely engaged in rational marital discussion and now, we're ready to help."

"You aren't going anywhere," Aiden says to Kamari. "You will stay here with the baby on a Zoom call with my wife and the rest of the family to make sure nobody else escapes... or it'll be your ass on the line."

Kamari gives Aiden a look like she's about to question the fuck out of what he's saying, but he doesn't budge and after assessing the situation, she clearly decides that fighting him isn't worth the effort.

"Fine," Kamari says. "But I don't regret helping them get her away from him. I still don't know his intentions."

She's obviously referring to my intentions. I understand Kamari's concern about Nik, along with everyone else's, but if only they would trust that nobody cares about her well-being as much as I do.

"If you hadn't involved yourself, she would be fine," I say to her bitterly, considering the ways I could punish Kamari properly if given a chance. A *real* beating would be a nice start, not whatever happened between her and Darragh in that bedroom. Darragh gives Kamari a hard and intentional pinch on her ass, which makes her squeal but in a way that suggests she enjoys it far too much.

"What I mean to say is… I will be respectful but cautious," Kamari says. "I won't let anyone else get into trouble and trust me, I am taking this seriously. That girl is only a freshman in college and she's not like us. She's innocent."

I struggle not to smirk. After all the ways I've had my tongue and fingers inside of Nik, she might still be a virgin, but she's the furthest thing from innocent.

"Thank you," Darragh grunts. "And I would really appreciate it if you could keep your ass out of trouble for a day or two."

"Hey, I wasn't the one who kidnapped her," Kamari says. "I only helped. Promise you all will get her back, quick, okay?"

That would be a lot easier if Kamari hadn't put her in trouble in the first place, but Aiden promises and his promise to her makes me feel a lot better. Darragh's wife appears to have a strong sense for bullshit, so if she thought Aiden weren't telling the truth, I'm sure she would have said something completely out of place.

"Get the ammunition out of the safe," Aiden instructs Darragh before turning to me. "Put my guns into your car."

"Any of them will recognize our cars," I point out to my brother.

"Good," Aiden says. "Then there won't be any mistake that this is a punishment for disobedience and that there is only one ruling family in Boston."

Chapter Twenty
Onika

"I want her ruined. I don't care about some stupid fucking Irish ritual. I didn't bring her here so you could work on some dumb plan."

It's dark. It's so dark and cold, but neither of those things wake me up. What jolts me awake is Six's shrieking, her shrill voice snapping me out of what I thought was a horrifying nightmare. This is the real nightmare – whatever and wherever this is. It's too dark for me to see at first, but I am definitely not in a safe house anymore.

"I'm not fucking raping her, Six," a man yells back at her. I don't find his words comforting, even if I agree with his disgusted tone about the matter. I don't want him touching me.

I don't want that to be my first time. I still can't even feel my body, all I have is consciousness and some vague awareness that I'm trapped.

"Why not?" Six yells back. "I went through all this trouble to torture her fucking roommate and track down the only yellow Mercedes with those three numbers on the plate and *then* I went through the extra effort to take Maura's car out there and cut the power lines to grab her. I deserve payment."

Her voice trembles with anger, but the person she's speaking to doesn't sound moved at all.

It doesn't make me feel better that she broadcasts exactly what happened to me. I still don't know what happened to everyone else. My sister is *pregnant*. The last thing she needs is trauma and stress, it's not good for the baby. While aware of the conversation and possessing vague notions of my own consciousness, I'm not all the way back yet. They must have drugged me.

"Your payment is coming, you stupid slut," the man says, barely raising his voice despite Six growing more shrill. "But you can't stomp around like a brat. You have to wait. This isn't a stupid fucking college ritual. It's our heritage. It's Irish pride."

"Well is there any part of the ritual that says you can't rape her first?" Six says.

By the time Six gets to this horrifying sentence, I realize that I'm not only completely bound up and unable to move, but also where I am and just how goddamn impossible it will be for me to get out of this. I don't even know what happened to my sister or her friends. For all I know, they could be dead and these psychopaths could have killed them. For all I know, they could be part of this "ritual" too.

My best guess is that Six is speaking to her brother. I don't know, but I know family is important to Odhran and I presume it's important to the rest of the mob.

"It's a waste of time and I don't want to do it," the man complains, sounding bored rather than offended.

That only gets Six angrier than before.

"You're a pussy," Six says. "I should have known you wouldn't have the balls to do it."

"You're a sick little bitch," he growls. "I'm not obligated to obey my little sister. *You* on the other hand are obligated to help me gut her and drink her blood."

Panic overwhelms me at first, but panic makes the pain worse and I picture myself as one of my characters determined to make it to the end of one of my horror short stories no matter how many slashers and jump scares and gross encounters. Horror is about grappling against the darkest parts of the human soul. Facing them.

Odhran might not even know I'm in danger. Rylee, my only other hope under normal circumstances has probably been tortured to the brink of death somewhere. I have to face this impossible situation alone and try to get out of it – even if it's clearly hopeless. Awareness of my body returns to me with a sharp jolt, but it doesn't matter. They clearly drugged me, and bound me, and now… I'm pretty sure I'm in the trunk of a car. It's not even a big car, because I'm not scrunched up that much but *damn* my arm hurts.

Maybe Odhran was right about my writing. I need to experience something real to get better. But I don't think I need to kill so I can get into a character's head or become a better artist. I just need to survive.

Odhran's face popping into my head does way more to soothe my panic than I expected. I can almost hear his voice as if he's speaking directly to me.

"Calm down, Nik. I told you, I'll handle it."

Stupid Odhran. He was always so confident about everything to the point of arrogance. I could use some of that blind confidence in myself now that I'm stuck here. My breathing steadies and I try to adjust to the darkness and my inability to move. Their arguing continues, although I must have lost the plot of it a bit, as I soak in every detail of my surroundings, running through every possibility of escape in my head.

"You are such an asshole," Six says. "You promised you would do this for me."

Her brother raises his voice for the first time during their argument, "I'm not raping a damn nigger, Six, so shut the fuck up. You're here because we needed her for the ritual and you had a fucking axe to grind."

I hear another male voice, which definitely makes my situation a *lot* worse. I could possibly handle one guy and Six, but now I don't know how many people there are out there waiting to kill me. Fuck, I don't even know where I am. Sure, I'm in the trunk of a car,

"Listen, Six," the second voice says. "You aren't important to this, unfortunately. You're just a woman. Thank you for your assistance but don't expect us to dirty our cocks because you couldn't keep Odhran satisfied."

"Fuck you!" Six yells. "This isn't about my ability to keep him satisfied. It's about... It's about... I deserve something! I'm not the least important because I'm the youngest and I'm not the least important because I'm a woman. I can hurt her."

The second brother chuckles. "Then hurt her."

BY THEN, I don't have a plan to get out of the trunk, but I sense once I get out of the trunk, I can get a better idea of my odds. Two men, Six and probably Maura simpering around somewhere. I wouldn't mind those odds in Call of Duty, but it's not like I have an M4 with an aim-OP V4 optic and an echoless-80 muzzle. That would make my life a lot easier. I'm sure a real gun is a bit harder to operate but... maybe not.

The trunk pops open and a brilliant light from a nearby street light blinds me instantly. I try not to scream. My kidnappers left my mouth uncovered and as far as I'm concerned, this is a miracle and I don't intend on losing the privilege. I have to think like Odhran. Feel what he would feel. *Probably completely calm like a freak.* I might not be able to be completely calm, but I can pretend, just like I pretend to be my characters when I need to write them out of a sticky situation.

"Fuck, she's fat. How did you get her in there?" the second voice says. My vision focuses as I turn my gaze away from the light and see Six shoving her brother hard and out of the way. She's the only one towering over me now and the part that hits me like a gut punch is that she doesn't look like a monster. Six looks like a regular girl about to get iced coffee from Starbucks with a pair of leggings, gray Ugg boots, and an oversized lilac Victoria's Secret long sleeved shirt. She even has her hair thrown up in a messy bun like in the memes.

Her eyes are the only part of her that betray her as something other than a regular Boston girl about to run into Dunkin' and those eyes bore into me like she wants to kill me with them and not the

Chapter Twenty

knife she wields. My stomach drops as the knife glints in the brilliant street lamp.

"I stuffed her in," Six says. "Maura helped."

Maura sidles into my view, leaving Six's brother flanked by the two of them. The taller brother appears behind them, his menacing eyes look almost black as he gazes over Maura's shoulder.

"Come on, Brian," the taller brother says. "Let's get her out."

"Fuck off, Cian," Brian says. The name sounds really funny, like the word *keen*. Most of the students at our college have Irish names that are difficult to pronounce and even more difficult to spell.

I wish I could jump out and run away on my own, but my mouth is the only part of my body not restrained. I still don't know why, but considering what Six asked of her brothers, I don't know if I want to consider the potential horrors they might unleash.

Cian pushes everyone out of the way so he's the only one standing over me. I assume he's in charge of whatever happens here because even Six defers to him and I never see her defer to anyone, even when pressed. Cian pushes his blond hair out of his face and stares at me like I'm a gross bug stuck to his windshield.

Brian steps up and he moves my legs while Cian grabs my shoulders. As they drag me out of the trunk, I get more information about our location than the pavement and street light. But I just feel worse. We're in a second location where they can easily kill me and I know it's what they want. This isn't just about scaring me. This is real. And terrifying.

I learn that we were in a parking lot behind a large stone, gothic church. It's definitely a Catholic church, but I don't recognize it, probably because I'm about as Catholic as I am Muslim – not at all. They rest me on the ground and I roll over onto my back, pretending to be limp and disinterested so I can take in more information.

Do what Odhran would do. Just stay calm…

BRIAN AND CIAN speak to each other in a language that I neither understand nor recognize and then Six interrupts them with an infuriated shriek. Her and Maura seem far less formidable in the presence of her brothers, but their refusal to rape me doesn't give me any additional hope that I'll make it out of here alive.

If they don't want to rape me, they must want me for something else, or they wouldn't have gone through the trouble to fuck with Six and get her to bring me here. Six snaps me out of my failed efforts to understand their conversation from context clues or the English words peppered throughout their interaction typical amongst bilingual people.

But the English words don't help me feel any better. *Ritual. Knife. Bleed her dry.* The younger one isn't very good at the language they're speaking considering how much he lets slip. And it's more than enough to send my panic through the roof again. My desperation gets to the point where I decide to roll away and using as much momentum as I can muster, I begin rolling away from the car until I feel a foot slamming into my ribcage with enormous force.

For the first time since they removed me from the car, I cry out loud. Six laughs and another foot lands against me. The pain is intense – far more intense than whatever spanking Odhran could come up. Heat and blood rush to my face as I scream out in genuine pain.

"Stop it, you fucking slut," Brian yells at his sister, which is admittedly odd. "We need her alive when the others get here."

"I don't see why she needs to be alive," Six says. "You aren't doing what I asked and I'm not going to help you anymore. I don't care about stupid mob politics. I want her *dead.*"

Cian storms over to Six and shoves her away from me. Maura steps back in fear – she poses absolutely no threat to Cian because he's enormous. He obviously scares me far more than Six does, especially since he has a body that looks like he consumes steroids and growth hormone for breakfast.

I shudder as I work through the pain, trying to get my breathing to steady again and trying to get myself to believe that I can find a way out of here. Two more cars approach the parking lot and since everyone with me barely reacts, I assume that the two cars contain the rest of the Cunningham family, joining together for a pleasant family reunion where they all get to participate in a bonding activity. My ritual murder.

"You shut up," Cian snarls at Six, acknowledging the cars that just pulled up. "Get her ass in the chair and if you're lucky, we'll include you in this."

Six still holds a knife, and judging by the expression on her face which I can barely make out from the position on the ground, she looks pissed off. Her body language reveals more than her face, each one of her fingers the color of Vienna sausages from the tight ass grip she has on the knife. Her body shudders with a mixture of loathing and frustration.

"I can't believe you're going to let Rory and Senan participate in this and not me. It's not fair. It's not fucking fair!"

Cian proves to me that I shouldn't underestimate him. Without hesitating he wraps his hand around his sister's throat so quickly and tightly that she can't cry out. A strangled exhalation barely escapes her lips. Maura yells at him to put her down, but Cian clearly doesn't give a single fuck.

"If you say another word," he says. "Our plans will change tonight and I'll make sure Rory and Senan have your cunt instead of the nigger's. Does that sound good?"

I can imagine Six turning red, but I can't see enough of her face to tell. Her legs thrash about madly as she drops the knife straight in front of me and claws desperately at her brother's tight grasp on her neck. Even if Six's life isn't exactly my top priority, there's something sickening about watching her own brother put forth such a strong effort to squeeze the life out of her. Just as her legs slow down their thrashing, Cian releases her neck and throws her a few feet away.

Six can't balance herself without oxygen in her lungs and tears pierce her eyes as she stumbles backward. Maura doesn't stop screaming at Cian as car doors open and the rest of Six's brothers join the circle forming around me. Oddly, no one pays much attention to me anymore. Maura is busy arguing with Cian, who appears completely unbothered, while Brian stands back, waiting patiently for his brother's commands.

The other brothers crowd around me, but I'm not paying any attention to them anymore. Six dropped her knife. And maybe if I roll my body on top of it, they'll all be fighting so hard they won't notice. I can move my fingers and *maybe*, just *maybe*, I can cut my way loose and then run like fucking hell. While they exchange greetings and argue, I roll over until my body covers the knife.

I can't move the knife precisely, but I think I can get the blade to cut the layers of duct tape joining my wrists together. There's a chance I could cut myself, but honestly, I don't even think about it. I'd rather cut myself a few times and live than die here, surrounded by racists and murdered by a girl who hates me. I didn't ask for any of this.

You can do this, Nik. Against all odds, you can do this. And once you're free, you use all that damn training Odhran put you through and you run like hell.

Chapter Twenty-One
Odhran

Nik's life hangs in the balance and if this gamble doesn't pay off, I'll have no choice but to unleash my fury on everyone in the Cunningham family. I know the bloodshed ritual – a powerful Irish ritual to call upon our strongest ancestors for an exchange of power. Every ritual requires sacrifice and this ritual requires you to sacrifice those of lesser blood.

In the original Gaelic text, the ritual calls for gypsy blood, but we don't exactly have a plethora of identifiable gypsies running around Boston. Dad always thought I looked like one with my dyed black hair, but I think he just preferred me and everyone else on the blonder side.

Impatiently, I hang out of the passenger seat. Aiden drives, which he doesn't normally when we're out together, but this is a matter for the boss. Murder. Not just any murder, annihilating an entire family. Aiden has spent all his time as the boss desperate to avoid a conflict just like this one – one that threatens to split our family apart.

Those stuck in the past and those ready for the future.

AIDEN PARKS three blocks down from the church where every Cunningham baptism has been held since 1845. The church has been part of our mob family tradition for years, although my grandfather split off and began going to St. Mary's instead of St. Joseph's years ago.

St. Joseph's Cathedral is an impressive and gothic church,and when the Irish first built this church in Boston, we had to fight against the local Bostonians who were decidedly Protestant and judged our families of presumed dirty, poor Irish Catholic immigrants to the point where we all had to work for each other. Hire each other. Look after each other.

Part of me will always believe that we are stronger together as Irish folks but... My brothers have a point. My loyalty to my family and heritage has very little to do with the sorts of women my cock prefers. *Woman.* There's only one woman and she had me completely wrapped around her finger from the second I saw a picture of her.

I tell myself that this wasn't love, but a sick murderous obsession that got twisted up with my sexuality. But Nik is more than that. She's like... love walking around. Pure love. Sweet. Innocent. Fascinated by darkness, but nowhere near it.

I WAS wrong to think she needed more darkness. I'm the one who needs more light. I've always been the one who needed her...

RIAN GETS out of the car first. He hates not being behind the wheel. I take responsibility for waking Callum up since Darragh refuses to risk being the one to do it. He grunts and then paws at me like an angry bear before I poke him in the side really hard like I used to do when we were kids. Callum is (thankfully) a lot less aggressive now than he was when we were younger, but he still sleeps like a hibernating bear.

"Get your ass up. We're there..."

Callum grunts and hops out of the car, his feet landing with surprising lightness on the gravel for a man so big. He thumps me on the back as he wipes sleep out of his eyes.

"We'll get her back. Don't worry."

I wish I could stop myself, but I can't. My worries get worse when I hear a loud, blood-curdling scream.

Nik.

I DON'T THINK or wait for orders, I just act on my impulses and run towards the sound of her screams. My instincts are too powerful to leave her unprotected. *I love her. I love her so much it hurts.* My heart bursts with adrenaline as I sprint towards the sound. Nik allows another shriek and I tell myself that this is the last one – that they've killed her.

I don't know how the fuck my feet move me so quickly. I load my gun as I run, not something as complicated as it sounds considering I just have a semi-automatic pistol and by my estimates, I'll only need two to three bullets before my brothers follow me. I can hear Aiden calling my name, but everything blurs together as I stumble upon the horrific scene.

Without thinking, I shoot at the first two blond heads that I see. The first bullet hits dead-on, causing complete pandemonium as my victim's face shatters in front of all of us. I ignore the loud screams and within seconds fire the second shot, which hits the second motherfucker in his cheek, enough to blow his jaw off in an explosion of blood and teeth.

I exhale and glance around. Three more brothers. Maura. Six. And there she is. Nik, lying on the ground next to a metal fold-out chair with ropes and blood all over it. *She's dead. Holy fuck she's dead.*

But then Nik rolls over. Before I can get too excited that she's alive, I hear another gunshot. I glance down at my chest, assuming that the bullet entered me, since I have no defenses.

"ODHRAN!" Nik cries out and then I'm sure that I've been hit. But nothing happens to me. My ears are ringing so loud that I can't hear a fucking thing, but then I feel a hand on my shoulder, hear another gunshot and watch as the rest of the Cunningham brothers fall to the ground, laid waste by the Murrays in a matter of minutes. The only one left alive isn't here and Aiden will track him down and have him killed soon.

Six's shrieking draws my attention again. Maura lies on the ground shaking visibly with her hands covering her ears. If she's trying to play dead, she's failing. Six screams violently and then her gaze meets mine and locks with it. I notice the knife in her hand, although I should have noticed it glinting blatantly beneath the streetlight before.

My brothers could easily kill her before she gets to me. I know they could, so I stand still and patient, waiting for Aiden to issue his command before I run to Nik. She rolls back over again and every cell in my body tells me to break rank and run for her. A wad of spit slowly travels down my throat as I try to force my hearing back properly, so more than just Six's agonizing wailing pierces through.

"We should kill her," is the next thing I hear. "It's not a clean job but... look at the girl."

They're talking about Nik and none of them are acting because Six is screaming at me.

I can hear her mouth moving as she waves the knife around and I expect her to bolt towards me and go on a suicide mission. My brothers killed her entire family in front of her. It's what I would expect from a girl raised the way she was raised. To go down fighting. She surprises me and turns away from me, raising the knife and racing towards Nik's vulnerable body, lying on the ground. I level my pistol at her and shoot. But my hands shake and I miss.

"ODHRAN!" Aiden yells at me, fully aware that I just brazenly disobeyed a direct command in front of him. He told me not to kill her, but I didn't care. I still don't. I know I'm too far away, but I run towards Six, hoping I can get to her before she gets to Nik, knowing that I won't.

I watch her close in on Nik's limp body. I yell her name, but she doesn't move until Six hovers over her with a knife. I feel my throat closing as I anticipate the pain. White rose petals stained with blood. *No. I can't let that happen.* I push myself harder, but as Six raises the knife and prepares to plunge it into Nik, she kicks her feet out and surprises Six, shoving her away.

With that, Nik rolls over and hurriedly springs to her feet. She has just enough of an advantage to get a headstart towards me, but Six isn't completely disabled. And she's a varsity athlete. *Oh fuck.*

"Nik, run!" I scream at her, hoping that one of my brothers puts an end to this quickly. I expect Nik to run towards me, but she doesn't. She runs straight towards the remains of Fiach Cunningham and grabs the gun lying next to him.

"Nik, stop it!" I yell at her, frozen in place now, unsure of what to do and completely unclear why my brothers don't just stop her. Stop Six. Stop *any of this from happening.* But she doesn't listen. She grabs the gun, levels it at Six and fires. I can't stop myself from watching it. I thought I would enjoy watching something like this – the woman I love killing the girl that used to mean something to me. *Before she hurt me.*

That gets my brothers to act. Six slumps over and Nik drops the gun, which fires again, the bullet ricocheting off the street lamp and disappearing into some backstop somewhere that one of our men will have to find before the police come. I run towards her and wrap her in my arms. She yelps as I hold onto her and I let go quickly, examining her for damage.

AND HOLY FUCK, there's damage. My body trembles as I look at her, completely battered and bruised beyond anything I've ever seen. I couldn't tell from afar because of the darkness surrounding the parking lot and the utter chaos, but they tortured her. And judging by the looks of it, dislocated her shoulder.

"How the fuck did you do that?" I breathe, keeping a safe distance but also keeping my hand pressed directly to her cheek. My thumb runs over her lip as my chest heaves. I can hear Aiden giving loud orders behind me, but I don't hear my name, so I don't move.

"Video games are apparently very realistic," Nik says, but her voice sounds heavy and weak.

"You need medical attention."

"I'm fine."

"You have a dislocated shoulder, Nik. You're not fine."

She won't look at me. Why won't she look at me? I hold her chin and firmly guide Nik's gaze so that we're making eye contact. Then I realize why she won't look. *She's crying.*

I don't think I ever understood heartbreak before that moment. My last relationship had lost all the love in it years ago. It had become an obligation and an expectation more than something based in mutual attraction.

But Nik's tears. Holy fuck. They hurt.

"I killed her," Nik says and then she sobs so hard that it knocks something entirely loose in my brain. This girl is so fucking pure…

"I love you," I blurt out, at the absolutely fucking worst time. And Nik looks at me like I'm a monster. Which I probably am. I pull her chin towards me and I kiss her, tasting the blood on her burst lip, the salt and sweat that dribbled down from her cheeks. I taste her tears and I don't stop kissing her, because I mean every word out of my mouth.

I love her. She shudders as I kiss her, but she doesn't break away from me. Not immediately. Nik loves kissing. I could tell the first time I kissed her that she would. She has the perfect lips for it – utterly addictive, full in every way and now… they're even more delicious than normal because the fact that I can even taste all her pain means she's safe now.

And I can take it all away. *Soon.*

When she pulls away from me, her eyes are still sad and as black as the night around us. They're deep and gorgeous, and yes, it's a terrible time to freeze in place thinking about Nik's beautiful eyes.

"I love you too," she whispers, but then she keeps sobbing. "But I killed her…I killed someone…"

I want to hold her so badly and it hurts that I can't. Neither of us could wait any longer to say it, but that doesn't exactly make this the ideal time. She's crying, covered in sweat, blood, dirt, and snot, not to mention bruised all over and suffering from the dislocated shoulder.

She doesn't even cry about her own pain, but the fact that she hurt someone else.

"Nik," I whisper. "You were defending yourself. These people hurt you… *Look at you…*"

"It's my fault," she says, her chest heaving. "It's all my fault…"

I don't know how any of this could possibly be her fault. Her shoulder looks awful and she winces with every breath. I could set it back in place but I don't want to be the one to hurt her like that.

Callum interrupts us at just the right time. He can set shoulders too. We all can. Dad made us practice on each other – both the dislocating and the setting. He notices it immediately.

"Her shoulder is fucked. Hi. You're Nik, I'm guessing?"

Nik has to tilt her neck dramatically to meet Callum's gaze. I can tell that she finds him terrifying, although Callum is about as terrifying as a teddy bear compared to my other brothers. She's lucky he's the first one she gets to meet.

"Y-yes," Nik stammers.

"Nice to meet you. I'm Callum. Unfortunately, I'm going to have to make a terrible first impression."

Without being asked and without giving any warning, Callum grabs Nik and quickly sets her shoulder. She yelps in pain from both the suddenness and the experience of having the humerus shoved back into the shoulder joint, but then she gives him a look of both fear and gratitude.

"Th-thanks," Nik says, her body shivering, most likely from the shock of everything as well as her torn clothing. It doesn't matter what time of year it is, you rarely get a warm night in Boston. Callum immediately removes his flannel shirt and puts it over Nik's shoulders

I have to stop myself from getting irrationally jealous. I'm only wearing a t-shirt and that wouldn't help her much.

"No problem," Callum responds, turning his attention to me.

"Listen," he says. "Aiden and Darragh will deal with the bodies. Rian has to bring Aisling to the doctor."

"She's dead," I say bluntly to Callum, but he shakes his head. *Not dead.*

"Her friend took off," Callum says. "I'll be out looking for her but... don't be surprised if we can't find her."

"Maura escaped?" Nik asks, her voice trembling in terror. With her shoulder fixed, I slowly put my arm around her and draw her closer to me. She still winces, but at least she can tolerate my closeness now.

"Everything will be fine," I whisper, kissing the top of her head. "I promise."

Chapter Twenty-Two
Onika

I see the doctor at Odhran's apartment. I never expected to be in his apartment at all, but the circumstances are especially horrible. My mind is a scattered mess and I worry that maybe Odhran was right – maybe there were some parts of the human experience I couldn't write about without a little more darkness. I didn't really want to kill Six. I just wanted to stop her. But still. I pulled the trigger.

I'm not the angel Odhran seems to think. Even if I regretted it, for one split second, I did something that I knew could kill her and I didn't bother to stop myself.

I'm sure he would just blame it on the trauma. But I already hate the thought of calling it trauma. I already hate the thought of this... *stuff*... staying in my head. I want it gone and I just want Odhran, who is far too quiet for my liking. The most he's said to me since the drive over here was "I love you". The words are still heavy for me.

I love him, but I don't know what love means to Odhran or why he said it moments after he thought I killed his ex-girlfriend. There's a dark part of him that I feel drawn to, but after all this, there's another part of me that's completely uncertain.

What about years down the road when he's tired of me?

Odhran's inability to stop staring at me like he's about to eat me doesn't exactly help. He just gazes at me, completely silent as I wait for his mob doctor to visit me in his apartment. The doctor arrives and makes me strip down to nothing. The examination is uncomfortable, but thorough. I at least get the impression that the doctor is discreet. Unfortunately, the visit isn't without additional pain.

I need stitches and bandages. Odhran lets me squeeze his hand as the doctor gives me the stitches. I swear I squeeze so hard that I break his fingers, but he doesn't act like he experiences the slightest bit of pain.

"I'm here for you, Nik," he whispers. "Everything will be just fine."

He sounds so calm and in control that I absolutely want to believe him. It just doesn't feel like everything is in control, especially not with a needle and thread passing through my flesh.

At least the doctor thinks I'll be fine in three weeks as long as I take care of the wounds, don't allow any infections and use painkillers for a few days. Odhran doesn't even pay him before he leaves, although I guess I don't really know how mob doctors work. I sit perched on the edge of Odhran's glass dining room table when Odhran leads the doctor out of the apartment, exchanging basic pleasantries. I wish Odhran had a more practical table because balancing on this is extremely precarious.

At least he isn't gone for long.

When Odhran returns with a handsome face and dark hair falling over his brow, his jaw is tight and he seems almost impatient. He approaches me and puts his arms on the table as if pinning me there, before getting very close and pressing his forehead against mine. My breath catches.

"I almost fucking lost you," Odhran breathes. "That will never happen again, Onika. I wish I brought you here under better circumstances, but you will be living here from now on."

He kisses me slowly and I don't bother arguing, partly because of the painkillers and exhaustion, partly out of fear, and partly because I want to be with him. I don't know how Odhran got into my heart like this, but he's there… and I want to keep him there.

"Okay," I whisper.

"Perfect," he grunts. "But I have to warn you away from the bedroom at the end of the hall. It's not really a bedroom."

"Is it some type of weird sex dungeon?"

Odhran gives me a funny look. "No. It's a custom built enclosure for my pet anaconda, Killer Bee. I've raised him since I was fourteen."

He tells me he has a bedroom for his pet snake and then looks at me like I'm the weird one for suggesting a sex dungeon.

"Can it escape?" I ask Odhran.

"No," he says. "Nobody can get in there but me because of the handprint lock. Six had a habit of killing my pets so I had to be careful."

He doesn't sound sad, but his matter-of-fact tone disturbs me just as much as the information. Thankfully, Odhran skates past the topic.

"You would never do something like that," he says. "That's why I said it. It's not because you almost killed someone, Nik. It's because you feel. You care about other people. And... I didn't realize that I wanted that. I didn't realize I was drawn to it."

He runs his tongue over his lower lip and looks away from me as if he's just admitted something embarrassing. Odhran's black hair falls over his shoulders in a tangled, greasy mess. I can tell he's lost sleep over this and even if I'm battered and bruised on the outside, I can tell how hurt he's been.

He can't stop touching me. It's not sexual, or aggressive, just obvious. But he can't keep his hands off me, like he's afraid if I'm out of reach, I'll disappear. It's love. For all his monstrous ways, Odhran can't help but expose that he's still human in the littlest of ways.

"I didn't kill her," I whisper. "I wanted to for a tiny moment but... I'm glad I didn't."

He exhales sharply. How the hell does his breath smell good? And why do I want to kiss him when everything about tonight has been painful and horrible?

"You're an angel," he says. "I'm in love with an angel."

Then he kisses me and it's better than a warm sugar cookie. His lips taste like everything I ever wanted, everything I thought I was too ugly and weird to ever have.

"And a pretty good shot," he whispers, after pulling away. "Sorry. But it's true. And I'm sorry that you saw me... you know. I just... I would do it all over again if it meant saving you."

"I was getting out of there on my own..." I mumble, even if I totally wasn't. My efforts to use the knife to escape failed and only made my situation worse. I'm lucky I didn't end up with any broken ribs, judging by the way my torso aches from kicks and punches.

Odhran's fingers idle over to my wrists and he pins them to the dining room table. He's not trying to hurt me, just keep me firmly in pace. My breath catches from how close Odhran is to me. Through my pain, his scent still gets me high. I wish he would kiss me again, just to feel something warm and nice again.

It's like he can tell.

"What matters is you're safe now," he murmurs. "Now come to bed... Tomorrow, we start fresh."

Odhran doesn't drag me to bed and ravish me. We're both too exhausted and haggard from the night we've had. Odhran gives me a sponge bath, careful to avoid my freshly mended wounds. It hurts when he runs his washcloth over my body, but once we're done, I feel more human. He takes a shower afterwards, but I don't leave his bathroom – I just watch him.

He has a ridiculously luxurious shower that could easily fit six people – way bigger than any apartment bathroom I've ever seen. Odhran loves the audience and he especially loves my reaction to his body when he strips. I've seen him naked before, but there's something even more vulnerable about him now. I don't know how the hell he made it through the night without a scratch on him.

Water soaks through his black hair quickly, sticking it to his extremely pale neck, which does have signs of red irritation on it from hot water. He doesn't mind that I stare at his muscles or his tattoos. He doesn't speak until he starts soaping up and then he gives me a mischievous look.

"Like what you see?"

I squeeze my thighs together as I sit on his bathroom counter with a white fluffy robe wrapped around me tightly. It's hard *not* to like what I see. Odhran saved my life and everything about the way he's taken care of me just turns me on even more. It's not just his looks. It's his darkness. It's his everything.

"Yes," I answer. Odhran continues shampooing his hair and soaping up. His body looks even better with water and soap dripping all over his toned, rippling muscles. I still can't believe Odhran's body is real sometimes, even if I've seen him shirtless tons of times at the gym, this is different and way hotter.

Odhran smirks. "Want one?"

I'm too zoned out staring at his body to know what the hell he's talking about. I run my tongue over my lower lip unconsciously and pretend that I'm paying attention.

"One what?"

"A tattoo. You can't stop staring at them."

It's true, I can't stop staring at Odhran's tattoos, but it's mostly because he's the most tatted up person that I know and I can tell that each one of his tattoos has a special meaning to him. He's private with his own heart and he doesn't share much, but from all my so-called staring, I can tell that most of his tattoos are related to his Irish heritage. Whatever that means.

From what I've seen of Odhran's "Irish heritage", I'm not sure if I want to know more. I definitely don't know if I want a tattoo. Kalani has a couple, but she's the crazy and wild sister, I'm the boring sister. I wouldn't even know what to get.

"I don't know. I don't think so."

Odhran's face gets even more excited and I wonder if I should worry.

"I'll give you one."

"What?"

Odhran shrugs. "You're on painkillers. I have what I need. I'm good at drawing too."

"You can't just give me a tattoo. We're exhausted."

"True," Odhran says, stepping out of the shower and wrapping a thick white towel low around his hips. His dick sticks out through the towel, so big that it forms a permanent bulge between his legs, even when he's not hard and not trying to show it off. "But I don't care if I'm exhausted. I'll always have energy for you, Nik."

My thighs tremble again because that statement definitely feels like foreshadowing. Odhran follows it up with a deep, possessive kiss that sends a thrill straight through my core. I never feel like I have any control around Odhran and tonight feels so much worse.

I've stepped into the lion's den and... I love it here.

He pushes hair out of my face and kisses me again. I don't even care that he's getting me wet. I just love how he smells and tastes, especially how his shampoo smells. My arms hurt too much to rake my fingers through his hair, but I get hot and bothered imagining when I'll be able to move without pain again.

"It'll help you sleep," Odhran assures me. "I'm good with the needle and in the morning, you can see the result of my work."

"How will getting jabbed repeatedly with a needle help me sleep."

"There's still a part of you that likes pain, Nik. And the needle can be soothing. I fell asleep when I got that one and this one..."

He points to the strange mask on his thigh. It looks Asian, but I don't know what it means.

"What does that one mean?" I ask as his hand points to his thigh, which he bares to me through his towel. My chest throbs at how close he is to exposing his cock to me. Odhran loves teasing and I bet a part of him is trying to tease me with how close he's standing and how he's showing me his tattooed thigh.

"It's a hannya mask," he says. "It's a jealous female demon. But the ironic part is... you get it tattooed when you want to ward one off."

"Creepy."

"I did it on a dare," he says. "I like it though."

I reach my hand out to touch Odhran's thigh. He has gooseflesh all over, like my touch seriously affects him. Our eyes meet and then Odhran moves even closer, to kiss me.

"Come to bed," he whispers. "I'll give you a sexy little ass tatt."

"I can't get an ass tattoo!" I argue, my hand jerking away from Odhran's thigh, like that could possibly change his mind once he gets it set on something.

"Why not?" he asks. "You have a great ass."

"Thank you."

"It's hard to believe no one else has been tempted," Odhran says, touching my butt and playing with my soft flesh while it jiggles. "Are you sure you're still a virgin?"

I roll my eyes. He obviously knows the truth, but then I wonder if this is his weird way of asking if anyone hurt me. His tone isn't jealous this time, but concerned. He can't keep his hands off me and I love it. Everything about him is so warm and protective.

"I'm still a virgin."

Odhran's jaw doesn't relax. He runs his finger over my lips.

"Okay," he says. "I plan to change that. Come…"

ODHRAN'S SYRUPY voice has to be half the reason I do whatever the hell he says without protesting. His voice got me to drop to my knees on the cliffs. His words etched themselves onto my brain. Odhran's damn sexy Boston accent and his commanding tone gets me into his bed, face down, ass up.

He helps me position myself mostly naked in bed on top of a towel so I don't hurt my injuries with just my underwear on. As I sink into Odhran's fancy ass memory foam mattress, I feel like I'm floating on a cloud. I don't fight, I just let him peel the fabric away from my bare ass and then he puts something, probably a rubbing alcohol solution, on my ass because it stings a little and feels cold.

"Your ass is safe," he whispers. "I'm sure that's little comfort."

"I'm fine," I murmur, half-asleep because of the memory foam, painkillers and shower. I feel Odhran's hand rubbing my ass. He has such big, dominant hands. Our size difference is especially dramatic when you press our palms together. He's huge.

"What a great ass," he whispers. "I know exactly what you need here."

Onika

My throat tightens as I suppress the last bit of nervousness about letting my boyfriend give me a spontaneous tattoo. Is Odhran my boyfriend? He's something. Maybe something more than that.

"I love you," he says. "I want you to know that when you wake up."

"I'm not falling asleep," I protest, although I know my voice sounds suspiciously sleepy and this bed feels more like a cloud as time passes. I cast one last look at Odhran and he has a kit of tools laid out on the side table near the bed and a chair pulled up to the edge.

A bright lamp gives him enough light to work with. His blue eyes glimmer with excitement. I don't know how he's still so wide awake. It must be close to four in the morning. Maybe later.

"Okay," he says. "Whatever you say, Nik."

I HEAR A SOFT, buzzing sound, feel a light sting and then... I fall fast asleep, just like Odhran said I would.

Chapter Twenty-Three
Odhran

There was so much blood from the tattoo. The thin capillaries on Nik's ass didn't react well to the needle at first and I had a lot of cleanup, but I finished and her ass looks beautiful and even more like it belongs to me. *She's officially mine.*

I CAN'T STOP THINKING about Nik's ass that night, even though I last touched her and that perfect pair of cheeks three weeks ago when I gave her a tattoo. I felt like claiming her after everything that happened, marking her forever as belonging to *me*. I have no regrets and I think she's adjusting to her new ink.

A lot has changed since that night. Life has gotten better. Nik's wounds and injuries are healing and…

I just want to make love to her.

SIX DROPPED OUT OF SCHOOL. By some miracle, she survived that night and Aiden allowed her and her mother to escape into exile. The rest of the family – dead. But Six survives and apparently, Aiden will allow the two women of the family to live out their days in

Nunavut. It's the only place he promised they would be safe from his wrath. We don't have to worry about her anymore. Unfortunately, I can't say the same about Maura.

They still haven't found her and Aiden refuses to take my concerns seriously. He thinks without support from the Cunninghams a college girl is no threat. I hope he's right, but I don't want to take more chances with Nik.

I have completely eliminated any potential threat from Nik's life. As an English major, most of her classes are in a completely different building from mine, but I rearranged my schedule so that she doesn't have to go anywhere alone. When I can't be there, I have her friend Rylee walk with her.

Rylee is extremely strange. She turns red whenever I talk to her, stammers a lot and she says the most awkward things. But she does whatever I tell her to and seems to get along with Nik, so I accept Rylee's strangeness even if she makes me deeply uncomfortable with her staring and some of her questions...

Why does she need to know what size my pants are? She is *very* strange.

At least she's Irish and on the right side of the conflict. Aiden still has problems with a few other families, but most who side with the Cunninghams have left.

Rylee's mother comes from a mob family, but her father is a completely normal entrepreneur who owns a small brewery in Cambridge and pays Darragh $13,000 a month for protection.

For the rest of the semester, Nik and I get closer and our college routine becomes... *nice*. Nik agrees to partly move into my apartment, but she spends one night a week having a "girls' night" sleepover in her dorm room with Rylee. She doesn't want to lose her room & board money, so she won't move out completely until next semester. I use her girl's night to feed Killer Bee and work on my plans.

I still haven't slept with Nik. Her injuries won't heal until after final exams, so I have to wait, but that means I have to make our night together special. After waiting for so long, my desire for our first night to be perfect has been my primary obsession.

Chapter Twenty-Three

So I spend my time preparing for her. For us. For the ritual that will finally bond us together permanently – something that precedes marriage, something special that will be just ours. The tattoo was just the start of my plans for Nik. We have so much more to look forward to from each other.

I don't just mean having her lips around my cock or finally getting my cock inside her and feeling her tightness wrapping around me. My body aches with desire for her just concocting these plans. In the meantime, I keep it all a secret and maintain a normal routine with Nik.

We still go to the gym in the mornings, but I make her breakfast. Nik has a *very* unhealthy diet which I'm in the process of fixing. Normally, she eats whatever the dining hall has or disgusting frozen waffles *caked* in butter for breakfast. At my place, I make her freshly squeezed orange juice, toast from Evie's home-made sourdough bread (she gives me a loaf every week), three eggs so she can have enough protein, sauteed spinach and two strips of bacon.

Once we go to the gym and have breakfast, I attend my classes and Nik attends her. Nik thinks I'm "crazy" for cooking every day, so at least once a week we order her greasy, excessively salty Chinese takeout for dinner when we game together. Most nights we have dinner together, but when we don't Nik eats with Rylee and I have dinner with my brothers.

Days pass, Nik's wounds get better and the two of us only get closer. It's strangely beautiful to watch her change around me. She doesn't flinch when I come near her. She cuddles with me every night. She even agrees to look at pictures of Killer Bee and appreciate his glory.

"Maybe one day I'll meet him," she says. "I don't know."

But she smiles and my heart does the funny fluttering thing it always does around Nik. Her cheeks are so round and cute when she smiles and her eyes get all tiny and adorable. Every time I see her smile, I just want to kiss the top of her nose and pull her close to me. Her heart is so big that she doesn't even mind my pet snake...

It's as close to acceptance as I can expect for him. Six tried to kill him, but I try not to think about her.

My life and Nik's have become so intertwined that I forget what it was like to not have her, even if we haven't been together very long. When I'm away from her, I feel cold, desperate. I check her social media obsessively. By the time finals start, Nik is mostly better and I'm confident she could survive a night of making love.

But I want more than survival from her. I want her complete involvement, utter submission, and complete euphoria. Our first time together deserves to be explosive, passionate, and entirely ours. I can't wait.

Patience has never been my strong suit, but Nik's finals are very important. I have my math and economics final exams on the first day of finals, then I turn in my papers for Medieval Irish history and for my two economics electives early so I can dedicate the rest of my time to helping Nik write her final papers.

English majors have no final exams but a *lot* of writing. I've never seen Nik like this. It's both disturbing and fascinating to watch her utterly lose her mind in my apartment.

"IS THERE a reason you're staring at me?" Nik asks. There is *never* a reason. I don't need one. She's gorgeous, she's mine, and if I wasn't staring at her in person, I would be obsessing over the hundreds of pictures of her that I have saved to my cell phone.

"Thinking about your lips," I answer, which is partly true.

Nik rolls her eyes and tips a can of Monster energy down her throat. She called it a "nasty white boy beverage" the first time I offered her one, but now she has consumed all my favorite flavors in pursuit of better grades.

"No distractions, Odhran. You promised. Gemmell was really hard on my last paper and she expects something *outstanding.*"

"You're already outstanding," I tell her, pushing pretty, coiled, and very messy hair out of Nik's face. Her cheeks darken, and I know that I'm tempting her.

"Stop. This counts as distracting me."

"You look too cute for me to stop."

I approach her little perch at my kitchen counter and turn her away from her laptop to give her a kiss. Despite her protests, Nik eagerly abandons her work to kiss me back. Her fingers rake through my hair and her thick thighs wrap around my torso as she pulls me close.

"I love you," she whispers, resting her head on my chest and giving me the biggest hug. There's something about Nik's hugs that make me feel like a ball of fur or something soft... it's infuriating but... I like it a bit. I guess.

"We should have a baby then," I tell her, kissing the top of her head. Nik pulls away sharply and she looks at me like I have two heads.

"Where did that come from?"

"Babies? I think you know how babies are made... I mean... We haven't gone all the way but..."

"I know where babies come from, Odhran. Why did you suddenly bring up having a baby?"

"I'm Irish. It's what we do."

"That's pretty racist," Nik says, which is a thoroughly confusing statement.

"How?"

"It's a stereotype."

I fold my arms and raise an eyebrow. I understand Nik's point but my family history speaks for itself. I respond calmly, "I have four brothers and too many sisters. Stereotype or not... we love breeding."

"Don't call it breeding."

"Why? Isn't it a turn-on?"

Nik bites her lower lip and rolls her eyes again, a sure sign that it's a turn-on but she doesn't want to admit that she's incredibly dirty, so I'll have to force the filthiness out of her. Luckily, I absolutely love every aspect of sexually corrupting Nik.

"I think you like me talking about how badly I want to breed you.

All it would take is one night for me to knock you up with a tiny little caramel baby."

"Odhran!" Nik squeaks. "I'm trying to write."

I peer over her shoulder and look at her final essay for her creative writing class, which Nik hastily covers up, but not before I catch a few choice words. Cock. Ropes. Knife.

I smirk. "Were you writing something dirty?"

She sighs as I kiss her shoulder and eventually, after a few more kisses loosen her up, Nik responds. "Yes."

"Can I read it?"

"No."

"Can I act it out?"

"You already have…"

My cock nearly rips my pants. I don't even know what she's writing about, but my ego rises instantly at the thought that any of our encounters could be worthy enough for Nik to write about.

"That sounds very hot."

"Or horrific," she whispers. "Depending on your perspective."

I kiss her neck and she lets out an unwilling moan. Sucking on her neck makes that moan even louder. *Not tonight, Odhran. Patience.*

I PULL AWAY FROM HER, restraining myself at the last minute.

"Once you submit that final paper, you will come back here and we will finally, finally fuck the way we were meant to."

Talking about sex still makes Nik nervous. I haven't kept my hands off her entirely, but oral sex is different from what I want from her. I never had a woman who was entirely mine before. Not like I'll have Nik. She will never touch another man and she won't ever need to. I make her cum every day and I don't plan on stopping. *She tastes so fucking good.*

"Thank you," she whispers as I pull my lips away from her neck.

"You had better hurry," I tell her. "It's hard getting to sleep with your perfect ass pressed into me."

"And it's hard getting work done with your dick bulging through your pants right next to me."

"Fine," I tell her. "I'll go sit with Killer Bee and meditate."

"He's going to eat you if you do that," Nik says hesitantly, and I wonder if I should let him out into the apartment to scare her into my bedroom...

Unfortunately, she needs to finish that final essay.

"I'll be careful, my love. Now work. Text me if you need more energy drinks or a foot rub."

"I don't need a foot rub and this energy drink is probably going to stop my heart."

I kiss her and leave her alone for a while, walking into Killer Bee's enclosure where he lies curled up in the corner. He doesn't move for a while after I feed him, so I don't have anything to worry about, despite Nik's complaints. He doesn't make much of a mess and I have a little bench in his plant-filled enclosure with an incredible view of Boston.

"Hey buddy," I whisper. "I didn't think I was capable of love. Maybe I was wrong. Because I love her enough not to take her right there against the kitchen counter."

He doesn't answer. I probably shouldn't confess my sexual depravity to my snake where Nik might hear me. She already thinks I have "big demon energy". I sit with him for about an hour while scrolling idly through Nik's old pictures on social media in between chess matches on chess.com. When I check on her, she's slumped over the counter, fast asleep.

I guess she crashed. Poor thing. I whisper her name, but Nik just lets out a little snore. She's incredibly cute. I walk up to her and push her hair out of her face. She makes a little squealing sound. I wrap my arms around her, feeling her little head nestled against my chest as I carry her to bed.

She can finish her essay in the morning...

Chapter Twenty-Four
Onika

Professor Gemmell is old school, so I have to walk all the way to the English department to slide my printed final paper under her door. I've never written something so experimental or dark. I don't want to admit that Odhran was right about a brush with darkness bringing more depth to my writing, but it definitely feels that way.

It's the best paper I've ever written.

Since Odhran won't let me go anywhere alone, Rylee accompanies me to Gemmell's office, chatting happily about her plans for the winter break. Rylee loves Christmas and she has plans for her Christmas cookie baking schedule, finding a date to go ice-skating with and more.

Once I turn in my final paper… *I'm done.*

I don't have to come back to campus until next semester. Once I slide my essay under the door, I want to squeal with excitement. Rylee does it for me. After hugging her and finally letting some of my excitement show, my nerves set in.

"Oh my God," Rylee says. "What is it? Did you screw up somehow? We can break in and get it back."

I didn't know my roommate would end up being a ride-or-die like this, but I'm glad that she feels close enough to me to offer to break into a professor's office.

"No. It's not that. I'm fine."

I DON'T NEED my closest friend knowing that I'm nervous about what awaits me in Odhran's apartment. He's been on edge all day and more alarming than that is that he has completely slackened his obsessive levels of security around me. I don't mind that he hasn't sent me fifteen texts in the past hour, but when Odhran changes his highly regimented behavior, I start to worry.

"It's Odhran," she says, smirking as her cheeks get red. "What's wrong? Does he want you to give him a blowjob? I can teach you. I think I have a banana in my purse."

Rylee thrives on girl talk, sex talk, and everything having to do with getting guys. I'd rather not think about my roommate giving head, so I politely decline her offer. I would rather keep my vision of bananas entirely pure.

"No. I'm fine. Thank you…"

I like Rylee, but I don't need her knowing the details of my sex life. I distract her by asking her what sugar cookie recipe she settled on – the one from Martha Stewart or Rachel Ray – and she launches into a lengthy explanation about an Irish cooking YouTube channel she watches online.

She drops me off at Odhran's apartment without returning to the blowjob conversation. Thank goodness. We wish each other happy holidays and she promises to steal me away from Odhran a few times over the winter break. Hugging her goodbye, I feel lucky to have found someone at my college who I could bond with. I had prepared myself mentally to spend all four years alone but… Rylee doesn't care that I don't fit in, that I'm totally shy and antisocial, or that my boyfriend is a wild Irish mobster.

Your owner: I'm waiting.
Me: I'm outside.

Onika

Your owner: I know. I can't wait to taste you.

ODHRAN HAS NEVER HELD BACK his feelings for me, but I still feel insanely fluttery inside when he's so blunt about how much he wants me. After everything we've been through together, after falling for him and falling into trouble, I'm ready to embrace his darkness. I'm ready to fall in love with Odhran.

Me: I can't wait for you either, sir.

HE TOLD me exactly what to expect from this ritual, but now that I'm outside Odhran's apartment and it's freezing cold, I question my sanity. For a few weeks now, I've had palm-print access to both the building and the elevator that takes me several floors up to Odhran's penthouse apartment – something utterly ridiculous for a college student to own in the first place.

Once I step into the elevator, I obey Odhran's instructions and set my backpack down before stripping down to the lingerie he instructed me to wear under my clothes when I left his apartment. There isn't much time before the elevator gets to the top and Odhran made it quite clear before I left what would happen if I wasn't dressed exactly the way he wanted.

Easy.

I shed my white puffy winter coat, my ugg boots, socks, my thick black yoga pants and then my large red sweater in record time to reveal the red bodysuit with a thong that Odhran requested.

Of course, the elevator has mirrors, forcing me to look at myself exposed and barefoot. I look short. But I also look curvy, a little more toned than before from all of the gym time with Odhran and... *pretty.*

It has been more common recently for me to notice the good things about myself instead of the bad.

It's easier with Odhran pointing out all the things he loves about me. The elevator doors slide open into a dark room and my heart stops. He warned me that he was preparing for me, but he didn't tell me what to expect.

"Odhran?" I call out, taking one barefoot step into his apartment. My heart races. The elevator doors slide closed behind me, shutting my backpack and clothing behind me. His apartment is so cold – several degrees cooler than I remember when I left. I wasn't in lacy lingerie back then.

There isn't any response when I call Odhran's name.

"Odhran?"

I TAKE another step into the apartment and work my hand along the wall in an effort to find the light switch. Before I can reach it, and before I realize what's happening, a hand clamps over my mouth and a large arm wraps around me tightly, throwing me off balance and silencing any screaming sounds I would have made in surprise.

My back slams against a hard wall of muscle and my back lands right against a very thick bulge. How big is this man? *He is so damn crazy.*

Unceremoniously, Odhran runs his tongue from the top of my shoulder blade all the way up the length of my neck until he gets to my earlobe, which he sucks on until I squirm.

"You look fucking perfect," he whispers. "We have a long night together, Nik. I've been waiting."

He slowly creeps his fingers away from my lips, awaiting a response.

"Yes, sir."

I feel Odhran's big cock jerking against my ass. The first night I met him, he didn't hesitate to thrust every inch of that monster deep into my mouth. I choked on it. I tasted his flesh. There was a part of me that he cracked open that night – the darkest part of me. I might just be an artist, but I'm not afraid of the darkness anymore.

Like light, like words, like color, darkness can be controlled.

"Good girl," Odhran whispers and those two words get me instantly wet. "Before I push my cock past your tender hymen, I need your pussy nice and wet."

"Yes, sir…"

Odhran chuckles and sucks on my neck until I moan, distracting himself with my taste and forcing me to gush all over the red bodysuit plastered between my thighs by my wetness.

"You are so excited to have my tongue in your cunt. But that won't happen until you get my cock wet. I've been more than patient with you and right now, I need to fuck your throat until I cum, princess."

Again, my thighs are completely soaked, my pussy betraying all my moral senses as I lean into Odhran's game. It's more than a game for him. It's a ritual. Something special. Something new. Something that will be just ours.

He releases me from his tight grasp. I turn to face him, just to see him for the first time and his stern, sharp face almost terrifies me. It's like if I spend too much time away from him, I forget how terrifyingly beautiful he is. It's not just his gorgeous, insanely pale blue eyes or his skin. It's that silky hair and how he smells. His voice. His complete control over himself and every situation he finds himself in.

"On your knees, princess."

I drop to my knees as he unbuckles his black trousers and whips a thick leather belt from the loops. My stomach lurches in anticipation of Odhran possibly using that belt later. He's made a lot of promises – some of which could be considered threats. He planned all this, so I can't fathom the extent of what he has in store for me.

His cock wants to escape his pants desperately. He hurriedly removes all the clothing on the lower half of his body, obscuring his rock hard abs and gorgeous chest. I run my fingers over his bare thighs, appreciating his muscular, masculine legs and the sexy tattoo of the Japanese mask.

He removes his underwear and I sit back on my heels, patiently waiting for him. Odhran's cock is impossible to ignore once it springs free and he is far from patient once the monster escapes. My jaw tightens at the painful memory of the first time I took Odhran's gigantic cock between my lips. He eagerly sinks his fingers into my curly hair and tilts my head up so I can look at him.

He isn't smiling, just holding onto his cock with his other hand and guiding it towards my lips.

"Open your mouth like a good girl."

I open my mouth wide, hoping that I spread my lips big enough to fit his dick but knowing that it's impossible, even if I try my best. But I want to please him, so I keep my tongue out and wait for his dick to slide all the way to the back of my throat.

Chapter Twenty-Five
Odhran

Nik gags when I slide half my cock down her throat. The tip of my member scrapes the textured cavern and I nearly explode as she gasps for air and her throat tightens perfectly around my dick. Pleasure explodes through me and I groan.

"Fuck, I love your mouth."

I grab onto her hair and lose myself in the moment. I stop caring about the gagging or the spit or the tears. She has a safe word now. I can do this. My hips thrust forward furiously as I fuck Nik's throat like it belongs to me. Because it does. After tonight, every part of her will.

Every part of her.

Nik's lips spread wide around my cock as I pump into her mouth. As I take her completely, she gazes up at me from her knees, so fucking beautiful. As her dark brown eyes look up at me, I hardly have any restraint left. My cock bursts into her mouth and I fill Nik's lips with my cum.

It's like I haven't cum in a year. So much of my seed pumps down her throat and I can tell she doesn't want to swallow, but it's too late. I'm not ready to make a mess of Nik's clothes yet. Grabbing her hair to hold her in place, I indulge in the euphoric feeling of her tight little throat wrapped around a dick that is much too big for her.

Nik digs her nails into my thighs as I cum in her mouth. There's a touch of pain, but it hardly feels like a punishment. I would let her drive a screw into my palm if she wanted, as long as I still got to own her throat. But her pain won't go unrewarded. She's been an *incredibly* good girl, even as I rile her up every night, edging her to the point of orgasm and then taking it away, just so she's nice and soaked for tonight.

She hasn't cum in two weeks, even if I've had my tongue in her cunt every night. I'll even lick her asshole until she gets close and then leave her suffering from the confusion and pain of being teased.

Once I pull her mouth off my cock, I use her hair to guide Nik to her feet and then I let go. She looks at me with a mixture of love and hatred. My cock doesn't soften for a fucking second, even if I just unleashed the biggest load of cum I've ever produced down her throat.

"I drew blood," she says, showing me her hands.

"Good," I whisper, taking her fingers and licking the blood from my thighs off them. Her fingers taste nice, but they would taste better if she had pushed them into her pussy for a few minutes first. *We have time for that, Odhran. Be patient.*

When I let her fingers go, she drops her hands to her sides. Her lips are red and swollen. I run my thumb over her lips and as Nik shudders, I draw her against me and kiss her. My dick crudely pokes her stomach, but she doesn't seem to mind as she runs her hand underneath my shirt all over my abs.

I chuckle. She *loves* touching my stomach. It feels weird sometimes being with a girl who is this affectionate. I didn't grow up with a lot of touch like this. Relationships were more about duty than pleasure. This is more than pleasure, anyway. From the moment I touched Nik, the better word for what I feel would be euphoria.

She makes me downright euphoric, especially the way her fingers tease over my stomach. My nerves heighten as she gets to my chest, but I'm too busy enjoying her soft full lips to notice until her spit-covered fingers touch the raw part. I wince and she immediately notices and draws her hand away.

"What's wrong with your chest?"

"Nothing."

"You winced."

"It's a surprise."

She wrinkles her eyebrows in confusion, but seems to accept that this is her typical reaction towards me. "Show me the surprise."

"Is this just a cheap ploy to see me shirtless?"

"Show me," she says more sternly, folding her arms and trying to look as "strict" as possible. I love when she puffs out her chest like an angry little Pomeranian.

I'm more than happy to take my shirt off and earn even more praise and attention from Nik than before for my physique. But when I take my shirt off, it's still dark, so I put my hand on the dimmer and turn the lights up so she can get a better view of the surprise. I didn't expect her to be so handsy so soon.

I expected her to be more reluctant when it comes to what she calls "my games".

Her hands clamp over her mouth instinctively as she utters what I assume must be an admonishment.

"Odhran, you shouldn't have done that," she says, partly flattered and partly disturbed. I'm not ashamed of how much I love Onika. How much I would do for her. Tattooing her name is the bare minimum.

"Why not?" I ask her. I have tattoos that bring me less pride than this one.

"It's my *name*."

Nik just runs her fingers around the reddened skin, careful not to touch the fresh gooey Aquaphor covering the raised, injured skin this time. She gives me a look of deep concern.

"Did you do this yourself?" she asks.

"Yes."

That's the part I'm most proud of. I've given tattoos before, but I've never done something so complicated, so personal, or so difficult.

I just love that she can't stop staring at my chest. I would tattoo some-thing new for her every week if it would get Nik to keep looking at me like this.

"In the mirror?" she asks, still confused about how on earth I achieved *cursive* tattooing on my own chest.

"Yes," I answer calmly, even if I'm bursting with excitement at this demonstration of my commitment to her. "It was easy. Do you like it?"

There's a single rose underneath her name. I thought that was a nice touch, since they're her favorite flower. She nods and then pulls her hand away.

"I don't have your name tattooed," she says.

Nope. The butt tattoo I did for Onika is personal, but it's less blatant. I owe her this much. I owe her proof that she's the love I chose, and duty has nothing to do with why I'm with her. She's my choice.

"No," I answer. "But we can change that after we're married."

She smiles brightly and then, as if fearful about getting her hopes up, her smile falls away. I take her hand and press it to the bare part of my chest.

"I am yours," I tell her earnestly. "I am yours as much as you are mine. Tonight after we fuck, I'm going to drink your blood and you're going to drink mine, and the two of us will make this bond unbreakable."

She flinches when I say that, but I don't mind her reaction. I *expect* this reaction. Nik shudders as I take her hand and kiss it softly. Her gaze meets mine and again, my dick jumps forward. It's her turn to get naked now. Her turn to show me everything.

"Take your clothes off," I command her. "I'm going to put my tongue in your cunt before I put my cock in it."

Nik looks absolutely gorgeous in the tight red lingerie. Her dark, coppery skin always glimmers from her moisturizer. Everything about her is always so fucking alluring that I don't have any control of myself. All I feel with her is pure, unfiltered desire.

She slips one of the red straps over her cute little shoulder and my cock jerks at the thought of giving her another tattoo right where the strap falls. When the next strap drops, Nik exposes her breasts and I can't help myself. I kiss her neck repeatedly until she slides her lingerie off and it falls to the ground.

Her mouth tastes spectacular and her lips are definitely still swollen from the way I forced my cock into her pretty, tight mouth. Once she's naked, I break away from our kiss and my hand gropes her breast gently. She moans as my fingers graze over her perfect perky nipples.

I have never felt such large and sexy nipples with little bumps all around them and delicate, hardened nubs at the ends. The slightest touch is more than enough to make Nik moan like I've pressed my tongue against her clit. She has soft, sensitive breasts. Her curves are such that every part of her is soft. I can't choose between her tits and her ass.

Both of them turn me on for extremely different reasons. Nik's moaning just from my fingers teasing her nipples encourages me to go further. I bend my head to her full breasts and run my tongue over her dark, hazelnut-colored nipples. Her moans drive me wild. I slip my fingers between her lower lips as she moans just to feel how wet she is.

Nik cries out louder as my fingers force her thighs apart and her pussy is so damn wet that my fingers nearly slide all the way inside her. I move my fingers slowly between her thick lower lips and fixate my attention on her clit while my tongue roams over her nipples in teasing circles, sucking on her perky nipples whenever Nik seems most sensitive.

When she gets close to orgasm, I drop to my knees and move my hands to her thighs so I can spread her thighs apart and taste her pretty ass pussy. Her thighs are stuck together from her juices, making it almost difficult to peel them apart. Once I have her lower lips exposed, Nik's delicious musky scent hits my nostrils and drives me crazy with an instinctive lust.

I have been eating her sweet pussy every night to prepare for this, and touching my tongue to her clit and full lower lips just feels right. I'm ready for her. She lets out a soft moan and slides her fingers through my hair as I lick slow, purposeful circles around her clit. Nik holds onto my hair as I eat her out slowly at first, getting her even wetter with my tongue and fully losing myself in how good she tastes.

Nik can't hold herself back. I've kept her away from climax for so long that she moans and gets close to the edge within a few minutes. I put two fingers inside her as I keep teasing her clit and Nik's moaning gets so loud that I almost cum all over myself. Her pussy tastes like magic and I drive my tongue deeper until she finally reaches her first release for the night.

Having her cum on my lips is downright glorious. She shudders and keeps moaning as I drink up every drop from her pussy and keep teasing her with my tongue. Fuck, I want her so bad. Nik can't keep it together as I clean her pussy with my tongue. She climaxes again and tightens her grip on my hair. Her grasp hurts, so I remove her hands and turn her around so she faces away from me.

That's enough of that. I spread her ass cheeks apart and lick her clean from behind, taking my tongue along the length of her crease from her engorged clit all the way to her puckered backdoor.

Mine. Every inch of this woman is mine.

She no longer flinches when I put my tongue in her tight back door where it belongs. I kiss her perfect butthole and then her cheeks before murmuring, "I love your pretty black ass, princess. It's so soft..."

I run my fingers over Nik's tattoo. It's flawless, just like the rest of her, and it's my best work. A Celtic knot joining a rose and shamrock together. Underneath it, I etched an ancient Gaelic protection sigil into Nik's skin in script. My cock lurches as I kiss her tattoo.

I can't take it anymore.

RISING TO MY FEET, I wrap my arms around Nik and draw her tiny, soft body against mine, enjoying how that curvy ass nestles in my crotch. I bend over and whisper, "I'm going to give you thirty seconds to get in bed. One second longer and I'll spank you hard enough to bruise that perfect black ass."

"Thirty seconds?" she whimpers, nestling into my grasp despite my threats. "I can do that."

"Go ahead, princess. Run."

Chapter Twenty-Six
Onika

O dhran releases me from his constricting grasp and I run towards his bedroom. Thirty seconds is plenty of time to get from the living room to Odhran's bedroom. It's a penthouse, but it's not infinitely large. I run away from him, curious why I don't even hear him chasing me quickly. He walks behind me as I run, and I only see why when I get to the bedroom door.

It's locked.

I turn around and press my back against the door, giving Odhran a fierce look as he gives me the most annoying smug smile in the world.

"You cheater."

"That was a good one," he says, completely lacking remorse. "If it makes you feel better, I never planned on sparing your ass tonight."

He leans forward and turns a key into his bedroom door, opening it. *Oh my goodness.* I believed Odhran when he said he would make tonight special, but I could have never predicted exactly how far he would have gone.

There are mirrors on the ceiling. Candles everywhere. Rose petals. I glance over my shoulder and try not to worry about the belt Odhran brought from the living room. Instead, I think about how fucking sexy he looks behind me with his dominant, muscular body towering behind mine.

My pussy won't stop dribbling with excitement. I'm weak at the knees already from the way Odhran made me cum. I'm done questioning what's wrong with me or why I'm drawn to him. It's love. It's how safe I feel around him. There is something completely powerful between us that I don't want an explanation for. I just want to drown in Odhran's darkness and join my body with his.

I want to find out how far he'll push me with his ritual tonight. I trust him not to push me too far. *He loves me and I know it. It's not just the tattoo. It's everything.*

"Do you like the roses?" he whispers. "They always remind me of you. I kept white sheets in case you bleed."

Goosebumps spread all over my shoulders and neck. My pussy gushes again. Odhran has every inch of me under his control. Sex talk that would make me nervous before gets me completely wet now.

"I love the roses."

"Good," he whispers. "Then you will be more than happy to get into bed with them so I can spank your perfect ass."

"You tricked me. I don't think I deserve a spanking."

Odhran's belt suddenly becomes extremely prominent in my awareness. I don't like the way he's holding that thing, especially not when his grasp on the belt tightens.

"You may not deserve it, but I want to do it. For us..."

"What do you get out of it?" I ask Odhran for the first time, probing the dark part of his sexuality as I gaze up at his handsome, chiseled face.

"Control," he says quickly. "And... I get to prove to myself that you really love me. That you will do for me what I know I would do for you."

"You don't need proof of that, Odhran. You're... you. Gorgeous. Tall. Wanted by everyone..."

"Yet the only person who I ever got close to was a monster," he says. "She never loved me for more than what I could give her. I know that part of my life is over now but... your heart could wander."

"Never."

"How can you be so sure, virgin?" he whispers, taking my cheeks in his grasp and holding my face possessively so he's forcing me to look at him.

"I love you the way you love me. Completely. Madly. Deeply."

Odhran's cock jerks as he moves closer to me and draws my face to his so that he can kiss me again. I let his lips meet mine and as usual, kissing Odhran gets me soaked again. Juices spread across my thighs. I'm weak at the knees again and unfortunately, I moan. My moans send Odhran's desires into overdrive. He releases my cheeks from his forceful grasp and demands firmly, "Bed. All fours. I still want your ass."

I climb into bed naked and position myself on all fours. My initial thought is that the position is completely awkward, but I stop worrying about the awkwardness when I feel Odhran's weight sink into the bed. He presses one knee into the bed to balance himself and uses his free hand to gently touch my ass cheeks.

He absolutely *loves* playing with my butt. I never expected him to be this fixated on my ass, but Odhran has a complete obsession. He rubs my butt cheeks and then runs his thumb over my ass tattoo as if trying to soothe the skin. Healing that ass tattoo was difficult, but it definitely doesn't need soothing anymore, so I just enjoy Odhran's firm touch.

Excitement and fear course through me with equal force. I don't know what he will do next or how much pain he plans to cause with the belt. For now, he teases me but I know he's going to hurt me when he plants a kiss on each ass cheek.

"I love you, Nik," he says. "I fucking love you."

Then Odhran smacks my butt with his belt forcefully. I cry out as pain bursts through my body and a sharp sting surges throughout my body. Juices dribble out of my pussy but my ass feels instantly red and my body trembles from the pain.

"Fuck, you're red," Odhran grunts and then he hits me again without giving me a second to respond. The pain blinds me. It's not the worst pain I've ever felt and it's pain for Odhran. Pain for Odhran feels worth it because he's right – I know he would go through this much pain for me.

"Only three more," he says. "I love you, Nik."

One.

I cry out. The pain is incredible. My heart surges with a strange sense of pride from the bruises I know I'll wear for the next few weeks. Odhran's bruises. His sign of ownership and love.

Two.

That one hurts even more as my ass pleads for mercy, but I refuse to allow myself to say the safe word. I want this. I crave Odhran's bruises as much as I crave us finally having sex.

"I love you," Odhran breathes, out of breath from how hard he just spanked me. "I love you so fucking much."

"Then spank me, sir. Spank me…"

Odhran makes a low growl of pleasure in the back of his throat and then gives me one last spanking. The pain makes me see stars. Odhran drops the belt instantly once he finishes. I cry out as he touches my raw ass with his bare palm. His hand feels like it's made of fire. I flinch aggressively as Odhran touches me. It's so painful. My body feels completely aware of every sensation more than normal. Everything I feel for him is just so fucking intense.

"You were so good, little princess," Odhran says, holding me around my waist and carrying me out of bed before standing me upright on the bedroom floor. I wince as he sets me down and my ass jiggles painfully.

Once on my feet, my pussy drips again, continuing to coat my thighs. Odhran looks at me so seriously, his face almost concerned.

"Was I too hard on you?"

"No. But I'll have bruises throughout Christmas break."

"Good. I want you to think of me every time you're with Rylee Walsh."

I roll my eyes. Odhran won't ever change his extremely possessive ways, but I don't need him to change. I feel like I was waiting my whole life just to be his – and I'm happy that he will be the only man I ever touch. My wicked little muse.

Chapter Twenty-Six

"You are way too jealous."

"Yes," Odhran says. "I'm not sorry about it. Now… let me see your face."

It's not exactly a question because Odhran grabs my cheeks forcefully again. His cock is still incredibly hard. I don't think he would have been able to last this long if he hadn't put cum before. He examines my face closely. My cheeks warm instantly as he touches me. I can't wait for him to kiss me.

Just like I expect, he kisses me again and it is glorious. When he pulls away from me, Odhran's face is stern again.

"Lie back and spread your thighs. I need to look in your pretty dark eyes," he says. Odhran strokes my hair slowly as he says this and then twirls my curls around his fingers before letting go and nodding towards the bed.

This is it. It's finally going to happen, isn't it? Odhran's cheeks are completely reddened with desire already. I love that he wears his feelings all over his face. His skin is so pale… so pretty with all the veins beneath it and the redness. He makes his skin even prettier with the tattoos.

I bite my lower lip and obey Odhran, climbing into bed and sinking into the white sheets. The scent of rose petals are glorious. I don't even mind the stinging sensation in my ass. Odhran kneels on the floor between my legs as I lie back and he eats my pussy to orgasm three more times before he pulls away and throws me into the middle of the bed before positioning his body on top of mine.

I am completely vulnerable to him in this position, spread wide beneath Odhran's firm, muscular body. He is so goddamn sexy that my hands immediately rush to his back so I can enjoy Odhran's thick muscle development. He has a great back and better shoulders. His arms are perfect for me and I feel so safe pinned beneath him, even with a throbbing ass and an unreasonably juicy pussy.

Odhran pushes hair out of my face and kisses me as his hard cock touches my thigh. I can feel his dick drooling with desire over my thighs, but he doesn't rush. He just kisses me so slowly that I wrap my thighs around him and almost beg him to take my virginity.

I want sex so badly now that it hurts. The tight ache in my pussy won't go away unless I feel him inside me. I whimper and press my heels into the back of Odhran's thighs.

"Patience," he growls, pulling away from our kiss to tease my neck with his lips and tongue. As I moan and grasp at him desperately, Odhran presses the head of his cock against my entrance. I completely freeze as I feel the soft, large head of Odhran's dick against my entrance.

I've only had two of Odhran's fingers between my legs. The ache grows stronger as he rubs the head of his cock around my pussy entrance but doesn't drive the length inside me. He just teases me, preparing me for just how thick the head of his dick is.

"Your pussy is so small," Odhran murmurs, teasing me as he kisses my neck. "I'm going to get your blood all over my dick when I fuck you, princess."

I can't tell if this turns him on or if he's just trying to prepare me for the pain I'm about to feel.

"Yes, sir," I murmur. I close my eyes, but Odhran demands I keep them open. Our eyes lock as he pushes the head of his dick gently against my entrance as if to test how easy it will be for him to slide his monstrous pole between my legs.

My heart skips a beat. He's too big, isn't he? Odhran and I have a fairly large size difference and maybe we aren't ever meant to be together just because of that. I'm short and I have a tight pussy that aches when he slides two fingers inside me.

WHAT IF HIS dick doesn't fit? Nerves cause me to dig my nails into Odhran's back. He grunts and pushes forward a little more. Pain sears through me. Oh God. He's huge. Odhran's cock sends an immense burst of pain through me as he pushes an inch inside me. I have never felt a sensation so powerful in my life and I have also never felt so small in comparison to someone.

Odhran appears impervious to my nails clawing into his back. I gasp and spread my legs wider, hoping my splayed position and soaking wet pussy make it easier for him to drive his cock into me. Odhran's biceps explode into giant thick balls of muscle and they tense up and he plants himself in the bed to drive his hips forward.

The force of his hips finally splits me open. More pain surrounds my slit and spreads through my core as Odhran pushes forward. I cry out, pleading with him to go slower, but it's like he can't hear me. His pupils are so wide that the black covers the blue. I can't stop myself from thinking that he is an insanely hot demon. It's like he can't even feel any pain from my nails digging into his back.

"You're so tight," he growls. "Holy fuck, princess."

"It hurts…"

"Yes," Odhran says as he eases his hips out slowly, allowing me time to adjust to the small portion of his cock that he managed to fit between my legs. "It will hurt. But you can handle pain, Nik. You're so strong… so fucking beautiful…

Just as my heart flutters from Odhran's compliment, he cruelly thrusts the rest of his cock inside me. I cry out loudly as the intense pain turns unbearable. A hot gush of liquid spreads between my legs and I just know it's blood. My thighs tremble in fear and from the intensity of the pain, but despite all the pain, I associate Odhran with comfort and pleasure, so I cling to him furiously with both greedy hands and trembling thighs.

He runs his thumb over my lips.

"You're flushed," he whispers. "You look so pretty and… fuck, I love you."

Odhran presses his face into my neck and grabs some of my flesh between his teeth. The pain on my neck replaces the pain between my thighs. *Did he just bite me?*

"Shhh," he murmurs as my whimper turns into a pained and confused moan. "Just feel it babe. Your pussy is so tight. You're made for my cock."

I can feel blood dribbling from the bite on my neck, but the pain dissipates when Odhran takes his tongue and runs it gently over my nipple, dispersing the pain with a burst of immense pleasure. My nipples have never been more sensitive and with his cock buried between my thighs, I can feel *everything* down there as his tongue rolls slowly over my nipples.

"Those are pretty nipples," Odhran murmurs between slow licks. "They're so big... such a dark shade of brown..."

I moan loudly and feel an intense spasm between my thighs as my pussy clamps down hard around Odhran's cock. His tongue swirling all over my nipples is more than enough to drive me close to the edge of orgasm. He won't let me go all the way. When I get close to finally releasing, Odhran withdraws his hips slightly and moves his tongue away from my breasts.

"No," he says in a deep, growling voice. "You stay right there and let me fuck you to an orgasm. You need to learn that my cock is more than enough."

Odhran grips my hips, allowing his fingers to sink into my flesh. I can feel his cock stiffen inside me as he holds onto my curves and allows his hands to explore the softness of my flesh as well as how much there is for him to hold onto. Watching him grow more visibly aroused as he touches me sends a flutter of arousal through me.

Classmates always bullied me for how I looked. I never thought I looked as monstrous as they treated me. *I just wanted to end up with someone who could appreciate me.*

"You're so hot," he says. "I don't want to stop. I never want to stop..."

With that, Odhran moves his hips in a slow rhythm. My pussy still aches from the girth of Odhran's cock spreading me wide, but as he pounds me harder, the mixture of pain and pleasure intensifies as the large tip of his dick touches the back walls of my pussy with his deeper thrusting.

My first orgasm with Odhran's dick inside me comes without warning. The explosion of pleasure causes me to cry out loudly, my thighs wrapping more tightly around Odhran's firm, muscular body. His scent and his closeness draw even more emotion and intensity out of the climax. He kisses me so softly as I cum, taking the surprise orgasm in stride and treating me like I'm precious as I cry out for the big dick splitting my pussy in half.

"My sweet virgin," he whispers, kissing my neck. "Thank you. Thank you for the tightest pussy I've ever felt…"

I shudder and cry out again as Odhran holds me tighter, his cock swelling as our skin presses together.

"I can't breathe," I gasp, still struggling to come down from the intense euphoria of my climax.

Odhran moves one hand to my chest, right above my breast. His warm touch instantly relaxes me. Cruelly, he withdraws his cock and then slides it right back to its previous depths. I cry out again and my intense shuddering climax heightens. With his hand on my chest, I easily recover a sense of calm.

"You're hot when you cum," he says. "Sorry for the pain."

"You haven't…"

"No," he says. "Not yet."

My stomach lurches. Odhran and I have never had a proper discussion about babies or the future, but considering the strong beliefs he has about everything else, it probably shouldn't surprise me that he has strong beliefs about babies and family too.

"Okay," I whisper. "Should we have that conversation now?"

He's still inside me, which is definitely influencing my ability to think clearly. Right now, a baby feels like a very good idea. I hook my heels around Odhran's body and wriggle my hips a little, moaning and sighing as I successfully draw his cock deeper.

Odhran smirks and kisses me before responding, "No. Because we're not having a baby now. That's an entirely different ritual. I'll cum somewhere else…"

He pulls out of me and then flips me over unceremoniously before sliding back inside me with one forceful thrust. I moan loudly, lying on my stomach and firmly pinned down in Odhran's grasp. *Oh fuck…*

His fingers trail over my hips, along the side of my thigh and then around the curve of my ass cheeks until I feel Odhran's finger press against my asshole. He moves his cock a little and I feel my ass cheeks clench around Odhran's finger as he presses it harder against my back door.

"There," he says. "I think I'll cum there."

Onika

Chapter Twenty-Seven
Odhran

Nik squirms as I press my finger against her butthole and fight my desire to put the entire thing in there. With her pussy wrapped tightly around my dick, I know it would feel incredible. Slowly, I move my finger away from her ass.

It's so hard not to cum inside her. I want to save my cum for her pussy tomorrow morning. I know she thinks we'll have this long wait before I knock her up but... I don't have any more questions about how I want to spend my future.

I want to be with Nik forever – give her my babies, protect her, and have sex with her as much as humanly possible.

"Cum for me again, princess," I whisper, kissing her forehead and then moving my dick again. Nik doesn't take long to cum again. I slowly enter Nik from behind. Watching Nik's gorgeous ass bounce around my cock makes it nearly impossible not to cum inside her pussy. When I make her cum while pounding her from behind, I take my cock out and lick her pussy clean, getting her nice and wet while I tease her back door with my tongue, preparing her for what's coming next.

Once she cums a few more times, she barely flinches when I flatten my tongue and run it along her tight, puckered asshole. Her pussy is so pretty after it takes my cock. Crouched on my knees, I spread Nik's pussy apart and slide a finger through her slit. She shudders and her soft, pretty thighs squeeze together.

"Your pussy looks so good after I fuck it," I whisper. "It's all red and swollen from my dick."

"You're huge," she gasps earnestly. Her innocent voice saying something so fucking dirty gets me rock hard.

Her ass is about to find out just how huge I am. The thought of cumming in such a tight hole is enough to drive me into a frenzy, but because it's her first time, I calm myself.

"Yes," I whisper, kissing the base of her spine. "You took my cock well and you didn't even bleed that much."

Nik shudders and I kiss the backs of her thighs, running my finger through the remaining blood stains to clean them off her legs.

"I came so hard," she gasps, her thighs spreading apart unconsciously as she remembers the euphoria of her orgasm. It was nearly impossible not to cum with her perfect pussy gripping my dick so tightly. But I'm glad she had fun. Now it's my turn.

"Good," I whisper, kissing her ass. "I'll always make you cum first. But then, I'll take you however I want."

I tap her ass again and as her cheeks jiggle, Nik shifts her hips nervously.

"I'm cumming in your ass tonight."

She flips her hair as she looks at me over her shoulder. Her hair is a gorgeous mess of tangles, making her angry squint completely ineffective at chasing me away from her butthole.

"You can't fit a dick that big in there," she says.

"From virgin to expert in one night..."

Nik rolls her eyes. "I don't need to be an expert. I've had my butthole my entire life and your dick is..."

"It's huge," I finish for her, smirking and running my tongue over my lips excitedly. "Which means your ass is gonna milk the cum out of my cock in seconds."

"Is that some type of... kink..."

"*You* are my kink, Nik."

I spread her ass cheeks apart and press a slick thumb against her asshole. She squirms and inadvertently pushes her hips back to accept some of my finger in her ass. It doesn't appear to hurt her, so I push forward, which makes Nik moan my name disapprovingly.

As she moans my name, I push my thumb a little deeper in her ass, all the way past my knuckle. Her ass grips my finger so tightly that it nearly *hurts* my finger. Holy fuck. Nik's pussy is an absolute treasure, but her ass feels like a completely otherworldly experience. I push inside her deeper and Nik emits a hot little moan that almost sounds like a squeak.

"Fuck, you feel good," I growl. "Your ass is so tight…"

"It's so… much pressure," Nik whimpers, her skin turning a reddish copper color as a flush spreads through her.

"I can make you cum with just a finger in your ass," I whisper to her, kissing the base of her spine again. "Will you let me do that?"

She squirms a little more and makes a noise that sounds suspiciously like a "yes" to me. I push my finger inside her deeper, exploring her passage and paying close attention to exactly what Nik likes – what makes her moan, what makes her squeal and eventually what makes her cum.

I have always loved studying her, and watching her body respond to my teasing and touching has my cock stiffer and more impatient than it has ever been before. It's a fucking miracle I've held myself back this long. I can't wait to cum inside Nik's perfect round ass.

Exploring her ass with my thumb gets her aroused enough to squeak and moan with each thrust. Now that her body only responds with euphoria to my finger pumping into her ass, I suck on her pussy lips and Nik's responses to me kick into overdrive.

Her pussy gushes with juices as I pump my finger into her ass. I remove my tongue to let her juices drip onto her thighs so I can use those sweet, sticky juices to get my dick in her ass soon. When I finally get Nik to cum, her ass tightens hard around my finger and her pussy erupts with arousal.

She moans loudly and pushes her ass cheeks back against my face, nearly burying me between her fluffy, sizable butt cheeks. I know it's completely fucked up, but I absolutely love the way her ass smells. The skin on those plump cheeks is always soft and moisturized. I love bruising those cheeks as much as I love kissing and sniffing them.

Once Nik comes down off her orgasm, I remove my finger from her ass and rise to my feet to eagerly position my body behind her. I don't want her having too much time to come to her senses. Before Nik can return to her fearful state again, I use the head of my dick to take juices off her thighs before pressing the tip of my cock to her ass to help lubricate her tight, tiny back door.

"You are going to love my cock in your tiny little asshole."

"Odhran!" she gasps. "I came on your finger… I can't…"

She knows that she can use her safe word, but the word doesn't escape her lips. *She wants this.* My heart pounds with yearning for her. I love Nik so deeply and what terrifies me so much about loving her is how much she loves me back. She would do anything for me and that means it is my ultimate duty to protect her for loving me so purely.

My throat tightens with desire. It doesn't matter how much she begs now. My desire to penetrate her asshole is stronger than any other compulsion I've felt towards Nik. I have to own her asshole. *I need to cum there.*

I scoop her long mass of hair away from her back and neck, wrapping it around my wrist to hold her steady. Something about her squirming tells me I'll need to hold her in place as I take her ass from behind. Nik's back arches flexibly, presenting her tight puckered hole to me like a present.

Her slick, dripping and tightly puckered back door beckons to me and I eagerly press the tip of my cock against her ass, pushing in slightly. Nik squirms fearfully, but I hold her tight and steady with my hand wrapped around her hair. I don't want to hurt her, just keep her in place so I can slide my cock into her insanely tight ass.

The first three thrusts fail to get my cock in Nik's ass. She is just way too tight. When the head of my dick finally enters her, she cries out so loudly that I nearly stop. Instinct propels me forward and I slide half my cock inside her with one thrust.

"ODHRAN!" she cries out.

Keeping one hand wrapped around her mass of curls, I run the other hand slowly over Nik's exposed, curvy spine. Her back is so sexy and I would *love* to add another tattoo back there to match her ass tattoo. *Maybe we can get matching back tattoos this time.*

"Almost there," I murmur, once stroking her back relaxes her a little more. She whimpers and I want to end her pain faster, so I thrust the rest of my cock inside her. As Nik yelps, the force of her scream causes her tight ass to clamp down around my cock, squeezing my dick perfectly.

Holy fuck.

"It hurts, Odhran," she whimpers.

I have to make her feel good. Moving my cock in her ass, I work her clit with my fingers as I slowly ease my dick out a little. She whimpers with a little less pain and a little more pleasure, her moans changing in their intonation as I thrust my dick into her tight little ass.

"I love your ass," I grunt. "Almost there, babe."

"I'm gonna cum," Nik gasps, surprising me with the admission after only a few short thrusts in her tight, lubricated ass. I thought this hurt her too much for her to cum, but maybe teasing her clit is plenty to numb the pain.

Her ass gets even tighter and I lose control of myself as my balls draw close to my body and an explosive orgasm utterly wrecks me. My cum bursts from my cock and I feel the thick white liquid coating the walls of Nik's incredibly tight back door. It's so tight that I feel like I can't pull my dick out of her ass. The constriction around my cock feels absolutely incredible.

I almost can't believe that Nik came too, but her juices drip down her thighs, leaving proof behind that my cock in her ass caused a forceful orgasm to wash over her.

"Your ass is so tight," I grunt. "I can't get my dick out."

"Good," Nik moans. "Fuck me again... Just do it..."

. . .

MY CHEST SWELLS and my cock instantly stiffens with Nik's command. This isn't how I expected her to react to having my dick in her ass.

"Did you cum hard?" I grunt as I move my hips again, getting my dick even harder as I move inside of Nik's well lubricated back door.

"Yes," she says. "I need more of your cum in my ass. *Please…*"

I grip Nik's hips with desperate lust and withdraw my cock slowly before slamming back inside of her constricted asshole. Nik moans with pleasure. I knew she would love this, but her ass is almost too tight for me to handle and she clearly appreciates this far more than I thought. *She loves pain, Odhran… it gets her off.*

Gripping Nik's sexy curves, I pump into her ass, drawing closer to an orgasm with each thrust and grunting like a beast as I push my cock into her tightest hole.

"I love your sexy ass," I groan as I feel another climax building.

"Yes," she gasps. "Oh yes… It feels so good…"

Her soft, gentle voice drives me wild. I hold onto her hips and thrust one last time inside her as I cum. My muscles tighten intensely and the eruption is even stronger than the first time. Nik's ass grips my cock and milks every drop of my cum out of my dick. I groan as I slowly try to withdraw my dick. Her ass grabs onto me as if it has hands.

Nik moans as I withdraw my dick slowly and I can feel her ass and pussy spasming in pleasure around my dick as I remove myself. Finally, I withdraw my cock from her backdoor, leaving the tight hole slightly widened so my cum leaks out. My cock jerks again, but for the time being, I'm spent.

I bend down to kiss Nik's ass cheeks, thanking her gorgeous ass for an incredible night. She shudders nervously as I kiss her ass cheek as if she's worried that I'm going to spank her again. I chuckle and kiss her again. This time she moans. More of my cum leaks out of her ass and drips down her thighs. I can't believe how fucking sexy she looks like this.

"Come," I command her, standing behind her and watching Nik roll over to face me, her hair forming a giant mane of curls around her gorgeous, curvy body. My cock jerks again. We're going to have this forever. She peels herself away from the bed, craning her neck to gaze up at me with those gorgeous brown eyes.

I touch her darker skinned cheek, running my pale thumb over Nik's cheekbones. The contrast between our skin colors is absolutely beautiful. It's hard not to look at her, how fucking different she is, and not want it. Maybe Nik would find it offensive, but I like that she's exotic. Rare. That nobody else has a girl like her – not even my brothers.

"Are you going to spank me again?" she asks suspiciously. Her breasts sway perfectly in front of her, making it almost impossible to listen to the words coming out of her mouth. She turns me into a goddamn animal and I'm not even mad about it.

"No. I'm ready to plan our future."

"Oh," Nik says, nodding along. "We can play video games in bed all day tomorrow until we go to the gym and then we get beef lo mein for dinner. That's easy."

"I mean *our* future."

"Fine," Nik says. "You can share some of my lo mein. But if you just got your own lo mein instead of a gross ass seaweed salad–

I stop her lips with my finger.

"I'm not talking about takeout. I'm talking about babies. Marriage. All that stuff."

I can't tell what she's thinking. But it doesn't matter, because our lives become incredibly inconvenient at precisely the wrong time.

My doorbell rings. It's loud enough that I can hear it in my bedroom. I freeze, and close my eyes, trying to suppress my outrage. Maybe we can ignore it. I lean forward and grab Nik's cheeks, pulling her naked body against mine and kissing her. She pulls away.

"Aren't you going to get that?"

"No."

The doorbell rings again. Repeatedly.

"We should get that," Nik says. "I'll get dressed."

"I don't want to answer the door. I want to get you pregnant."

Nik rolls her eyes and reaches for one of my t-shirts. Watching her put on my t-shirt instantly causes me to sprout a semi-hard cock. I don't even bother to dress as I watch her cover most of her body with my t-shirt so all I can see is her perfect ass with that sexy tattoo.

"Aren't you going to dress?" Nik asks.

"I told you. I don't want to answer the door."

The doorbell rings several more times in succession. Both our phones vibrate. Mine is on the nightstand, but I can hear Nik's phone vibrating in her backpack in the elevator – which is just the private entrance. *This is something serious, isn't it…*

"Get your damn clothes on," Nik says as she slips into a pair of my black Bruins sweatpants. Her curves make it easy for her to fill out the legs but she's so short that she has to roll the waistband several times.

"Fine."

I throw on a pair of gray sweatpants and don't bother with anything else. Nik's eyes widen significantly as I pull out a pistol from my nightstand.

"Seriously?"

"I have bullets in the dresser."

"Since when am I your ride or die?" Nik asks, walking over to the dresser obediently and moving aside starched white boxer briefs until she finds a small box with four bullets. She hands them to me with a raised eyebrow.

I kiss her precious forehead. "Since I fucked your ass."

"I hate you."

"I love you too. Now come. Stay behind me."

"Do you seriously think someone you had to shoot would use the doorbell?"

"I don't know."

I'm not taking any chances with Nik. Unfortunately, as we draw closer to the guest door, our visitor's identity becomes extremely obvious. I exchange a concerned glance with Nik, who clearly shares my concerns. At least I know I can lower my gun. Nik walks confidently towards the door and opens it.

But it's not who we expect.

Chapter Twenty-Seven

Chapter Twenty-Eight
Onika

Maura presses the "stop" button on her phone. The voice we heard outside vanishes immediately. It's not Rylee. And Maura isn't alone. I don't recognize the two men with her, but Odhran clearly does. I glance back at him, wondering what he'll do and to my surprise, Odhran lowers the gun.

"Come on in," he says. "I'd like to know what you've done with Rylee. Because I doubt she sent you that clip."

Why the hell is he so calm?

Maura enters the apartment smugly, followed by two men. They're both blond and they look angry. *Very* angry. Both of them are holding shotguns, a weapon I wish Odhran had within arm's reach. I still don't know why he lowers his pistol.

"You cleaned up nicely here," she says, glancing around the room as she struts around. "Does that little bitch know that the last time we were here together, you fucked Six again?"

It's obvious that I'm the "little bitch" she's referring to because she sneers at me as she says it. I'm not scared of her anymore. After everything that happened, after everything I've been through with Odhran, I trust him. Maura doesn't scare me, but the weapons definitely do. If the tension thickens excessively, bullets will start flying and my boyfriend just lowered his weapon.

Odhran responds to her calmly, ignoring the existence of the two men.

"Come up with a better lie, Maura. And hurry up and tell me what you want."

I give Odhran a dirty look. Should he really have such a slick mouth with people who are armed to the damn teeth? Maura confidently struts to the couch and gestures for the armed men to follow her. Using their guns, they lead me and Odhran to the living room. Maura sits on the three-seater couch, flanked by her two "bodyguards", who look a little nervous now that I have had time to observe them.

Odhran and I stand in the middle of the room in front of his floor-to-ceiling glass window with a skyline view. His penthouse is truly beautiful, so I guess it's not the worst place to die. I glance at Odhran quickly and hopefully, but he just keeps his hands at his sides and remains infuriatingly calm.

"You're not so smart-mouthed now, are you?" Maura says, glaring at Odhran. "I just wish Six could be here to see this. She won't talk to me anymore, or they won't let her."

"I don't see how that's any of my concern. You could always move to Nunavut."

"You are such a fucking cunt," Maura says. "Whatever. It doesn't matter. Before I kill both of you insufferable assholes, I want you to watch that piggy little bitch friend Rylee bleed. It's what Six told me to do if our plan went wrong. Fuck everything up."

"She's lucky to have such a loyal friend," Odhran says.

I officially want to kill my boyfriend. Maura is prancing around his apartment wielding firearms and threatening to kill my best friend, and he's acting bored. We were just talking about spending our lives together. Maybe Odhran is content if those lives end now, but I'm not.

"This is so stupid, Maura," I say to her. "Weren't you there that night? Odhran's family is crazy and even if you kill both of us, they'll hunt you down."

Odhran's jaw tightens and he casts a somewhat infuriated side-eye in my direction. Since when am I the problem here? He's the one talking to Maura like she just invited herself into his penthouse for afternoon tea.

Maura rolls her eyes and sneers at me, "You are such an insufferable, fat little troll. Honestly. I can't wait to send pictures of your bloody corpse to Six."

Odhran glances at his watch, which makes both of the men holding weapons nervous, but doesn't impact Odhran in the slightest.

"Three," Odhran says.

"Three what, you stupid fuck?" Maura says, becoming irritated. "Your arrogance is starting to piss me off. Kyle, shoot the girl in the foot."

"Are you fucking kidding me, Maura?" the guy says. "She hasn't done anything."

"Are you here to ask questions or do what the fuck I say?"

"Two," Odhran whispers almost imperceptibly. I'm completely tuned in to his voice, drawn to it above any of the others arguing.

"I can't just shoot her," Kyle argues. "She's like the size of a fucking child."

Okay, that's disrespectful as hell, since short women are whole, complete *adult* women even if we can't reach the top shelves. I can't really help but let it slide considering the situation.

"Shoot her or I will," Maura says. "Why the fuck are you here if you aren't going to shoot them?"

"Because you promised–

"Give me the fucking gun," Maura says.

"One."

The lights in Odhran's apartment shut off suddenly. The blinds in front of the window shutter closed automatically, even without Odhran activating the system. *He knew this would happen.* Maura shrieks. I stay quiet, even as I feel a large arm wrap around me and drag me away from the center of the room.

"My brothers are here," Odhran whispers, keeping his hand clamped over my mouth so I don't scream. "It's a trap. Drop to the floor and crawl to the bedroom. The lights will come on in ten seconds."

I obey. Thankfully, I know Odhran's apartment like the back of my hand and even in the dark, I can get out of the living room in ten seconds. By the time the lights come on, I'm in the hallway and I can stand to run to the bedroom. I don't have any intention of staying out of the action, but I may not have a choice. I hear Aiden's voice. Then another voice as I start to open the bedroom door, maybe Rian's.

Maura says something loud, but a gunshot cuts her off. I swing the bedroom door open and launch myself inside. I know Odhran well enough to guess where he has another gun. I run to his closet and grab a shoe box from the bottom. It rattles around suspiciously.

I take off the lid to discover a pistol. I can count on Odhran to have guns stashed in more than one place at least. There might not be any ammo nearby. Odhran doesn't keep his ammo with his guns but I wish he gave me a map. Maybe just the threat of another weapon will be enough.

I throw the box to the side and press my ear to the bedroom door. I can't really hear anything and there hasn't been another gunshot. With a racing heart and the gun unsteady and cold in my hands, I hold it up and press my back to the hallway walls. It's quiet. *Too quiet.*

I come around the corner with my gun raised, the sound of several guns clicking instantly freezing me in place. I didn't think I was gone long enough for our circumstances to change so completely, but Maura is no longer in control. Odhran remains just where I left him when the lights went off, standing in the middle of the room. He doesn't stand alone. Aiden stands next to him while Rian and Callum hold Maura's accomplices at gunpoint. The intruders' weapons are on the ground and their hands are up in the air. Both of them glare at Maura, who Darragh Murray holds partly at gunpoint, but partly by the forearm.

"You can put the gun down, Nik. Everything is fine," Odhran says. I take another look around the room to make sure. One of the many lessons you get from first-person shooter games is that your enemies can burst around the corner and shower you with bullets when you least expect it. But that doesn't happen and Aiden Murray nods at me gently when I make eye contact with him. Instinctively, I defer to Aiden's authority without question. Once I lower the weapon, which isn't even loaded, Odhran crosses over to me and takes the gun from my hand, replacing it with his warm fingers.

"That was a close call," Odhran murmurs, kissing the top of my head.

The living room isn't brightly lit, even with the lights on, so the men in the living room who would normally all have pale-colored eyes now have eyes as black as a reptile's. Maura and her friends look like they regret what they've done. The color leaves Maura's face and she hasn't said a word since I entered the living room.

But what about Rylee?

I want to ask, but Aiden begins speaking once he seems satisfied that Odhran has the pistol out of my hand and in his control.

"Maura, the penalty for what you have done is death," Aiden says calmly. "But as you well know in our culture and amongst our families, men do not kill women."

Odhran's brothers all have a different reaction to the statement. It's hard not to notice Rian's visible discomfort as he shifts his weight from one hip to another and rolls out his shoulders. Darragh scowls more deeply and his grasp on Maura tightens. Callum doesn't budge and he doesn't seem like he's listening.

Maura makes an irritated shrieking sound like a spoiled kid holding a temper tantrum and attempts to break free from Darragh, apparently taking Aiden's statement as an invitation to escape. "We should probably just kill her since she pops up repeatedly like a weed," Odhran murmurs so that I'm the only one in the room who can hear him. Darragh doesn't let that happen. Pointing the muzzle of his weapon at the ceiling, he easily restrains Maura, pushing her against the living room wall and then pressing the barrel against her head. She yelps again and closes her eyes, shaking and begging Darragh not to kill her. I wish I could be emotionless watching her plead for her life, but I'm not.

Even if I should hate her and even if she walked in here intending to kill both of us, I don't want to watch her die. Odhran and his brothers seem too calm and I wonder if I should have stayed in Odhran's room if I didn't want to witness another assassination.

"Stop crying," Aiden says. "Or Darragh will give you something to cry about. Your family has disavowed you and your association with the Cunninghams. For as long as you have been gone, they have worked to prove their loyalty to me and they have given me complete permission to do with you as I see fit."

Odhran leans over and murmurs to me again, "He loves to hear himself talk."

I dig my fingernails into the back of Odhran's hand. This is serious and even if he might have a point, we can't get through this unless Aiden finishes.

"You're going to Ireland and when you get there, my cousin on my mother's side, who you might have heard of, Sean O'Sullivan, will take you to the church and you will marry him."

Darragh removes the barrel of the gun from Maura's head and even lets go of her hand, keeping the gun pointed at her, but giving her space to react. Her friends stand there in silence with their hands up still. Odhran doesn't flinch. Are they seriously talking about an arranged marriage?

"You can't do that," Maura says, but the force has completely vanished from her voice. I've never heard her sound like this before – downright terrified. Well, she might have heard of this Sean O'Sullivan character, but I haven't. Arranged marriage would be terrifying regardless, I suppose.

"Your family agreed to it in your absence. This was your choice when you chose loyalty to the wrong people. Marriage will remind you of your role in our family."

None of the men in the room flinch. I feel horrified on Maura's behalf, but not horrified enough to act. It's better than death. I hope so, at least. Honestly, if she gets any more pissed off, she might just come back and finish us off. Odhran clearly expected her to return.

"That man is twice my age," Maura says to Aiden, her voice shaking with each word even as she gets louder. "He's as old as you."

"Enough," Aiden snaps. "I don't want to hear any fucking complaining. You put me in a ridiculous position with your antics and you are a goddamn embarrassment. Without this, you would be cold in the fucking ground, so you will get on that plane and you will marry the *boss* of a proud Irish family so that your parents can walk around this city without shame."

"I won't get on a plane to marry some old man."

"Yes, you will. Because if you don't... my brothers will kill your friends."

Maura's eyes flicker directly to Aiden's. The man sure knows how to hold the attention in the room. Everyone stares at him waiting for his word. She takes a few seconds to consider. Her friends seem nervous, but they would probably be nervous anyway because of the guns.

"I'll go," she says, her voice barely audible. "Just don't kill them. Don't kill them in front of me."

Everyone in the room relaxes. Aiden gives Rian a look and makes a hand signal, which causes Rian and Callum to lead the men out of the room with their weapons. Odhran puts his arm around my shoulder. His closeness makes me feel comforted – like everything will be okay, even if I still have questions about Rylee.

Where did Maura get that recording of her? *Is she safe?*

"Smart choice, Maura. Tonight, Darragh will take you to a safe place where you can say goodbye to your family and we will get you a ticket for the next plane out of here. First class."

"Yes, Aiden," she says after a long, pained silence. I can tell it hurts her to say it, but what choice does she have.

"Darragh, take her to the car and tell Rylee she can come upstairs. I offered to take her home but... she insisted on coming along."

I can tell from the way Aiden's cheeks turn slightly red that Rylee probably irritated him until he dragged her here. Hearing that she's just downstairs makes me want to break away from Odhran's grasp and run to her, but as the room clears out and it's just the three of us, something tells me that Aiden has serious business to discuss. At least with Odhran.

Aiden walks over to his brother and puts his hand on his shoulder. "Thank you for keeping your cool."

"I'm not a kid anymore. It's time I grow up."

Aiden nods. "Excellent. Here. I brought this from mom's place."

He gives Odhran a brown parcel from his pocket and then looks both of us up and down.

"What are the odds?" Aiden mutters rhetorically. "It's a good thing dad's dead."

I IGNORE THE STRANGE COMMENT. Odhran never mentioned his dad and I didn't even know he was dead. Aiden steps aside as Rylee comes flying into the apartment at top speed. Rylee is about as curvy as I am and not exactly an expert runner, so she nearly trips over herself as she attempts to leap over the arm of Odhran's couch to pull me away from him and into a tight hug.

"You're alive!"

"You're the one who I was worried about," I say to her, holding her in a hug as relief finally floods me. She was right that I would need to see her to believe she was okay.

"Your boyfriend wouldn't let me hang out with you unless I agreed to put a tracking device in my phone. I guess it came in handy."

I give Odhran an angry side-eye, but he points to his chest and feigns innocence. I'll never get a confession out of him. Rylee doesn't seem to care. She grabs my hands and squeezes them.

"That bitch thought she had me, but I watch True Crime. I knew everything would be okay."

"So she kidnapped you?"

"And tortured me again!" Rylee says. "But that doesn't matter because I survived. Look at these."

She excitedly shows me her burns and our reunion goes on for several more minutes before Aiden gruffly reminds Rylee that her parents are worried about her since she went missing on a walk half a mile away from her house. Reluctantly, we say goodbye to each other and then the chaos settles into silence and a strange sense of peace settles over me.

This is what closure feels like, isn't it? And safety? Odhran comes up behind me and puts his arm around my shoulder again once we say goodbye to Aiden and Rylee. He kisses the top of my head and then presses his nose into my hair.

"Come to bed."

"More sex?"

"No," Odhran murmurs. "More sleep. Sex in the morning. We have a busy day ahead of us."

"We do?"

"Yes. I'm not done with you or your pussy. Now come."

He smacks my ass possessively and stalks towards the bedroom, expecting me to follow him and not bothering to turn around to double check. I hurry after Odhran, unsure how he expects me to sleep after the night we just had.

Once we're alone in his bedroom again, Odhran makes his plans clear and he eats my pussy until I fall asleep. I never experienced anything like it, but knowing Odhran, he'll probably do it again. I just remember soft orgasms, his tongue in slow circles around my clit and floating like a cloud as his tongue explored every crease.

I love being his.

Chapter Twenty-Nine
Odhran

I let Nik sleep in and skip the gym. We'll both get plenty of exercise before the end of the day. While she sleeps, I feed Killer Bee a frozen mouse. I keep them wrapped in brown paper at the bottom of my freezer so Nik won't run across them. I've had some close calls with the frozen mice since Nik moved in.

After feeding the snake, I do a few hundred pushups and several pull-ups until I work my muscles to failure. Nik is still sleeping by the time I'm done, so I have a protein shake and take a shower. She shows signs of waking once I'm out of the shower. I walk over to the bed and plant a wet kiss on Nik's cheek.

I think she's had enough sleep. She looks way too sexy right now for me to leave her sleeping. Nik grumbles and pulls the blankets over her head. I touch her ass through the sheets and she groans. Fuck. Her ass is so sore at just the slightest touch. Her response causes me to instantly sprout a semi.

"Wake up," I whisper, kissing her cheek again. "I want to make you breakfast."

She appears to stir a little from my kissing and makes a soft whimpering sound again. I palm her ass more forcefully and drag the blanket away from her head, ignoring her little groans of protest. Poor thing must be exhausted, but I can't allow her to sleep any longer. I'm not patient enough and neither is my cock.

"Nik. Breakfast," I say sternly.

She ignores what I say, still half asleep. Nik wriggles in bed a little and her ass jiggles, making my erection almost impossible to ignore. I don't know how much longer I can endure not feeling her pussy wrapped around my dick.

"No gym," she whines. "My ass hurts..."

At least she's more awake now, even if she still has her eyes closed and she's still wriggling in her burrito of blankets. Part of me wants to smack her ass to wake her up faster but... I want her to remember this morning forever.

"No gym," I assure her, pushing some of the curls out of her face. She is so fucking pretty when she sleeps. My muscles tighten as I look at her and wait for her eyes to flutter open. My semi-hard dick turns into a full-blown erection. Fuck cooking breakfast for Nik. I want to eat her pussy for breakfast. I wouldn't mind tasting some of her ass too.

One eye flutters open. When she makes eye contact with my abs, both of her eyes snap open and Nik quickly throws the blankets off, exposing her cute little outfit.

"I love seeing you in my clothes."

"I love seeing you without clothes," she says, a tiny smirk crossing her face. I love when I can get her to admit her attraction to me. I put my hand on the knot in my towel and Nik sits up all the way.

"Are you trying to see my dick?"

"No," Nik lies through her teeth. "I was... making sure you weren't going to smack me in the face with it."

"Right. You weren't staring at my abs or my tattoos or anything like that."

"No."

"Come on. Get clean and by the time you're done, I'll have breakfast ready."

She obeys without questioning. I love feeling like she trusts me enough to listen to me without fighting back all the time. But I love everything about being with Nik. It's peaceful. With a family like mine, you can easily think that relationships and everything in life is an adrenaline rush. Maybe I'm maturing...

I'm starting to like the quiet. Like Rian.

NIK ENTERS the kitchen dressed like an angel when she floats in. By that time, I'm dressed in a pair of black trousers and a white button-down shirt. Today is important to me, even if I'll have my clothes off again within an hour or so.

My heart stops as she walks into the room. *Nik is so damn gorgeous.* I love how thick and pretty she looks. Her curves get me hard instantly and her smile twists my heart into a knot.

She has her thick mass of curls parted in the middle and twisted in a curly bun at the nape of her neck. Her burnt cinnamon skin glistens with cocoa butter lotion and I can smell her before I hear her tiny feet padding across my apartment floor.

"This smells *amazing,*" Nik says.

"Crêpes were my favorite breakfast. My eldest sister Evie would make them for me when she babysat me over the summer."

I set a plate in front of Nik and she does a little happy dance in her seat, her boobs bouncing as she smiles. My dick grows in my trousers. I drew a little heart on her crêpe with melted chocolate and arranged bananas and strawberries in little designs around her plate. Pure Grade-A Vermont maple syrup sits in a little ceramic dish next to her plate.

"You made this?"

"Yes, gorgeous."

I set my plate down and sit across from her, watching Nik gleefully examine the plate.

"This looks good. I thought we weren't eating all these carbs anymore?"

"Today is different. Special."

Nik grins and we dig in. It's hard for me to focus on eating when I want to watch her eat. Her cheeks look so cute when she puts food and fruit in there, like a little chipmunk. She doesn't notice me watching her, I don't think. Maybe she does. The contents of the package Aiden brought me last night burn a hole in my pockets. I just want to say something.

"Odhran. You've barely touched it," Nik says once she finishes.

Fuck. I guess I did get too distracted.

"No appetite."

"You just said they were your favorite," Nik says. "Is something wrong? You make fancy breakfast and you don't even eat it and now you look… suspicious."

It's like she can read my mind. I understand why I know everything about Nik, but that doesn't explain how she knows everything about me. She understands me better than anyone else ever has, even if she's not Irish.

"It's because I want to ask you something," I blurt out. Nik looks at me suspiciously. I was stupid to think I could eat breakfast before asking her. I'm too excited. I want her too badly.

"Ask me what?"

I reach into my pocket for the emerald green velvet box and get out of my chair before getting on one knee. I assume that initial action would make my next one obvious, but Nik continues looking at me like I have two heads.

Here we go.

I open the box and flash the ring to Nik. She gasps.

"Odhran, is this an engagement ring!?"

It's a solid 24K gold ring with a twisted band and four emeralds surrounding a brilliant diamond in the shape of a shamrock. The custom, vintage engagement ring belonged to my great-grandmother on my father's side and I inherited it when he died. I thought I lost it, but before Six went to Nunavut, one of my brother's men recovered the ring from her things.

The ring means something to my family. It's from the old country, except for the gems, which our ancestors allegedly bought off some Scottish pirates who brought them up from Africa.

"Yes. I want you to marry me, Nik. I don't just want you to be my girl. I want you to be my family."

"But Odhran… You can't be sure. You dated someone for your whole life and–

"Don't argue," I respond sternly, flashing Nik a serious and incredibly sincere glare. If she rejects me for her own reasons, I could find a way to accept that. My past is my past. I don't want either of us to go back there.

"You're sure?"

"I am completely in love with you."

"I love you too," she says softly. "But… I know there are things we don't talk about Odhran."

"Like what?" I ask her, my chest tightening. I want her to take the ring. The hesitation makes me impatient. If I could hold her down and slip the ring on her finger, I would. Maybe I'll have to ask Rian for help. If my brothers can get Callum married, they can help me.

"Race."

"Oh."

I run my tongue nervously over my lips. I don't know what she wants me to say. She's right that we have never talked about it. What does she want me to say? I still have certain beliefs that she won't agree with but… I'm different. Can't she see that I've done this for her because I value her.

"We have to talk about it."

"I don't see why we do."

"Because you're asking me to marry you," she says. "And I know you take that seriously."

She's going to say no.

"Okay. We can talk about whatever you want," I say to her, meaning every word of it, wanting to unravel myself for Nik if it would make her happy.

Her hand touches my cheek. Simple contact sends a surge of desire through me. I love her so much it hurts. I want to do anything she asks. *Everything.* But there are some parts of myself I can't ever give up. My pride. My family. My love of Ireland and all things Irish. My brothers.

"Do you hate black people?"

I swallow slowly. What a fucking question.

"I don't hate you."

Nik looks visibly uncomfortable, but she doesn't drop her hand away from my cheek. Her gaze is downright unnerving. I don't want to feel like I'm under attack any more than I want to lose her.

"That's not what I asked."

"I don't," I answer firmly. "I don't hate Asian people either."

She appears slightly satisfied. I still would feel better if she just slipped the ring on her finger.

"Okay. But what about Six and Maura and their beliefs. And all that stuff," she asks. Nik is a smart girl. She might not have direct involvement in everything that has happened, but she has definitely paid attention. I can't hide from her, nor do I want to. That doesn't make me eager to expose parts of myself that I know she won't approve of.

"My brothers are different. I want to be different too. I'm not perfect."

"So you have a mild case of racism?" Nik asks, raising an eyebrow suspiciously. She drops her hand from my cheek naturally, but the action hurts. I take her hand and kiss it. Nik doesn't pull away.

I answer her, "Maybe. I don't want to be that person. I'd rather just... be myself. A fucking weirdo."

"I want you to heal that part of you, Odhran. For me."

"I would do anything for you."

"I know. That's why I'm asking. I don't expect you to be perfect today. But I expect you to change," she says seriously. She doesn't ask me for much, but she's always so hesitant about asking. Doesn't she know that I would do anything for her? I nod slowly, appreciating her closeness and wanting to indulge in more of it.

"Like you changed for me," I whisper, inhaling Nik's scent and wanting so badly for her to just agree to be my bride. No more arguing, no more waiting. I want the certainty and security of a future with her. Nothing about commitment scares me as much as spending a life-time without Onika by my side. I want her to be a Murray. *To be mine.*

"Yes," she says, nodding and biting on her lower lip as if expecting more reluctance and hesitation from me.

"If you marry me, I'll be whoever you need me to be. Your lover. Your protector. An educated philosopher on matters of race and gender."

Nik smiles and rolls her eyes.

"Then yes."

"Okay."

"I'm saying yes to your proposal. Yes, Odhran. I'll marry you."

Fuck. She didn't say no. Nik's response finally hits me. She just said yes.

"Are you fucking kidding me?"

"What type of response is that?!"

"Sorry. I'm just… I'm surprised."

"What? Why are you surprised after last night? We talked about having babies."

"Yes but…"

"I know you are dead serious when you bring up stuff like that. For some weird reason… I get you. I just… I love you…"

She grabs my cheek and pulls me forward, kissing me forcefully. Nik never takes the lead like this. I fucking love it. Her lips taste deli-cious. I kiss her back but mostly, I allow Nik to take the lead. When she pulls away, she's grinning and then she puts the ring on and I feel our bond strengthened already just from the small gesture.

"Does that mean we're having babies, then?"

"As long as I can keep writing, we can have babies," Nik responds, unconsciously admiring the ring. She makes me smile like an idiot all the time. I thought she would ask for a lot more than time to write.

"That is… not much of a request, Nik. Of course you can keep writing. I'm your biggest fan and your sexiest muse."

"Who said you were my muse?"

"I edited your essay while you were sleeping."

Nik's eyes widen with frustration. She looks like she's going to hit me, which automatically makes me smirk. I love when she gets all feisty...

She swats at me as she chastises me, "I told you not to do that!"

"I wanted to make sure you passed."

I won't apologize for looking after Nik.

"I have 101.5% in the class. I don't need your help."

She's right. She doesn't need my help. Nik is competent at pretty much everything and she's beyond competent at writing. She is profoundly talented. I think she could be famous one day.

"You're right," I whisper. "But I need your help for my life plans."

Nik's stare makes me feel so intensely. I want to make love to her so badly.

"What *are* your life plans?" Nik asks. "I've never even seen you attend classes."

Of course I attended *some* of my classes, but I don't really need to attend them regularly to maintain my good grades. Nik knows I have good grades, so I understand her confusion. Aside from the gym, I've rarely shown much interest in anything other than her.

"Being a good father," I tell her honestly. If we have children, that's the most important job I would have.

"That's it?" Nik asks.

I shrug and push hair away from her face. I bet we'll have pretty kids.

"It's more than what I had," I tell her. "Come. Kiss me."

She kisses me like I command. Her lips taste incredible. I want more.

"I love you," she whispers. "I want to be your wife and I want your babies. Is that crazy? You're basically an unhinged mobster who stalked me and captured me and took me to your lair."

"Just like your fantasy horror stories," I whisper, taking Nik's lower lips between mine. "I told you I was your perfect muse."

"Shut up. Let's just... make a baby."

It's exactly what I want to hear. I carry Nik back to our bedroom and lose control of myself once we're alone. She is so fucking sexy and the thought that making love to her will also fulfill some duty to my family only heightens my desire to be with her.

"I love you," I murmur. "I love you so fucking much."

She pulls me into bed and spreads her legs to take me inside her.

This is perfect. This is everything.

"I LOVE YOU TOO," she whispers. "My beautiful, twisted muse."

THE END

Click here to order Book #1 in my next series:
Varsity Possession
https://bit.ly/mcgrawcollege1

Click here to receive text message updates when the next Jamila Jasper book releases:
bit.ly/textjamila

Turn the page for more dark mafia romance reading...

About Jamila Jasper

The hotter and darker the romance, the better.

That's the Jamila Jasper promise.

If you enjoy sizzling multicultural romance stories that dare to *go there* you'll enjoy any Jamila Jasper title you pick up.

Open-minded readers who appreciate **shamelessly sexy romance novels** featuring black women of all shapes and sizes paired with smokin' hot white men are welcome.

Sign up for her e-mail list here to receive one of these **FREE hot stories**, exclusive offers and an update of Jamila's publication schedule: bit.ly/jamilajasperromance

Get text message updates on new books: https://slkt.io/gxzM

Dark Mafia Romance Preview #1

Sample these chapters from my Amalfi Coast Brotherhood Italian mafia romance series while you wait for the next mafia romance series.

If you enjoy dark & twisted mafia romance stories, you can binge the entire completed series on your eReader.

Enjoy the free chapters.

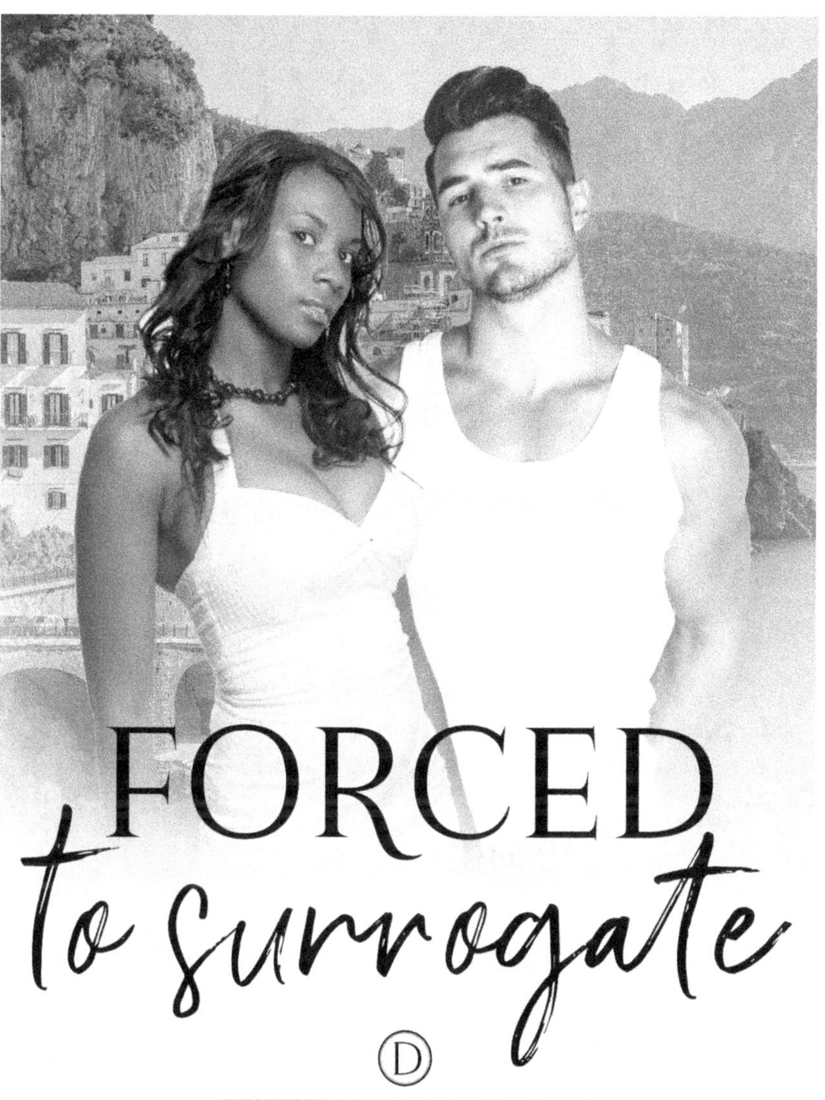

FORCED to surrogate

the amalfi coast mafia brotherhood #1

JAMILA JASPER

Description

The last thing Jodi remembered was a shot of tequila.
Next thing she knows,
Italian sociopath Van Doukas has her chained in his basement...
And he's claiming she agreed to become the mother of his child.

There's a detailed contract and everything... with her signature.
Jodi will do whatever it takes to get away from him...
But she doesn't count on the 6'7" Italian Stallion being skilled with his
tongue and excellent in bed.

Series Titles

Forced To Surrogate
Forced To Marry
Forced To Submit

Content Awareness

dark bwwm mafia romance

This is a mafia romance story with dark themes including potentially triggering content, frank discussions and language surrounding bedroom scenes and race. All characters in this story are 18+. Sensitive readers, be cautioned about some of the material in this dark but extremely hot romance novel. The character in this story is *forced by circumstance* into her situation.

Enjoy the steamy romance story…

Chapter 1
Produce A Pure Italian Heir
Van Doukas

There aren't enough cigarettes in the world for meetings with my father. The boss. Tonight, I meet with him to discuss something 'very important'. He calls everything 'very important', but tonight, I know exactly what he wants from me.

He wants me to kill again, this time for my foolish sister, who can't seem to keep herself out of trouble. Everyone in the family heard about what happened to Ana by now. That idiot Jew was foolish enough to put his hands on her with witnesses and expect nothing to happen? That's not how the Doukas family works, which he'll soon learn.

You mess with the Doukas family, we retaliate. If the Jew had any wits about him, he would disappear from the Amalfi Coast and head for the mountains or Sicily, or somewhere we don't have ears. He could go to Albania like Matteo. Maybe then we wouldn't find him. But fuck, I don't want to carry out another hit. Why can't that lazy fuck Enzo do it? Or better yet, Eddie. I carried out my first hit when I was two years younger than him. We spoil the new generation and wonder why our family falls apart.

None of this would be my responsibility if Matteo would get over himself and come down off his fucking mountain.

I stop my motorcycle and approach my father's front door. The all white old European style mansion sits on an excessive and opulent lot on the coast, right above the cliffs with a long path to the beach, a 'fuck you' to the tax collectors and the government who want to stop us from doing business.

Most of my siblings still live here, but I prefer keeping myself far away from papa and his… associates.

I can hear the party from the entrance. Seriously? On a fucking Tuesday afternoon? I assumed he called this meeting because he was working for once. He's intertwined in a different business based on the noise filtering outside. Please, Lord, let me not walk in on my father having sex with a model… *again.*

I open the front door to our old family home without knocking and immediately regret it when a completely naked foreign woman runs giggling toward the door, too high and drunk to feel self-conscious, exposing her completely nude body to a stranger. At least I didn't find her twisted in bed with papa, although this isn't much better.

"Oh! Good afternoon, sir!" she teases me in crude Italian, spinning around to show off her assets. *Whore. Foreigner. Her tricks possess little interest to me.* My brothers Lorenzo and Matteo would sway more easily.

"Where's my father?"

She giggles and spins around again. Fucking hell, I wish the ground would swallow me up. My father's prostitutes do not interest me.

"Your papa?" she says, standing to face me with her legs slightly apart, daring me to ogle more of her body. I have no interest in whores and I want her to answer my fucking question.

Before I can answer, another one of my father's toys saunters into the foyer, naked. This one is young—she looks eighteen just about— far too young for my father. I grimace and keep my gaze firmly fixed away from the nude females. Just because the men in my family are bastards doesn't mean I have to follow suit.

If we don't conduct ourselves with respect, how can we expect the respect of the Amalfi Coast?

"Yes. My father. Sal," I grunt, failing to hide the irritation in my voice.

The woman ignores my irritated tone with her response.

"Oh, he's in the back with Boyka. I can take you there after we take you to bed upstairs."

How much is he paying these women? We're still struggling to get Jalousie off the ground and he spends all his money on Slavic hookers.

"Not interested. I have a meeting with him."

"Are you sure?"

I don't dignify them with a response. I walk past the girls, keeping my eyes away from their bodies. Where the hell is my father? I pass the long hallway with the family portraits and follow the loud music and the louder giggling from near the pool. The familiar sound of pool jets betrays papa's location.

He's in the fucking hot tub again, I know it. He spends all fucking day in the hot tub, dishing out orders and expecting work to happen without him lifting a fucking finger. It's a fucking miracle anything gets done around here.

My father chuckles loudly, and I brace myself before approaching him. He's the boss and you don't question the boss, even if he's your father and even if he cares more about partying and women than our family — than our future.

When I enter the back patio, the pungent smell of tobacco and marijuana surrounds me. Judging by the bottles of vodka on the ground, the piles of cigarette butts and the other piles of detritus, they've been at this fucking party since last night.

Fuck. I put the cigarette tucked behind my ear into my mouth and approach my father's outdoor speakers, unplugging them and stop-ping the little dance party happening around his hot tub. Three women, each wearing next to nothing with their tits out belly dance for him while he chuckles loudly, his fat stomach causing waves in the hot tub. When the music stops, they stop too and look up at me indignantly.

They don't have to ask who I am. The ones who don't know Van

Doukas can tell that I'm related to Sal. I have my father's eyes, but thankfully, I don't have his overweight body or his bald head. The girls make booing sounds at me, but I brush them off.

"I'm here for our meeting," I say sternly to papa.

He chuckles and nods. "Yes. The meeting. I almost forgot."

Almost? He doesn't look like he's fucking prepared for a meeting.

Papa dismisses the girls, except for one — Boyka. She slides into the hot tub next to him, twirling his thick plumes of chest hair around her fingers and sliding his freshly cut cigar between his lips. Nauseating. Papa coughs after a puff and taps the cigar over the edge of the hot tub.

"You're early."

"I'm twenty minutes late."

"Oh?"

"Papa, you said it was important. Shouldn't we conduct this business alone?"

None of the girls are dumb enough to rat on Salvatore Doukas, but unlike my father, I don't see the sense in taking risks.

Boyka's hand moves down my father's chest and I don't want to imagine what sorry shriveled part of him she touches next. I just want my orders so I can get the fuck out of this bachelor pad.

"I'm getting old, Van," he says. "I'm getting old."

He didn't call me down here to bitch about his old age. I furiously puff on my cigarette, waiting for him to get to the fucking point. Papa grunts as Boyka touches something... sensitive. Cristo...

Watching my father grunt through a hand job might be the only thing worse than watching him stick it to a woman.

"Do you mind postponing your fucking hand job until later?"

Boyka's hand rises guiltily from the water and I choke down bile. She really was touching the old fuck. I shouldn't swear at him or set him off. Papa might seem old, but he can have me killed. Any of my brothers would do it if he gave the command. Tread carefully, Van.

"Maybe I should leave," Boyka says, giving me a flirty glance as she plays with her tiny pink nipples.

"Yes," I snap. "Please get the fuck out of here."

Papa scowls. "Be respectful, Van. Boyka is a very dear—"

"I said please."

Papa smirks. "Boyka, return in thirty minutes. If we're not done…"

"We'll be done," I interrupt, glowering at my father. I don't have all afternoon for his games when I have the club to attend to.

Boyka reluctantly leaves.

"Are the women in this house allergic to fucking clothes?"

"None of them are allergic to fucking anything."

I'm not doing this with the old man today.

"Why did you call me here?"

I start another cigarette. I keep swearing I won't touch another, then I spend five minutes around papa and change my mind.

He leans back in the hot tub, displacing several pints of water over the edge.

"I'm tired, Van," he groans, leaning back and rubbing his forehead.

"From working?"

My father doesn't pick up on the sarcasm. He hardly leaves his fucking hot tub anymore, and he hasn't done anything even remotely resembling working at either of the nightclubs, restaurants, apartment complexes or construction sites around town.

If it wasn't for me and Enzo, he wouldn't have the fucking time to boink Boyka or whatever the fuck he does with all these young Slavic women.

I still have to tread carefully around him. He's still my father, my boss, and I must obey him.

"Yes," he says, coughing. "From working. I need someone to take my place and lead the family soon. I want to retire, Van. You and I both know I need a break."

He spends every fucking day on vacation while his sons and nephews run his businesses. Vacation? We're the ones who need a fucking vacation.

"Perhaps you should contact Matteo about that."

My older brother spent his entire life preparing to be the boss. It's not my fault he fucked off, leaving his worthless children with us, I might add. I'm already halfway through my fucking cigarette and he hasn't closed in on the point.

Papa scoffs. "Matteo hasn't left Albania in four years. He left his children, his business, his fucking money, and he's not coming back. Give up on him."

"You're the one who trained him for the role. Send Enzo after him. Better yet, send his fucking son."

I don't want to go into the mountains to bring my jackass older brother back and I don't want to have this conversation with my father.

"Why don't you go to Albania?"

"Every time I'm in the same room as Matteo, he tries to kill me," I remind papa. I love Matteo, but he isn't exactly easy to get along with.

I'm surprised a woman tolerated him long enough to allow him to give her Eddie.

"Fair. But I need a replacement, Van. I don't want to be the boss anymore. I can't take the stress much longer."

Stress? What stress? Does my father seriously think sitting in his fucking hot tub banging whores counts as a job?

"Have you considered the role?" He asks before I can spew something disrespectful in my father's direction.

"Why would I want to be the boss of this fucking family? It's filled with degenerates, fuck-ups, people who need more violence to be kept in line. I kill enough as it is. You don't want me to be the boss and nobody in this fucking family wants me as the boss."

"People respect you, Van."

"People fear me. There's a difference."

Papa nods. "Exactly. Personally, I think you would make a good boss."

"I disagree."

But I don't completely. Yes, the job would be horrific and I'd have even more blood on my hands than I do now by the end. I could bring honor back to our family, clean the streets of our scum, stop the Jews from fucking with our shit... but I can't. Not with Matteo gone. Even in the fucking Albanian countryside, he would find out what I did and Matteo would kill me.

"No," Papa replies calmly. "You don't. But I agree with your assessment that you're not quite ready."

"I never said that. I said I didn't want the job."

Nobody smart wants my father's job. He spent twenty years walking around with a target on his back before he built up enough trust, enough loyalty, enough captains in the streets of Italy to ensure his safety. I don't want to lose my freedom.

"You didn't have to say anything. I know my son."

"Hm."

Arguing with my father is entirely senseless.

"You need an heir, Van."

"What?"

"I will give you the leadership of this family without the ritual, without the sacrifice and without the financial investment required. All I want is an heir."

"Why don't I go up to fucking Albania, then? Because I can't produce a child out of thin air."

Papa chuckles. "Don't you have women? If you want a woman... I filled this house with them. I have very young ones too. Eighteen. Nineteen. They make good mothers."

"I am not interested in fucking teenagers."

"Then find a whore like that old Greek Pagonis fuck. I don't care how you get the heir. You can prove how serious you are by giving me a child. I'll be generous. I'll give you a year."

"I don't want this role," I snap. "So the likelihood I'll produce an heir is slim."

Papa laughs, which only infuriates me further. There's nothing funny about bringing a child into the world.

"You can't lie to me, Van. You were always the most ambitious child. Maybe it's because you were smack in the middle and we didn't pay any attention to you. Who fucking knows?"

My father spent little time raising any of us, except for Enzo, and look how that fucking turned out.

"Thank you for the psychoanalysis."

Every time I visit my father, my desire for alcohol increases exponentially, along with my cravings for nicotine. He brings the worst out of everyone, especially me.

"No problem," he says, again ignoring my sarcasm.

"What happens if I don't produce an heir? Eh? You still need someone to take your place."

"I make this offer to Lorenzo if you don't produce what I want."

"What?" I would have at least expected him to mention one of our cousins, one of the very obedient captains from the northern coast, or even fucking Eddie, Matteo's 18-year-old son, would be better than my irresponsible fuck of a brother. That old fuck really knows me well because he just said the only thing that could get me to reconsider his stupid fucking offer.

"You heard me."

"Lorenzo would ruin this family. For fun."

"I know. And it would become your responsibility to save it. You would have to act as the boss to save Lorenzo from himself. You might as well earn the position."

Fuck this old man...

"I don't want a family life, papa. I don't want the fucking wife or the fucking family. I want this life. It's what I'm good at. Business. Killing. More killing. That's who you taught me to be."

I'm not a man who can picture himself kicking around a football with my children or taking them to the beach. I'm not built for seducing women for more than a night and dealing with the danger of introducing them to my life or worse, hiding it the way papa did with our mother.

He can pretend it's not his fault what happened to her, but we all know the truth. No woman deserves our life. I can't afford to react. He loves when he can draw a reaction out of me.

Papa continues, as if my reaction is irrelevant. "Part of this life means having a family. I can't expect my other children to carry on my bloodline."

"Matteo has a son. You have a fucking bloodline. Why don't you make him the fucking boss?"

"Eddie? Eddie will not survive long the way he lives."

"That's a way to talk about your grandson, eh?"

"Have another cigarette, Van."

I'm already on my fucking third. But I'm not in a position to turn down his offer, considering the shit he wants me to deal with right now. An heir? I thought he wanted me to kill someone. Producing an heir in a year… It's just fucking impossible. I stick the cigarette in my mouth and light it.

"You can't let the family fall apart. We aren't the only people who would suffer. What would happen to our people, good Italian people, when the only people around they can get money from are the fucking Jews, who hate our guts?" He says.

I can't let his guilt trip work on me.

"I want an heir."

"Hm."

"Consider what you would sacrifice by turning down my offer, Van. It's not just about the family. It's power. You act like you're a fucking saint, but you are my son. You enjoy power. You're just too much of a stuck up cunt to let yourself enjoy it."

"Thanks papa."

"You're welcome. Now, onto the matter of the Jew."

Fuck. I hoped my father would only piss me off one way today, but if we're discussing the matter of the Jew, I won't leave here tonight without an assignment. Someone else could easily do this job, but he wants me to kill. Because I'm good at it.

"I suppose none of my other brothers have the free time to do this?"

"I don't care. I need you to do it. The cunt offended this family."

"Perhaps we waste too much time retaliating for every offense. Ana told you to drop it."

I'm taking a risk just questioning his order, but he's pissed me off so much that I stopped caring.

"Decision making isn't women's work. It's our work. The man

signed his own death warrant. I want it done soon. Call me when you finish the job."

"Hm."

"If you don't like the way I run this family, Van, you know what to do. I want to retire. Make an old man happy."

Drugs and whores are the only things that make my father happy.

"An heir," I scoff. "You want me to have a fucking bastard child to continue your bloodline? A bastard won't have any loyalty to his family. Children have a mother and a father, a mother they spend all their time with. If I fuck some poor woman, you won't have an heir. You'll have a problem on your hands."

"Then get creative. If you need to get the baby and kill the mother, do what you must."

What's happening to this family? When did we lose our way and talking about murdering women for our own ends? Papa... This life changed him. It was slow, but it changed him completely. Too bad there's no getting out.

"Thank you for the advice."

"You're welcome. Now get Boyka back in here and get the fuck out. I need relief."

"Good evening, papa."

I drop my cigarette on the ground without bothering to step on it. Maybe my father's right — it's time for him to retire. But how the fuck will I get an heir? I need help.

There's one person I can call on for assistance in these matters. I don't like involving the Greeks in Italian business, but... they're our cousins. She answers after a few rings and it sounds like she's at a nightclub. She has an inordinate amount of time for parties...

"Ciao?"

I can barely hear her over the sound of the music.

"Miss Pagonis. It's Van."

She giggles. "Duh. What's happening? You finally have work for me?"

"How soon can you come back to Italy?"

Produce A Pure Italian Heir

Chapter 2
Single AF On The Amalfi Coast
Jodi Rose

I'm the last single woman in my family.

Three months in Italy, and I haven't had so much as a kiss, but my younger cousin Raven gets married to her college boyfriend and he looks like a dream. I drop a congratulatory comment on her photo, but my heart sinks.

You ugly, Jodi. Get used to it and stop chasing all these men out of your league. Settle with Kyle. He's the best you can do. Maybe mama was right. I'm not the marrying kind, anyway. I spent all my dating years focused on school and look at where that got me…

"Edo!"

The bartender gives me a sympathetic look. Ugh. Edo is so hot. Too bad all the hot guys are gay, especially in Italy, apparently.

"What happened?"

"Look at this."

I show him my phone and Edo cracks a smile. "Beautiful! Is she your sister?"

"No, my cousin. She's getting married and here I am… single… again."

And I'm running away from my problems with a one-way ticket to

Italy. When my family finds out I'm not coming back, they're going to lose their minds. Everyone already thinks I'm crazy for leaving Kyle...

"Fuck your ex, Jodi. Seriously, fuck him," Edo says with all the passion of a best friend, even if we barely know each other.

I have major regrets about getting drunk my first night here and spilling all the drama about my ex-boyfriend to a bartender, but at least it made us fast friends. Although I'm not sure if Edo just likes the fact that Americans tip, unlike our Italian friends. He always has a way of scamming some extra euros out of me. At least he's a damn good listener.

I groan and dramatically lean against the bar as I make a proclamation that I wholeheartedly believe.

"I'm never going to get with another guy again. This is it. I'm dying alone."

I've read the statistics. Or at least I've read what women on Lipstick Alley say about the statistics. I'm a thick, well-educated black woman who is tired of the dusties and has real ass standards — according to the internet, I'm dying alone.

Edo grins and shakes his head. Since he learned I was American, he's done everything in my power to take me under his wing since I got here. I just hate getting too far out of my comfort zone, so I've ditched all his invitations to visit the local clubs in favor of spending my nights drinking cocktails alone and checking social media. I'm in Italy. I should have daily adventures and bread. I can't forget the delicious ass bread.

"You will not die alone," Edo says. "At least not without trying... my latest cocktail creation."

Edo does a dramatic dance before revealing some clear beverage that looks like some horrible mix of vodka, vermouth and orange juice.

Good. I want to get completely fucked up.

"That looks... clear."

"You'll love it, I promise."

"Will drinking really make the pain go away?" I muse, twirling the glass around so the little orange peel swirls inside it. Kyle. Why do you always miss the ones who fuck you up the most?

Hopefully, this drink will get my ain't shit ex off my mind, but let's be real. What I really need is a summer romance. Ha. Like that's going to happen in a country where half the people think I'm a prostitute because of my skin color.

"Yes. It will. Absolutely." Edo replies with a wink.

"Cheers." I swirl the drink around despite Edo's repeated claims I ruin his creations by doing that. I pour it down my throat and taste a pleasant citrus flavor before a powerful vodka burn. It takes everything in my power to get the rest of the drink down my throat. Whew! That was a damn burn.

"What the hell did you put in that?"

Edo winks, but offers no response. Tricky ass Italian.

"My shift ends in ten," he says. "I'll take you out tonight to Jalousie. No getting out of it this time to watch *Empire* in your apartment."

How the fuck does this skinny ass white boy know me so well already? I shake my head, prepared to reject his offer to take me to the club, but Edo won't let it go. He wriggles his brows suggestively.

He loves regaling me with stories about all the shenanigans that go down at the Amalfi Coast nightclubs. I'm not really a nightclub girl. Small bars like this one fit me better, but didn't I come to Italy to have fun? Meet someone? I should put in some effort.

The only men who give me any attention are the creeps on the beach who say so much nasty shit to me in Italian that I'm glad I don't understand.

Maybe I'll meet better men at the club, especially a club with a fancy ass French name like this one. Jalousie. Wait... Edo's mentioned Jalousie to me before in the past.

"Ain't that the club with the mafia shootout you told me about?"

I don't believe half the shit that comes out of Edo's mouth, but he loves regaling me with stories about the real Italian mafia, which he claims is apparently far worse than any mafia in Long Island or Staten Island. How could anyone who lives in one of the most beautiful parts of the world hurt and kill other people? I think he likes telling tall tales to impress tourists.

I get people on Staten Island killing each other, but the Amalfi Coast? Hell fucking no. The sea is perfectly blue, the air smells fresh constantly, and it's plain peaceful out here. Italians have a rich culture, amazing food, better wine and the guys here are hot.

Not every guy, but when you walk down the streets here, you definitely encounter more than a few hotties. They all dress like supermodels, too. I've never seen so many regular ass people sporting Gucci and Fendi.

"Yes," Edo says. "But you're here for 9 more months, right? Have a fling. Don't tell him your real name... and disappear. You can find a hot and incredibly rich man to spoil you during your trip."

"Wait... is this a gay club or my type of club?"

Edo chuckles. "The guys are hot. I didn't say they were gay. You haven't earned your way into going to a gay club with me yet."

"Wow, Edo. I thought we had something going here."

Edo shrugs. "My private life is my private life. That's how it is in Italy. Your private life, on the other hand, is my playground. I'll introduce you to people. I know people who frequent Jalousie."

"Hot guys?"

"Eh..."

"Hot straight guys?" I correct myself before he answers. I don't want Edo tricking me into going out for nothing.

"Not exactly... I have a girl friend in town who goes all the time — Cassia Pagonis."

He says the name like I'm supposed to know who the fuck that is.

"Who the fuck is that?"

Edo chuckles. "A very fun girl with very hot brothers."

I perk up a little until Edo tells me they're all married. Great.

"Great. They're married..."

Before Edo can reassure me (again) more customers wander into the bar and Edo scurries to the other end of the bar to take orders.

I gaze into my phone again, looking at pictures from Raven's wedding. My cousin looks gorgeous, but I can't help a twisted pang of envy. I know it's wrong but... will that ever happen for me?

My homegirls from college keep sending me articles about the sorry state of marriage for black women. Alyssa says that we need to divest completely from marriage and just have fun.

My idea of fun isn't keeping a collection of all "my dicks" in a private folder on my phone. I want the real fucking thing! Even if the world loves reminding me that 'the real thing' only happens for white women or black women with the lightest dusting of melanin... I want to believe in love.

I scroll past Raven's pictures and my feed is all babies, new puppies, new jobs, new houses, new apartments, new husbands... new everything. Before Italy, I was just doing the same old shit. I wanted to shake things up. I don't know why my life hasn't trans-formed entirely. I'm in the prettiest place on earth — the Amalfi Coast.

Edo's shift ends, and he calls my name from the other end of the bar, beckoning me over to the cash register.

"Any tip for me today?"

"I saw you slip that five euro note out of my wallet. I think we're good."

Edo shrugs. "Sorry, this job doesn't pay well."

"I get it. I'll pay for our drinks tonight. Happy?"

"Incredibly."

I shouldn't be offering to pay for anyone's drinks, honestly, but I tell myself that I'll worry about all the damn money I'm spending once I get back to America. I have nine months of freedom and then I can worry about these damn bills and loans and everything else.

Edo drags me off my stool, and we step outside into the cobble-stone street. I'll never get over how beautifully blue everything is here. The streets smell like the ocean, pastries, wine and cigarettes, of course. People sell jewelry and fruits on the streets and the Italian accents are... gorgeous. My Italian's still crap, despite Edo's best efforts to teach me a few phrases.

At least I don't have to hear all the street harassment thrown my way, which is plentiful. Edo replies defensively to a grey-haired man who calls something lewd in my direction and grabs me tighter. "Fuck these guys," he says. "You aren't that fat."

I swear, I'll never get used to how fucking blunt they are. But I appreciate Edo doing his best to defend me. We can hear the music from Jalousie echoing down the street before we get close.

"Isn't it early for the club?"

"Why are you so fucking American?" Edo asks, linking arms with me. "Relax."

"EDOARDO!" A shrill voice with a strange accent calls from across the street. I know Italian accents by now, at least how people from the Coast sound when speaking English, and this girl sounds different.

"That's Cass," Edo says to me, a smile breaking out across his handsome face. "Chin up. She'll love you."

Edo waves to the girl across the street and she struts over to us, sticking her hand out to stop the cars making their way down the cobblestone streets. They don't even honk as she passes.

The first thing I notice about her is how striking she is. She's tall, with curly dark brown hair pinned up out of her face and flowing down her back. She's wearing crazy high heels, like all the European girls do, a short leather skirt and a tight black leather crop top.

With her dark red lipstick, she looks like a film noir femme fatale… and she stares like one.

"Edo… is this your American friend?"

She turns to me and smiles. Shit, her accent might be strong, but her English is perfect. Cass's hair falls over her shoulders, her curls carrying a soft eucalyptus scent.

"Jodi Rose," I say, happy to have some female company around here, not like there's anything wrong with Edo. "Nice to meet you."

She takes my hand, three silver Cartier bracelets sliding down her wrist. Wow. Her bracelets aren't the only expensive item of clothing she has.

"Cass Pagonis. I'm sure Edo has told you all sorts of horrible stories about me."

"I did not!"

Edo definitely did. But Cass doesn't seem like a crazy party girl. She rolls her eyes and brushes him off.

"I'm here on the Coast working for my cousin's family," Cass says. "I'm from Thessaloniki. My idiot brothers want me back next week, unfortunately. But I could use a night out before I go."

Edo claps his hands. "Yay! Party time. Too bad Jalousie only caters to the most chauvinistic mafia pigs you can imagine."

"I thought you said they were hotties?!"

"They are," Edo says. "But they might be assholes."

Now he tells me. Edo would have said anything to get me out of my damn apartment. I hope I don't regret it.

"Watch it," Cass cautions, an impish smile on her face. "Those chauvinistic mafia pigs are my cousins and brothers."

Edo shrugs. "Fine. Fine. But I need dick too. Gay rights."

Cass swats his shoulder.

"Edo, why don't you let me take her for the night? There's no one at Jalousie for you, and you can go meet up with Klaus or… that other one."

Edo suddenly straightens his back and reminds both of us that just because he's gay doesn't mean he's given up on old world chivalry.

"I can't send Jodi off with a stranger," he says.

I appreciate the sentiment, but I don't know if Edo would do much damage against… any man who weighed more than his slight 108 lb frame.

"I'm fine," I tell him. "Seriously."

"I'm armed anyway," Cass says. I think she's joking, but neither of them laughs. Is she serious? She doesn't look armed, and she looks more like a model than someone who knows how to use a weapon.

I could use a female friend in my life over here. I've got plenty of female friends back home, but they all want to talk about Kyle and my "healing journey". They don't want to hear that I'm still lost after all these months.

Edo shrugs. "If you insist."

"I insist," I tell him. "You've done enough taking care of me. Plus, I'll get to know my new friend… Cass."

"Exactly," Cass says. "Jodi… I think we can become wonderful friends. We can swap stories about Edo."

"There are no stories about Edo," he chimes in. "Because Edo is an incredible friend and a better bartender."

"Shoo," Cass says. "I can handle things from here."

Edo doesn't quite walk off, but he checks his phone and begins texting furiously to plan his next move.

"It's the last time they have DJ Fat Camel playing here. We'll dance, drink and later, I'll take you home, yes?"

"That sounds good to me."

"Well, you have my number if Cass abandons you on the top of a Ferris wheel," Edo says as he swipes four times quickly across his screen and then shoves his phone into his pocket.

Cass rolls her eyes. "I have done nothing of the sort. Get out of here, you big drama queen."

"Ciao!"

Cass and I say "Ciao!"

Edo walks down the cobblestone streets and lights a cigarette before disappearing around the corner. Cass breathes a sigh of relief and turns to me.

"I just think you're perfect," she says.

Weird comment to make, but I mumble a gracious thank you, assuming something got lost in translation.

"Do you have friends with you?" Cass asks, taking out a hand mirror and fixing her bright red lipstick.

"No. I'm here solo tripping. Had a quarter life crisis and… here I am."

"Do you like Italy?" she asks genuinely. Her eyes are so intense.

"It's beautiful."

"Not as pretty as Greece," Cass says. "But I agree. Shall we go in?"

"We should head to the back of the line," I say, my stomach knotting as I see the line stretched around the block. I hope we can even get into the club.

Cass grins, unperturbed by the growing line outside Jalousie.

"My cousin owns the place. Come on, we go in through the back."

Before I can protest, she takes my hand and we walk around a back alley that smells like trash, vomit and again — cigarettes. Cass drags me over to a door and surveys me once before touching the handle.

"Very proper outfit. Excellent. Let's go. Ready to dance?"

I nod, even if I'm nervous. Sure, I'm trying to have an adventure tonight, but I just met this chick. How do I know she isn't crazy? Well, she has Edo's backing, so at least she'll be a good time. Edo definitely knows how to have fun if his clubbing stories are even 55% true.

Cass punches in a six-digit code and the back door to the club opens. I can smell the club before I hear the music and Cass drags me in through the back before I can second guess myself. What am I really doing? I don't know this chick at all and I agreed to go clubbing with her? Is Edo's word really enough?

Once we're in the back door, a man appears. He's tall, with dark brown slicked back hair, tattoos all over his arms and grey eyes. He has broad shoulders, but is otherwise lean and very muscular. He's handsome, but it's too bad he smokes. I can smell the cigarettes from a distance.

"Cass? What the fuck are you doing here?" he asks, seeming genuinely upset.

"Shut the fuck up, Enzo," Cass snaps, her expression changing suddenly into a disapproving scowl. "I have business here."

The man smirks. He's around Cass' height, but he looks... greasy.

"Is that her?"

"Mind your fucking business."

Cass pushes him hard so we can get past him. The grey-eyed man's eyes land on me and he runs his hand over his jawline before snickering.

"He's going to kill you."

"Shut up," Cass snarls. Enzo laughs and raises his hands in defeat.

"Enjoy your night," he says to me in a sing-song voice. For the first time, I feel real hesitation. But Cass grabs my hand and drags me inside of the club.

Cass drags me all the way to the tables and chairs surrounding the dance floor, chatting excitedly and peppering me with questions about

America. I struggle to understand her accent at first, but then I get into the rhythm of her voice and it's easier for us to communicate.

I have to listen in so hard that I barely scan the room we enter. At least the nightclub has a nice interior, and it doesn't seem like any ghetto shit might pop off. Another Edo exaggeration, it seems. I relax as Cass sets me up at a small, two-person table.

"I'll get you a drink. Wait here. If anyone comes to talk to you, tell them you are with Cass Pagonis. That will shut them up."

Before I can protest, or offer to come with her, Cass disappears. Shit. I guess I have to wait here. I already have five texts from Edo about the hotties he met at the club a few doors over. Damn, he moves quick. I've been here for weeks already and I still haven't met a heterosexual male who hasn't been an incredibly old and excessively horny man offering for me to be his 'African prostitute' — offers I have obviously declined.

Cass returns quickly, before I have any time to worry with two shots, each one with some blue flavoring at the bottom.

"Okay, Jodi. This is to a long and beautiful friendship between us, starting with one crazy night, yeah?"

I nod. "Hell yeah. I've never done anything like this before."

I blurt out the last part nervously, but Cass has a way of soothing me. She just smiles and nods. "Don't be scared! I'm a good Greek girl. Now come on... we'll take the shots together."

She counts us down.

"1... 2... 3..."

I take the shot — and it's the last thing I remember about that night.

Click here to keep reading:
https://bit.ly/amalficoast1

Extremely Important Links

ALL BOOKS BY JAMILA JASPER
https://linktr.ee/JamilaJasper
SIGN UP FOR EMAIL UPDATES
Bit.ly/jamilajasperromance
SOCIAL MEDIA LINKS
https://www.jamilajasperromance.com/
GET MERCH
https://www.redbubble.com/people/jamilajasper/shop
GET FREEBIE (VIA TEXT)
https://slkt.io/qMk8
READ SERIAL (NEW CHAPTERS WEEKLY)
www.patreon.com/jamilajasper

JAMILA JASPER

Diverse Romance For Black Women

More Jamila Jasper Romance

Thank You Kindly

Thank you to all my readers, new and old for your support with this new year.

I look forward to making 2022 an INCREDIBLE year for interracial romance novels. I want to thank you all for joining along on the journey.

Thank you to my most supportive readers:

Cortney, Yolanda S., MonaGirl, Dianna, Mary, Nysha, Fayola, Ty, Shyra, Andi-Mariee, Keisha, Jennett, Fredericka, Candece, Lydia, Sabrina, JM, Jackie, Mo, Ashaunte, Tolu, Lori, Dionne, ZLB, Nicol, Elbert, Jesi, Brenda, Desiree, LaShan, Only1ToniD, Debbie, Tiffanie, Shawnte, Lisema, Christine, Trinity, Monica, Juliette, Letetia, Margaret, Dash, Maxine, Sheron, Javonda, Pearl, Kiana, Shyan, Jacklyn, Amy, Julia, Colleen, Natasha, Yvonne, Brittany, June, Ashleigh, Nene, Nene, Deborah, Nikki, DeShaunda, Latoya, Shelite, Arlene, Judith, Mary, Shanida, Rachel,Damzel, Ahnjala, Kenya, Momo, BJ, Akeshia, Melissa, Tiffany, Sherbear, Nini, Curtresa, Regina, Ashley, Mia, Sydney, Sharon, Charlotte, Assiatu, Regina, Romanda, Catherine, Gaynor, BF, Tasha, Henri, Sara, skkent, Rosalyn, Danielle, Deborah, Kirsten, Ana, Taylor, Charlene Louanna, Michelle, Tamika, Lauren, RoHyde, Natasha, Shekynah, Cassie, Dreama, Nick, Gennifer, Rayna, Jaleda, Kimvodkna, Jatonn, Anoushka, Audrey, Valeria, Courtney, Donna, Jenetha, Ayana, Kristy, FreyaJo, Grace, Kisha, Stephanie E., Amber, Denice, Marty,

LaKisha, Latoya, Natasha, Monifa, Alisa, Daveena, Desiree, Gerry,
Kimberly, Stephanie M., Tarah, Yolanda, Kristy, Gary, Janet, Kathy,
Phyllis, Susan

Join the Patreon Community.
www.patreon.com/jamilajasper

Patreon

Instantly access all six seasons of *Unfuckable* (Ben & Libby's story) with 375 chapters.

For a small monthly fee, you get exclusive access to my all this & my recently completed serial Despicable (275 chapters) ⬇️

www.patreon.com/jamilajasper

Patreon has more than the ongoing serial and previous serial releases...

INSTANT ACCESS

- NEW merchandise tiers with **t-shirts, totes, mugs,** stickers and MORE!
- **FREE paperback** with all new tiers
- **FREE short story audiobooks** and audiobook samples when they're ready
- #FirstDraftLeaks of Prologues and first chapters **weeks** before I hit publish
- Behind the scenes notes
- Polls and story contribution
- Comments & LIVELY community discussion with likeminded interracial romance readers.

LEARN MORE ABOUT SUPPORTING A DIVERSE ROMANCE AUTHOR
www.patreon.com/jamilajasper